JACOB'S CHOICE

"The story transports the reader to a time in Pennsylvania history when the area was beyond the edge of the frontier, a place steeped with great danger. The account is accurate and uncomfortable. You can almost smell the smoke and feel the pain."
   —**C. Rusty Sherrick, interpreter of Delaware Indian history**

"Using historical facts and a vivid imagination, Ervin Stutzman does a beautiful narration of nonresistant Amish life."
   —**Sam Stoltzfus, Old Order Amish historian**

"This novel of Amish life in eighteenth-century Pennsylvania allows us to imagine the joys, tears, doubts, and religious devotion of the earliest Amish immigrants. In retelling the story of the Hochstetler massacre, Stutzman reminds us that the family was real and that their sacrifice was both a human tragedy and a triumph of faith."
   —**Karen Johnson-Weiner, coauthor of *The Amish***

"Ervin Stutzman's recounting of this tragic event demands soul-searching. Written with honesty and grace, *Jacob's Choice* draws the reader into the story to feel the angst of the Hochstetler family. A must-read for all of us who strive to live out our faith."
   —**Becky Gochnauer, director, 1719 Hans Herr House & Museum and the Lancaster Longhouse**

"Ervin Stutzman understands that a good story is the most powerful rhetorical form to bind communities together, pass on traditions, and ultimately to understand the triumph and the tragedy of the human condition. In this dramatic and accessible tale of how one Amish family faced a horrific crucible of their nonresistant faith during the French and Indian War, Stutzman puts 'flesh on the bones' of known facts. He also creates a searing virtual experience that challenges us to see how extraordinarily difficult it is to follow Jesus Christ and love our enemies."

—**Susan Schultz Huxman, president, Conrad Grebel University College**

"Ervin Stutzman has composed an incisive historical novel dealing with Amish courage and forgiveness during the turbulent period of the French and Indian War. His narrative on how Jacob Hochstetler dealt with an Indian attack on his family, related indignities, and his own tribal captivity and escape—coupled with a tender romance and other matters of the heart—provide for a truly edifying and rewarding read."

—**William Unrau, distinguished professor emeritus of history, Wichita State University**

"Ervin Stutzman has written a fictionalized yet historically accurate story of an eighteenth-century Amish family's nonresistance in the face of attack, murder, and captivity. Jacob's subsequent sojourn with Native Americans in a Seneca village is authentically portrayed. Stutzman brings characters from the past to life!"

—**Beth Hostetler Mark, Messiah College librarian and descendant of Jacob Hochstetler**

"Stutzman's keen knowledge of time and place brings to life the Hochstetler family's testing through the Indian attack and captivity and their commitment to Anabaptist values. Nonresistance, forgiveness—and romance—are just some of the choices this most widely known family in the original pioneer Amish settlement must make."

—**Daniel Hochstetler, cofounder of the Jacob Hochstetler Family Association**

JACOB'S CHOICE

Return to Northkill, BOOK 1

ERVIN R. STUTZMAN

HERALD
P R E S S

Harrisonburg, Virginia

Herald Press
PO Box 866, Harrisonburg, Virginia 22803
www.HeraldPress.com

*The Library of Congress has cataloged the hardcover expanded edition as
follows:*
Library of Congress Cataloging-in-Publication Data
Stutzman, Ervin R., 1953-
 Jacob's choice / Ervin R. Stutzman. -- Expanded edition with photo-
graphs, maps, and historical background.
    pages cm. -- (Return to Northkill ; bk. 1)
 Includes bibliographical references.
 ISBN 978-0-8361-9875-1 (hardcover : alk. paper) 1. Amish--Fiction. I.
Title.
 PS3619.T88J33 2014
 813'.6--dc23
                            2013041014

JACOB'S CHOICE
© 2014 by Herald Press, Harrisonburg, Virginia 22801. 800-245-7894.
    All rights reserved.
Library of Congress Control Number: 2013041014
International Standard Book Number: 978-0-8361-9681-8 (paperback)
    978-1-5138-0168-1 (hardcover)
Printed in United States of America
Cover design by Kirk DouPonce, DogEared Design;
    interior layout and design by Reuben Graham
Cover photo by Kirk DouPonce

Unless otherwise noted, Scripture text is quoted, with permission, from
the King James Version.

21 20 19 18 17   14 13 12 11 10 9 8 7 6 5

To Rachel Weaver Kreider, the centenarian whose unflagging energy, irenic spirit, scrupulous Amish genealogical scholarship, and interest in the Jacob Hochstetler family story inspire me to follow in her footsteps, although I hardly dare hope to live as long as she has.

Contents

Author's Note

Jacob Hochstetler of the Northkill stands tall as a hero of faith among the Amish, largely because he stood the test of nonresistant Christian faith during the French and Indian War. The story of his family has been recounted through various media over many generations. Although the primary event in the narrative has often been referred to as "the Hochstetler Massacre," today's sensitivities beg for a softening of that language. I have chosen to simply call it an attack. There were indeed many massacres during the war, larger-scale hate killings perpetrated by European whites as well as Native Americans. One of the most egregious was the massacre of the peace-loving Conestoga Indians by the Paxton Boys in December 1763.

I chose to write the first novel in the Return to Northkill series from the viewpoints of Jacob and his daughter Barbara. Although their Anabaptist understanding of Native Americans was considerably more compassionate than that of many of the Pennsylvania settlers, they did not have the deep concerns about justice for Native Americans that many of us do today. Descriptions of the "red man," "natives," and "braves," as well as other characterizations of Native Americans contained in this novel, reflect the common preconceptions and prejudices of the colonial era. This novel would be very different if it had been narrated from a Native American point of view. The next two novels in this series will more fully explore that perspective. Readers who wish to explore Native American issues from a contemporary justice perspective may benefit from reading the series of essays in *Buffalo Shout, Salmon Cry: Conversations on Creation, Land Justice, and Life Together* (Herald Press, 2013).

As much as possible, I used the known names of the people in this story. I used my imagination to put the flesh of this story on the bones of known facts to create a plausible account of what may have happened. Any errors or conflicts with known facts are mine.

—Ervin R. Stutzman

PART I

-1-

June 29, 1757

Jacob and his sons were harvesting barley in the field next to Northkill Creek when they received the dreadful news about their neighbors. Humming a Swiss tune, Jacob raked the cut stalks of barley into piles while three of his sons gathered and stacked them. With good effort, they could get the golden grain into shocks before supper. Fritz, the sheepdog, lolled in the shade of a huge chestnut tree at the edge of the sun-baked clearing.

Suddenly Fritz jumped up and ran barking to the corner of the field. He stood by the wide path to the rutted road, yapping at something Jacob couldn't see.

"What's the matter, Fritz?" Jacob said. He wasn't the kind of dog to bark at just anything. Jacob tossed a sheaf of barley onto the pile and cocked his head to listen. Soon he heard the sound of pounding hooves.

"Fritz! Come here." He snapped his fingers and the dog came bounding to his side. A few moments later, a rider came into view, his hat askew as he leaned forward on his stallion. He looked like one of the provincial soldiers stationed at the Northkill fort.

"Hey there! There's Indians nearby!" The soldier rode across the stubble to where Jacob was working. Christian, the youngest boy, only eleven, was working beside his father and stepped up to listen as the rider dismounted. Jacob beckoned toward his sons Jakey and Joseph, and they hustled over to hear the news.

"You're Hochstetler, right?" the soldier asked.

"*Jah*. Jacob Hochstetler."

"My name's James Adams, from Fort Northkill. Indians were just over a mile north of here, murderin' and stealin'.

13

Killed the whole John Reichard family, 'cept for an eight-year-old boy, who they took captive."

"No!" Jacob glanced toward the garden where his wife, Lizzie, and six-year-old daughter Veronica, whom they called Franey, were working. "Today?"

"This afternoon. After Reichards, they pounced on the Frederick Meyer family. Mr. Meyer was mowing in the meadow and the missus was plowing nearby. Them demons shot her through the heart and then scalped her."

Nineteen-year-old Jakey's face paled at the news. Joseph, thirteen years old and fast becoming a man, tightened his jaw and leaned forward.

"They shot Mr. Meyer as he tried to get away with his little boy, then they tomahawked and scalped their little tyke and threw him into the creek. Took the rest of the children as captives."

Fritz sniffed at the horse as the soldier continued, "The Meyers' neighbor—Jacob Kauffman—heard the shooting and came to see what was happening, but by then the savages was gone. He found the little boy, 'bout two and a half years old, throw'd in the creek with just his head out of the water. They'd scalped him and left him for dead, but he was still 'live and crying for his papa. Musta' been a pitiful sight—"

"You can't live after you've been scalped," Joseph said. He was often sure he knew more than the grownups.

"Well, that's what they said. The neighbor found the boy and thinks he just might live. Someone will need to take him in, though, seein' as both of his parents are gone."

"Do you need our help?" Jacob said.

"Nope. Just bringin' a warning. I'll be obliged if you let the neighbors know just south and east of here."

Jakey crowded in closer. "Where'd the Indians go?" It was the question on Jacob's mind as well.

"No one saw 'em leave. They have a way of disappearin' in the woods so you cain't find 'em. You never know where they'll show up next. You might better come to the fort for the night."

"Thanks for bringing us the news. We'll pass it on to others," Jacob said. The four of them watched as James mounted his horse and urged it back toward the path.

"We must tell everyone right away," Jacob said. "I'll go tell Mother. Jakey, you go tell John's family. Joseph, you let Barbara's family know."

The boys took off running to their siblings' homes while Jacob walked to the garden with Christian at his side. If only he didn't have to tell Lizzie, who was already so frightened of the Indians that she begged to move to a different settlement.

Lizzie was hoeing beans and Franey was pulling weeds in the tomatoes as Jacob and his young son neared the garden. Lizzie straightened up and gripped the handle of her hoe so tightly that her knuckles were white. Her face was drawn.

Jacob cleared his throat. "Sad news. The Indians attacked two neighbors this afternoon."

"I knew that's what you were going to say. I saw the soldier come and go. Who did they hit this time?"

"The Reichards and the Meyers."

"No! I was just at the Meyers' house three days ago. I could've . . ." Her voice trailed off.

They stood trembling in silence. What had prompted the Indians to kill their Amish neighbors? Didn't they know the Amish were peaceful people? Maybe they weren't as safe as Jacob had thought. Franey clung to his arm as he gave Lizzie more details about the afternoon's attack.

"I sent Joseph to let Barbara know, and Jakey went to John's house. You better go inside. I'll do the chores now. We'll make plans at the supper table for what to do next."

"Papa, can I help you with the chores?" Franey asked. Jacob nodded. There wasn't much she could do to help, but she might feel safer near to Jacob. Lizzie moved toward the house as Jacob headed for the barn, scanning the woods for any sign of movement.

❖

It was a lovely day to pick lettuce in the garden. Barbara bent over the row, fingering the fragile leaves as she nudged them from the soil. Her husband, Cristy, liked it in his salad.

"Barbara! Barbara!"

A young man raced down the path onto Barbara's little farm. Her brother Joseph pumped his arms as he ran, holding his straw hat in his left hand.

"I'm over here in the garden." Barbara stepped over a row of radishes and moved toward the path. "Is something wrong?"

"Indians killed a couple of our neighbors this afternoon—the Reichards and Meyers. Took some of their children captive." Joseph's tenor voice was pitched a little higher than usual.

"No! It can't be! I just saw the Meyer family last Sunday." Barbara ran over to her three little girls who were playing by the raspberry patch. Scooping up two-year-old Annie and one-year-old Mary in her arms, she shouted at her four-year-old, who was stuffing raspberries into her mouth. "Magdalena, come with us, we're going into the house."

There were no Indians in sight at that moment, but who knew where they might be hiding? "Joseph, go tell Cristy to come in right away. You can tell us the rest of the story inside."

A few minutes later Barbara's husband came into the house with Joseph. "Bad news," Cristy said, as he hung his hat on a wooden peg. "This is the closest that Indians have come since the beginning of the war."

Joseph fidgeted with his hat. "The soldier from the fort says we'll need to be on the lookout. The Indians could strike again at any time."

Barbara shivered as he shared more about the attack on the neighbors. "We better go to the fort to sleep tonight," she said. "I don't want the Indians stealing my children in the middle of the night."

Cristy's face tightened into a frown. "We better talk to your *Dat* before we do that. After he begged for an exemption from helping at the fort, he won't feel right about seeking their protection."

Barbara cleared her throat. "Joseph, what do you think? Won't *Dat* listen to reason? The proprietors built the fort for our safety. Why shouldn't we use it?"

Joseph's face was sober. "No. You know how steadfast *Dat* is in his convictions. Even when the Indians were burning farms in the next township last year, *Dat* kept us all at home, even though *Mam* wanted to leave. He made John's family stay too, 'cause they live on our property."

Was Barbara the only one who could stand up to their father? "We should go regardless of what *Dat* thinks," she said. "Joseph, tell *Mam* we're coming over right after supper. We can all go to the fort together—*Dat*'s family, John's family, and ours."

Joseph picked up his hat and headed out the door. "I'll tell *Dat* you're coming."

Cristy lifted his hat off the peg. "I don't want to get cross-wise with your *Dat*," he said. "I'll be in for supper as soon as I finish that patch of grass I was working on. It's right close to the house, so I'll keep my eyes open for any signs of trouble."

"Cristy, first go tell your mother what happened this afternoon. I'm going to stay inside with the children. And I'm going to lock the door, so you'll need to knock when you want to come in."

"Okay, I'll tell *Mam*, but I can tell you now that she won't go to the fort with us."

Cristy was probably right. Mother Stutzman was a tough woman. Who could help but admire her? She had lost her husband at sea on the trip to America and then cleared the land for farming with only her young boys to help. She farmed her own place for years until Cristy's older brother Hans built a house next door to hers. Barbara and Cristy named their firstborn, Magdalena, after her.

Barbara served the first asparagus of the season for supper, along with fresh lettuce and boiled potatoes. She waited for Cristy to comment about the good meal, but he was quieter than usual. Barbara could have predicted it, since he didn't want to hear her arguing with her father about going to the fort.

Magdalena broke the silence. "*Daati*, what will we do if the Indians come to our house tonight?"

Cristy didn't bother to look up, so Barbara answered. "We're going to go to Grandpa's house after supper, and then to the fort, where it's safe."

Magdalena's face wrinkled into a frown. "What's a fort, Mama?"

"It's a place where people go inside for shelter during a war. There are walls to keep the enemy outside." How could she make it clear that they were in danger without frightening Magdalena too much?

Annie and Mary jabbered at each other, free from the cares that gnawed at their mother's stomach. How could Barbara ever forgive herself if they were scalped or stolen away like the Meyers' children had been that day? With that kind of warning, it gave them a chance to make sure that never happened.

Cristy and Barbara had talked more than once about moving to an Amish settlement some miles south, farther from Indian territory, but Mother Stutzman would hear none of it. They felt obligated to stay close to her, since they were living on land she'd given them to farm. Besides, Cristy wanted to farm alongside his brother Hans, who tilled the piece of Mother Stutzman's land on the other side of Wolf Creek.

And then there was Barbara's father, who wasn't about to move even though her mother would gladly have put more distance between them and Indian territory. So if they were to have moved away, Barbara couldn't have lived next door to her mother. She depended on Lizzie to help bring up her children, along with other helpful things like canning and butchering. So there they were, stuck in the Northkill, right in harm's way.

After supper, Barbara packed for the short trip to the fort by gathering a couple of blankets and a few things to eat. Then she and Cristy walked toward her parents' house, each with supplies in one arm and a child in the other. Magdalena walked ahead of them, carrying a bag over her shoulder. It should have been a pleasant walk, especially because a gentle breeze sifted through the warm summer air. But Barbara was shivering inside. She glanced here and there into the woods as they walked, looking for any trace of Indians.

Barbara's parents lived about a mile north of Barbara's place. Not far to the west of them stood the house of Barbara's younger brother, John. He had moved there a few years earlier after taking over part of their father's farm. John had married Bishop Jake Hertzler's daughter Katie in the fall of 1752, just a few weeks before Barbara married Cristy Stutzman. Within a year, they had both given their folks a grandchild. John and Katie's baby, Jacob, had been born just a month before Magdalena came along. Now both families had given the folks several more grandchildren.

"Looks like John is taking down more trees," Cristy said as they approached the property. "More land for farming, I suppose."

"That's because he has *Dat* and the boys to help him," Barbara said. "If I'd have been born a boy instead of a girl, I'd be living on that land."

A wry grin spread over Cristy's face. "With someone else besides me."

Barbara rolled her eyes. "I guess you're right."

"Besides, we have all the land I can handle. Why would we want that piece?"

Cristy was right. It was just that Barbara's *Dat* seemed to favor his boys. He wanted to make sure that all four of them got land to farm. Even after the aggrieved Indians started attacking settlers in 1755, Jacob added a 112-acre plot to the two plots he'd been farming.

"Makes it handy," Barbara's father had said after the deal came through, "'cause that plot ties the other two together." It was an oddly shaped property, stretching nearly a mile from north to south, and about half that far from east to west. Its fifteen angled borders zigzagged through trees and clearings from one stone marker or stake to another, 253 acres in all.

"Your *Dat* told me he chose this place because of the walnut trees," Cristy said. "Now John is taking them down."

"*Dat* doesn't like walnut trees, because you can't grow things under them. He only liked them 'cause they show there's good limestone soil for farming."

"He sure likes fruit trees."

"That's true. I helped him plant them when I was barely older than Magdalena. Hoed and watered them too. That's how I came to learn about different kinds of fruit trees." Soon after she and Cristy had gotten married, she helped him get started with their own little orchard.

"Don't get your hopes up that *Dat* will go to the fort tonight," Cristy said as they approached her parents' house.

Barbara sighed. Cristy knew her father all too well. Even before *Dat* planted trees, he had planted himself on this plot in the Northkill. Now he was as rooted as a stump. He tilled the soil as part of his service to God the Creator. He felt led by God to come to that plot, and he wasn't planning to leave unless God directed him away. Farming was for him like midwifery was for Barbara's mother. The fertile soil dropped its fruit into his waiting hands.

Barbara's *Dat* swung open the door of their two-story log house and stood at the threshold, waiting for them to arrive. His broad forehead reflected the evening sun, partly shaded by his brown hair cut at mid-temple in the manner of a monk. Strands of silver-gray glistened in his thick hair, permanently flattened in a band against the back of his skull by a hat that was too tight.

"Joseph said you'd be coming," he said in his deep baritone voice. "We were expecting you."

Barbara's heart quickened. "We brought things along so we could stay in the fort tonight, *Dat*. You can take us in your wagon. There'll be room for John's family too, I would think."

Her father cleared his throat and then spoke softly. "Well, well. It's not often that you and *Mam* find the same way to disagree with me. Here, let me take Annie." He reached out for his granddaughter, who flung herself into his arms, and then he turned to go inside.

"Huh!" Barbara said under her breath. Her *Dat* seemed to have his mind made up. She and her mother would have to work together if they were going to change it.

-2-

About the time that Barbara's family got settled in, John's family showed up at the door. On any other day, the older children would have run outside to play. But after the news about the neighbors, they knew it was not safe. So the grown-ups sat on chairs and the children sat on the floor. Franey sat sideways on Jacob's lap and laid her head on his shoulder.

"I can hardly believe what happened today," Jacob said. "I had thought surely the Indians would leave our people alone. They attacked the Meyers in broad daylight."

"Why are the Indians so mad at us?" Christian asked.

"It's as much the French as it is the Indians," Jacob said. "Both of them are fighting for land. The French got the natives on their side because the British are moving into Indian territory. The Delawares used to live on the land here at—"

Barbara's dark brown eyes were filled with worry. "Let's not talk about the war. I want to know what we can do to keep our children safe tonight."

"Me too," John said, with a furrowed brow.

"I'm still trying to make sense of it," Jacob said. "Things have definitely changed. When we settled here in 1738, it didn't matter that we lived just three miles from Indian territory. We didn't worry when the Indians wandered onto our land, or into our house."

Lizzie cringed and shook her head. "It didn't always work out that way. Remember that time a couple of years ago when—"

Every time they talked about Indians, Lizzie brought up the time she had an unpleasant run-in with the natives after she refused them food. "That's true," Jacob said, "but most times it did. But now that they've killed other Amish people, we'll have to be on the lookout. From now on, none of us should work in the fields by ourselves."

"*Dat*, let's go to the fort right now. I'm sure most of our neighbors will be there. They can tell us what they're planning to do." Barbara's face was pinched and drawn as she spoke.

Lizzie hugged little Mary to her chest. "I'd hate to have something happen to the children."

Jacob felt a tug-of-war inside of him about going to the fort. His wife, children, and grandchildren all pulled on one end of the rope. They deserved his best efforts to keep them out of harm's way. His father and the principles of nonresistance pulled hard on the other. How often had he heard the bishop say that we must put our trust in God, not in the provincial army? Jacob Hertzler was not just the bishop of the fellowship but a personal friend to whom Jacob Hochstetler looked for spiritual guidance. He wasn't anything like the Catholic bishop back in Alsace, who dressed in fine clothes and lorded it over the parish. The bishop, whose daughter had married Jacob's son, was a gentle man people usually called by his first name, Jake.

But Jake could be stern when needed, and he enforced the rules of the church with some strictness. What would he say when he found out that Jacob had helped take his grandchildren to the fort? On the other hand, what would he say if the Indians attacked John's family in their home when they could have sought safety?

Jacob released a breath. "Maybe we can go. This once."

Lizzie's face softened in relief. "Thank you," she said. "I'll feel much safer tonight."

Barbara echoed her mother. "Thanks, *Dat*."

"Jakey, you go hitch the horse," Jacob said. "We can all go in the wagon."

Lizzie stood up and began to gather provisions as John and Katie headed back to their home for a few things to carry with them.

"Let's do one more thing," Jacob told Lizzie when she was ready to leave. "Get some dried apples and peaches to put on the table. If the Indians come, food might help them feel better about us."

Lizzie furrowed her brow. "We're running short of apples. It will be another few weeks before the new crop comes in."

"Yes, but it might help. Christian, go to the cellar and get some apples and peaches."

Christian scurried off and was back with the dried fruit in a few minutes. Lizzie laid them out on the table.

"Jakey and I have the guns," Joseph said, as they headed out the door. He had his own ideas about the proper uses for a gun.

Jacob frowned. "If you must."

Jakey drove the horse and wagon up to the house. Sixteen people crowded in and headed for the fort—Lizzie and Jacob with the four children who lived at home with them; their son John and his wife, Katie, along with their three children; and their daughter Barbara with her husband, Cristy, and their three children. It was risky to ride together, but Jacob was the only one with a wagon. Two miles was a long way to walk with so many small children.

"*Dat*," Barbara said. "What's so wrong about using a gun to stop the Indians from coming onto our property?"

"The Bible teaches us not to kill. You know that." Jacob kept his eyes trained on the rutted road ahead.

"But last week you shot a fox that was stealing your chickens. Why wouldn't you shoot at an Indian who wants to scalp or steal our children?"

"That's different. Foxes weren't created in the image of God. Indians were."

Franey nestled on the wagon seat next to her father. "What's a scalp?"

"It's when the savages cut a piece of skin off the top of your head with your hair still on it," Joseph said. "It's a war trophy."

Jacob gave him a stern look. "Joseph, we don't call the Indians savages. Besides, white people take scalps for bounty too. Last year, when Governor Morris declared war on the Delaware people, he offered 130 dollars for the scalp of an Indian man or boy above twelve years of age, and fifty dollars for the scalp of an Indian woman. That sounds savage to me."

Franey's brown eyes grew as round as walnuts. "If they try to scalp me, I'm going to run and hide in my tree."

Joseph raised his rifle with one hand. "If Indians try to scalp us, I'm going to shoot them."

"Me too," Jakey said.

"That's not the way you were taught," Jacob said. "If that's the way you boys are going to use our guns, I'll have to put them away."

Joseph glowered at his father. "But we can't just let the Indians come and—"

"Joseph!" Jacob looked hard into his son's eyes until he dropped his gaze.

Holding onto two of the little ones in the wagon, Lizzie changed the subject. "I wonder who's going to take in little Frederick Meyer."

Jacob nodded slowly. "Maybe we should. The Stehleys took in little John Glick when the Indians killed his family last year, even though he wasn't Amish." The jostling of the wagon through the ruts threatened to jar his teeth loose.

"Maybe someone who wants children will volunteer," Lizzie said. "A younger couple like Ulrich and Anna Yoder. Of course, now that Ulrich passed away suddenly, it would be too much for Anna."

Franey clung tightly to her father's hand as they drove through a section of woods where undergrowth crowded the path. Perhaps she realized, like Jacob did, that it was a likely place for an ambush. She'd heard too many stories of Indian attacks over the past two years.

In 1756, when the Indians started attacking the settlers along the frontier, dozens of families had gone to one of the forts along the Blue Mountains during raids like the one against the Hochstetlers' neighbors. Many of them left ripe crops in the fields and moved away for fear of the Indians. Although the Indians burned the settlers' crops and buildings in surrounding counties, the Amish people had been spared. Jacob stayed on the farm all summer and filled their small barn to the rafters with the fruit of the land. He gave glory to God for teaching the principles of nonresistance. He knew that's what had saved them.

The family was getting close to the fort now. It looked familiar to Jacob, as he had once stopped by to watch it being built. It was a small wooden structure, perhaps thirty-two feet square. The few soldiers who were stationed there told Jacob that they scoured the area for Indians every day.

"Who goes there?" the watchman called.

Jacob walked toward the fort with his lantern held high. "The Hochstetler family," he shouted. "There's a wagon full of us. Got room?"

"Yes, come on in. You'll need your own provisions."

"We brought food with us. We'll only stay for the night."

A soldier swung open the gate and let them in. Lanterns glowed like small dots around the open space. As the family walked toward an open spot, Jacob recognized the faces of a few neighbors in the light of his lantern's glow. "Hello, George. Pete."

Lizzie and the other women spread out some blankets, and the family found places to lie down.

"Can I sleep beside you, *Daati*?" said Franey. "I'm scared."

"*Jah*, but you don't need to be scared. The Indians won't come into the fort. We'll be safe here."

"What if they come to our house when we're not there?"

"Let's not worry about that."

Despite his own advice, Jacob slept fitfully that night. Had he done the right thing by coming to the fort? How could he justify such forthright dependence on guns for defense?

The next morning, people gathered in little clusters to talk about the latest attack. Jacob overheard someone say there'd be no funeral for the Reichards or the Meyers. Because of the danger of further attacks, both families were buried in haste without public notice.

In his conversations that morning, Jacob chanced to meet Thomas, a man he'd seen not long before at the blacksmith shop. There Thomas had bragged that he'd killed two Indians and was ready to kill more.

Now Thomas swaggered up to Jacob. "Did you hear about the killin' over at Allemangel in Albany Township?"

Jacob shook his head. "Recently?"

"Last week. Them bloodthirsty savages broke into Adam Trump's cabin. They killed him and took his wife and son as captives. They say the lad was about nineteen years old. The mother fled from them as they was tak'n her away. An Indian threw his tomahawk at her and she was badly wounded in the neck, but she kept runnin'. She might live."

Jakey and Joseph leaned in to listen. "What did they do to Adam?" Joseph asked.

"They tomahawked and scalped the man and left a knife in his body. The knife was tied to a pole about four feet long. Left a halbert too."

Joseph looked puzzled. "A halbert?"

"It's like a pike or a battle ax," Thomas said. "And I suppose you all know about Pete Geisinger being killed and scalped right here near the fort last Wednesday. And Thursday, Balser Smith's daughter, 'bout fifteen years old, was captured by two Indians."

James, the soldier who'd notified Jacob's family of the attack that day, came up to add his view. "I say the only good Indian is a dead Indian. 'Specially now that they've sided up with the French. Good thing the gov'nor put a price on their heads. Lets 'em know they ain't welcome 'round here."

He looked closely at Jacob. "I told you about the Reichards and the Meyers this afternoon. Aren't they some of your people?"

"*Jah*, the Meyers belong to our fellowship."

"I thought so. He wore whiskers like yours." He motioned toward Jacob's untrimmed beard. "Ain't that part of your religion?"

"*Jah*, we men wear beards. These boys haven't joined the church yet."

James glanced at Jacob's three sons with their clean-shaven faces. His chin jutted out. "They said Mr. Meyer didn't have a gun with him. You Amish folk don't use guns, do you?"

"Sure, we have guns," Joseph said. "My *Dat* is the best shot in the neighborhood."

"But not against our fellow men," Jacob said.

James glared at him. "Not even against them murderin' savages?" His voice trembled.

"No," Jacob replied. "The Bible tells us not to kill."

"But what will you do when the Indians come to your house? I suppose you're gonna let them tomahawk and scalp your family while you stand back and do nothing?" Thomas's eyes blazed.

Jacob took a deep breath. His throat was dry. How could he possibly explain nonresistance to a soldier while standing in a fort under his protection? "We believe the Lord watches over us," he finally said. "He won't allow anything to happen to us that's not part of his will."

"But we'z in a war. The French and Indians are hell-bent on driving us off this land," James said. "If you won't defend your land, it puts an extra burden on the rest of us. Why are you here now, depending on the rest of us to keep you safe?"

Jacob winced. He fell silent for a moment, then said softly, "But I won't shoot my gun at the Indians or the French. Jesus told us to love our enemies."

Thomas shook his head. "You're making it easy for the red man to rob our land. This ain't a good place for people like you to live, 'specially these days."

Jacob pulled a large handkerchief out of his pocket and wiped the sweat from his forehead. He could see his wife, Lizzie, watching them from a few feet away.

"Well?" Thomas said.

Jacob took a deep breath. "Our people came to this settlement from the old country because William Penn invited us. He knew we were nonresistant people. He told us he'd made peace treaties with the Indians and that they were our brothers. They've never made any trouble for us."

"What do you mean? Them red devils just murdered one of your 'nonresistant' families." Thomas spat out the word. "We cain't build this country with people like you."

Jacob shrugged and turned away from him. What good would it do to argue?

"Come Lizzie, let's go home." Jacob gathered the family and rode away from the fort. It was mostly silent except for the hollow sound of the wagon bouncing over the ruts in the path. Thomas's words ran through Jacob's mind as he steered the wagon toward home. "We cain't build this country with people like you," the soldier had said. *We cain't build this country with people like you.*

-3-

When they got home from the fort, Jacob and his sons headed for the fields. They worked until Lizzie called them for dinner. They sat together at the table, but no one talked much. Jacob needed some time to think, and that worked best when it was quiet.

The clock struck one o'clock. "Time for us to get back to the field," Jacob said, rising from the table. "The sun will be down before we know it."

Jakey pushed back his chair, followed by Joseph and Christian. Jakey's willingness helped set the mood for his two younger brothers, who weren't as enthusiastic about work on the farm. At nineteen, Jakey was thinking about marriage; he knew that hard work might earn him a plot on the farm.

"Thanks for the good dinner," Jacob told Lizzie. He took his straw hat from the peg on the wall and headed out the door.

The boys picked up their hats and followed Jacob into the bright sunlight. The almanac said they had just passed the summer solstice. Why not take advantage of every ray of light on the longest days of the year?

Jacob watered Blitz, their only horse, and guided him back to the field where the plow had rested over the noon hour. Now that they were done harvesting the barley, Jacob could plow a small patch nearby. He hitched the gelding to the implement, threw the loop of the reins over his shoulders, and guided the shank into the rich limestone soil. Blitz leaned into the work.

Jakey made his way back to the hay field with a sickle in his hands. It worked better than the scythe around the fences. The hay was tall and thick, so it took more than the usual effort to swing the blade through it. As Jacob expected, Jakey brought it to him before long. "*Dat*, I wish you'd sharpen this sickle." Jacob stopped his work for a few minutes to grind a sharp edge on the tool.

Joseph hefted the handles of the wooden wheelbarrow and headed for the field where Jacob was plowing. Along with Christian, he was gathering up stones in the field and carrying them to the stone pile. The stones would be used to lay the foundation of the next building on the farm, just as they were under the house.

Jacob made a turn at the end of the field and sank the plow back into the moist soil. "Giddup, Blitz." The horse put down his head to pull. Turning up the rich limestone soil settled Jacob's nerves a bit. Something about the patterns in the soil, the slight wind, and the smell of earth calmed him. He was making such good progress that he entertained the happy prospect of finishing the field before dark. There was a cloud bank forming to the west. Wouldn't it be nice to get the work done before it rained?

Jacob didn't get done plowing that day, even though he worked for a couple of hours after supper. He didn't dare push Blitz too hard, lest he'd go lame. When he finally sat down to rest that evening, he was tired to the bone.

Franey was playing on the floor with a couple of wooden toys. "*Daati*, make me a little sheep."

"No, Franey, I'm too tired right now."

"You did it after supper before." She must have remembered the carving Jacob did the previous winter when it was blowing snow. He had made a number of little wooden figures for her—a dog, a cat, a horse, and a cow. Ever since he was a boy, Jacob knew he had the knack for whittling.

"That was in the wintertime when I wasn't plowing all day."

"Please, *Daati*, please. You make such nice things. None of my friends has animals like these. Can't you just make one more?"

"No, Franey. Don't ask again."

Franey sighed and focused her shining brown eyes on her father, trying to melt his resolve without words. Jacob was about to give in when he noticed that Joseph was watching them. Twice that week he'd complained, "You treat Franey different than us boys. It's not fair."

"Girls' feelings get hurt more easily than boys."

"So they get whatever they want?"

"Of course not."

Joseph shook his head. "Franey does."

"Son, don't argue with me." It was no use trying to convince Joseph about Franey or anything else. He was becoming deaf to Jacob's instruction.

The next morning, Jacob woke up with the sunrise as usual and then dressed and went outside to do the chores. He drank in the fragrance of the mown meadow hay, cut several days earlier. It was time to gather it into the barn. He glanced around at the woods. The Indians had attacked the neighbors while they were in the hay field. Perhaps he should leave the hay down for another day or two to make sure the Indians were gone.

Either way, the chores had to be done. Jacob tied their Swiss cow, Bessie, to a post, tossed her some fresh hay, and then sat down to milk her. Two cats came running when they heard the milk streaming into the metal pail. They were spoiled, standing on their hind legs and begging for a squirt of milk into their open mouths. Jacob sent them both a solid stream, which landed only partly in their mouths. He chuckled as they licked their paws and faces clean. The cats didn't seem to mind having a bath and breakfast at the same time.

Fritz was waiting too, so Jacob poured a little milk into a dish for him. As soon as he was finished milking, Jacob carried the pail over to the spring house. He covered it with a cloth and set it into the cool water. How gracious it was of God to have given them a fresh spring, about the only way to keep things cool in the summertime.

When he returned to the house, Jacob woke the boys, urging them to get ready for a big day of work. It still hadn't rained, so it was the perfect time to get the hay into the barn.

"What if the Indians come?" Christian said.

"We'll just have to be on the lookout. We can't just let the hay lie in the field."

After a quick breakfast, the menfolk headed for the field. Joseph went ahead, raking the mown hay into windrows. Christian drove the horse and wagon along the rows while Jakey and their father pitched the hay onto the wagon.

They had just finished unloading the third wagonload when Lizzie rang the bell for dinner. They washed up at the spring and then went to the house to sit down at the table with Lizzie and Franey.

Jacob bowed his head, and the others followed suit. They paused in silence, all making their own prayers until Jacob cleared his throat and raised his head.

Lizzie pushed a dish of steaming potatoes toward her husband. He served himself and passed it on to Jakey, who sat next to him. The boys passed it around the table, filling their plates heaping full. "I wonder if we shouldn't keep a rifle with us on the wagon," Joseph said. "It might discourage Indians from coming our direction, or at least slow them down."

"No, we won't be taking a gun with us to the field," Jacob said. "It wouldn't stop an attack anyhow."

Christian swallowed a mouthful of potatoes. "If I see Indians coming while we're working in the field, I'm going to run to the fort as fast as I can."

"That's a good thing to do," Jacob said. "But most of all, we have to trust in God."

"I don't understand why the Indians think they own this land," Joseph said. "We bought it, didn't we?"

Jacob nodded. "The Iroquois sold Pennsylvania some of the land that belonged to the Delawares in these parts. That's why the Delawares resent us white settlers. How would you like to have someone claim the land where you had grown up and called home? That's what the authorities did to our people in Switzerland. But I've always said that if we treat the Indians fairly, they'll leave us alone."

Yes, that's what he had always said, based on what he had heard from Bishop Hertzler and others who read the newspapers. But now that a family from their fellowship had been attacked, he needed more assurance that nonresistance was the right path to follow during the war. He needed more strength to stay on his land. Maybe it was foolish to think that the Indians would treat the Amish differently than they treated the other settlers.

Jacob glanced at the clock. "It's time to go, boys. We've had a whole hour off."

They worked hard all afternoon in the hot sun, with little time to rest. Jacob's father had taught him that idle hands are the devil's tools. If they all kept busy, they'd have less time to worry about the Indians.

The sun hung low in the sky when they came in from the field. They were approaching the front door when Jakey punched Joseph on the shoulder. It looked like sport, but Joseph yelled and jumped on his brother. Soon they were wrestling on the ground, both vying to pin the other to the ground. The two of them rolled around in a grassy patch near the front door, first with Jakey on top, and then with Joseph.

Joseph grunted out loud as he put a lock on his older brother. "Say 'uncle.'"

Jakey shook his head and struggled to get free, to no avail.

"Stop it," Christian said. "You got him down, now let him go."

"That'll teach you to punch me," Joseph said as he released his grip on his brother. The two of them got up and straightened out their tousled hair.

"I'll race you to the springhouse and back," Jakey said.

"Hold it; let me get these shoes off," Joseph said, still panting from the wrestling match. He bent down and untied the leather work shoes that cramped his feet. He had outgrown them a few months ago, but Jacob and Lizzie hadn't yet gotten a new pair stitched up for him. All of their children preferred going without shoes whenever possible, but some of the farm work, like mowing hay, was too dangerous without shoes.

"All right, let's go," Joseph said, heading for the spring-house. Jakey was taller and a bit slighter, so he should have had the running advantage, but Joseph reached the spring-house ahead of him. He brushed his hand against the corner and came rushing back, his long hair streaming behind him. By the time they got back to the house, Joseph was several long strides ahead.

Joseph had a look of triumph in his eyes. Last fall, Jakey would have won both contests. But Joseph was a teenager now and his body showed it. His muscles bulged against his sleeves and black stubble was showing up on his face.

Jacob stepped inside and breathed a sigh. A knot in his right shoulder protested the long hours of tossing hay onto the wagon. He'd leave it to the boys to wrestle and run.

"Maybe I'm not working you boys hard enough," he said. "If you feel like you need something more to do, I could find more work for you." His mouth twitched upward around the edges.

"No, *Dat*," Joseph said. "We're just having a good time."

"I used to do the same thing with my brothers," Jacob said. Winning against one's brothers meant more than just having a good time. Joseph was becoming the strongest and the fastest of the Hochstetler boys. That would shift things in the family.

Later that evening, the children were outside, enjoying the cool evening air. The house was so warm that the boys would have liked to sleep outside under the stars. Not now, not this summer, with threats of Indian attacks. It wasn't safe any longer.

Jacob and Lizzie watched the children from the front door of the house. "Lizzie," Jacob said, "I've been thinking about what happens if the Indians attack our place."

Lizzie's face looked drawn. "I worry about that every day," she said.

"Our cash isn't safe. I'm going to bury it outside. Right now." Jacob wasn't worried about the money in the jar that stood on the fireplace mantle. It was the easiest place to keep money for the occasions when he or Lizzie needed a few coins. If warriors came, they could have that money. But the cache in their bed had to be kept safe. Jacob lifted up the mattress to expose the coins they had been saving for the last several years. The money was wrapped in a piece of linen cloth, hidden even from the children.

Jacob laid out the cloth on the bed and counted out the coins to make sure none was missing. It was enough to help Jakey get started on a plot of his own. Then he wrapped the coins back in the cloth and headed out the door. It would be a good thing to bury them somewhere in the ground. Maybe in the floor of the barn or the distillery.

In the barn, Jacob found a small lidded tin container that the blacksmith had given him. He had been collecting some used nails in it, so he dumped them onto a shelf on the wall. The coins filled the box all the way to the top. The treasure would be safe and dry inside the box, since it had a good seal.

Lizzie joined him in the barn. "Where did you decide to put it?"

"In this little box. I'm going to bury it near a fruit tree." Jacob picked up a spade and headed for the orchard. Lizzie walked beside him.

"Put it where you'd naturally look for it," Lizzie said. Jacob had been thinking the same thing.

They walked to the edge of the apple orchard. Jacob pointed to a spot beside the tree that stood at the corner of the grove closest to the house. "Let's put it right there." That should make it easy to remember, since the orchard was laid out in a rectangle about the shape of the box. The little box would be buried in the corner of the larger box, the orchard.

The full moon shed plenty of light on the ground as Jacob dug the hole. He laid the box in the ground and covered it carefully with dirt, then spread some dead leaves on top.

"One less thing to worry about," Lizzie said with an exhausted sigh.

Jacob stood up and looked around the peaceful farm—at the fields, the barn, the corral, the orchards. He put a hand on the small of Lizzie's back. They definitely could use fewer things to worry about, Jacob thought as he and Lizzie walked back toward the house in the moonlight.

-4-

Rain lashed at the windows and distant lightning skittered in the south. Jacob slept fitfully, worried about what damage the approaching storm might do to the ripening crops. Then . . . *crack!* A bolt of lightning struck the yard. He jumped out of bed and rushed to the window.

"*Daati*, what was that?"

Jacob spun around to find Franey hovering by the doorjamb. She rushed into his open arms. "Lightning struck a limb on the old oak tree."

"What if it hits our house?" Her little body trembled.

Jacob stroked her hair. "The storm will pass quickly."

The rain fell in torrents, hitting the windowpanes with such fury it sounded like hail. The roof rafters creaked in protest to the wind.

"*Daati*, I'm scared. Can I sleep with you?"

Jacob lifted the covers and Franey crawled into the center of the rope bed. Lizzie, snoring loudly, stirred and rolled to her side. Jacob climbed into bed and put his arm under Franey's neck and placed his hand gently on Lizzie's shoulder. A flash of lightning lit the small bedroom. On its heels came booming thunder, followed by the eerie ripping sound of a tree branch. Finally, shattering glass.

Franey pressed tightly against Jacob. "Hold me tight, *Daati*."

"A branch must have fallen and broken a window." He pulled his daughter close. "Go to sleep now, honey. You're safe here."

Franey nestled her head under Jacob's beard and drifted off to sleep. Soon the storm moved off. But Jacob lay awake, listening to the rain as it slowed to a steady patter against the windows. Which of the trees had been hit? How badly were the crops damaged? The wheat was likely to be down, since the heavy wheat heads were nearly ripe. After a while, Jacob gathered Franey in his arms and carried her to her own cot, tucked her under the covers, and came back to the comfort of his own bed. Curling his body around Lizzie's solid form, Jacob willed himself into a fitful sleep.

A few hours later, the sun streamed through the windows, startling him awake. He dressed and hurried outside to survey the damage. A wooden bucket, emptied before he had gone to bed, held over three inches of water.

The oak tree nearest the house had been hit by lightning. As the severed branch fell, it poked through a windowpane in the house. The orchard was littered with broken limbs, but only a few sections of the wheat field were ruined. *Thank God it didn't hail, or we might have lost the whole crop.*

The rain was good for the flax crop. Jacob walked to the clearing near Northkill Creek, which flowed through the western edge of the orchard. The creek flowed faster than usual, swollen by the heavy rains. He drew in a deep lungful of fresh, clean air. There was no place he'd rather farm than in the rich limestone soil of the Tulpehocken Valley in Penn's Woods. If only his father could see what Jacob had carved out of this virgin forest, he would be pleased.

"Work hard, live simply, and pay attention to details." That's what his father had always said. It was the Swiss way. Although his father had farmed in the Alsace region of France, it might as well have been Switzerland. He cultivated his land in the manner of the Swiss, squaring the manure piles in the barnyard and maintaining everything in proper order.

Jacob planned the day's work as he walked back toward the house. The fields would be too soggy to work in, so cleaning up after the storm was the most important thing for that day. At the breakfast table, Christian asked if he could use the ax on the downed limbs.

"You can use it while we're using the bucksaw. Mostly I need your help carrying brush to the burn pile."

Christian frowned. "Joseph and Jakey always get to use those tools."

Lizzie reached over and gave his hair a tussle. "Soon you'll be grown up too. Then you'll wish you were a little boy who didn't have to work so hard."

"It will take some time to cut up the big branch that tore off the oak tree," Jacob said. "We'll split it for firewood."

"Save some kindling for the bake oven," Lizzie said.

"Did you hear that, boys?" Jacob said. "Only put things on the burn pile that can't be used."

By evening, they had cleaned up the branches and stacked the firewood in a neat pile.

"That saw gave me a blister today," Jakey said. He held up his hand to show Lizzie.

"If you'd told me sooner," Jacob said, "I would have asked Joseph to take a turn. But I'm pleased with what we got done today. You boys worked well together."

Lizzie nodded. "Maybe tomorrow we could go over and lend Anna Yoder a hand in her orchard. She stopped by for a visit today and mentioned that the wind took down some of her branches. What do you say, Papa?"

Anna Yoder was a young widow who lived alone next door to Michael Moser's property. At least she had help close by if something desperate happened. Since Anna's husband, Ulrich, had passed, Lizzie had befriended her. Jacob gave Lizzie a quick nod. "It's probably still too wet to work in the field anyhow." And helping someone else would be a good way to keep Lizzie's mind off the Indians.

As soon as the chores were finished the next morning, the family walked to the young widow's home. They carried a few tools, including a saw and an ax. Jacob slowed his pace to walk alongside Lizzie while the children ran ahead.

"*Naw geb auchdt* (Be careful)," Lizzie said to Franey. "We don't always know what's in the woods."

The recent attack had only increased Lizzie's worrisome manner, Jacob observed, but it hadn't dampened her generous

Jacob's Choice

spirit, which he had always admired. Underneath her worries flowed an undercurrent of compassion for those in need. No one cared more deeply for the widowed or poor in the Northkill neighborhood, or worked harder to assist them.

Anna clapped her hands with delight when she heard why they had come to her house on a sunny July morning. She walked outside with them, pointing out the downed limbs in the peach orchard and a pine tree that had blown over.

Jakey and Jacob trimmed trees while the boys carried branches to a pile in the clearing. Lizzie and Annie pulled weeds in the garden. Midmorning, Anna brought out a pitcher of tea she had steeped from spearmint in her garden. "This tea is good for you," she said, handing around mugs.

In the church fellowship, Anna was known as a healer and herbalist. She gave foot massages too, a common healing practice in the church. The boys gulped down the tea and Anna refilled their mugs.

By noon they had trimmed out all of the broken branches on the apple and peach trees and had chopped up the fallen pine. The roots would have to wait until more rain had washed the dirt out of the root ball.

On the way home, Christian tugged on his father's sleeve. "Anna taught me the names of the herbs in her garden."

"Good for you. What are they?"

"Basil, chives, dill, lavender, parsley, peppermint, rosemary, sage, and spearmint. See, I learned them in alphabetical order." He frowned as he counted on his fingers. "I must be forgetting one."

"I think you need another *s*," Lizzie said. "It's something Anna puts in her noodles."

"Oh yes, saffron. That makes ten." Christian held out his ten fingers. "Ten spices."

Lizzie eyed her own hands with a critical look. "I don't know how Anna keeps her hands looking so nice with all that garden work. I wonder if she uses some special herb ointment."

Jacob had noticed the same thing. When he said hello and shook hands with Anna, it had surprised him to feel how soft and uncalloused her hand was. From the way Lizzie was frowning at her hands, it was best not to mention it.

"I'll race you all back to the house," Joseph said. He dashed off and his two brothers bolted after him. Franey lagged behind with Lizzie and Jacob.

"You'd think the boys would be tired after all the work we did this morning," Lizzie marveled. "Joseph is always ready to outrun someone, regardless of how tired he is."

"Someday he'll be as happy as we are to rest," Jacob said. "We got a lot of work done." He looked at Lizzie with admiration as they climbed the rise of the hill toward their home. Her plump cheeks were pink with exertion and her brown eyes shone with the joy of accomplishment. She might not have hands as smooth as Anna's, but no one worked more efficiently. How often in the early days at the Northkill she had labored at his side to clear the land and bring in the crops. A true companion. No one could ever take her place in his heart.

One evening later in the week, Jacob and Lizzie and their family were just finishing supper when Fritz's barking announced the arrival of someone. Mindful of the threat of Indians, Jacob bolted out of his chair to reach the door, expecting the worst. But there was Anna Yoder, holding a peach pie in her hands, still warm from the oven.

"Come in, come in."

Christian crowded close to the young widow as she set the dish on the table. "Can I have some?"

Jacob frowned at him. "Just hold your horses, son. *Mam* will decide whether we eat it now or later."

Lizzie smiled at Christian. "We just finished eating, but I suppose it won't hurt for us each to have a little taste. It looks like a mighty good pie." She spooned slabs into dishes for Christian to pass around. Jacob leaned back in his rocking chair to enjoy the dessert. As soon as the children finished, Jacob sent the boys to the barn to feed the animals.

Anna helped Lizzie clear the dishes from the table. "I could give you and Jacob a foot massage while I'm here," she said. "You worked so hard for me this week that you deserve one."

Lizzie shrugged and looked at Jacob. "I don't think I want one. How about you, Papa?"

"Might as well. Can't hurt." Jacob had never tried a foot massage, but some of the people in the community practically swore by it. Hadn't Jake Hertzler once testified to the healing power of a foot treatment? The Amish settlement at Iris Creek had a healer who recommended it. How could one know without trying it?

Anna pulled a bottle of ointment from her bag and sat on a chair in front of Jacob's rocker. She spread a dab of ointment onto her hands and then lifted Jacob's right foot onto her lap. She rolled his foot in her hands and began to massage the sole with her thumbs.

"I'm going to push pretty hard in a couple of places," Anna said. "I might even use my knuckles to dig in a bit. If it hurts too much, you just let me know."

Anna had just the right touch—firm but gentle. After some time on his right foot, she switched to the left one. "The nerves in your feet are connected to other places in your body, so I can treat your organs right here on your foot. Can you feel it tingling in different parts of your body?"

"I felt something in my back a minute ago," Jacob said. "Now I feel it in the back of my neck."

A few minutes later, Anna stood up. "Are you feeling better now?"

"Oh yes, really good. Except for this little kink in my neck. I felt it after I chopped wood the other day."

Anna tilted her head toward Jacob. "When you were cutting up my orchard wood?"

"I'm not sure. But it's nothing to worry about."

Anna moved to the back of Jacob's chair. "Let me see if I can massage it out."

Jacob looked to Lizzie. She shrugged, as if to say, Why not?

Anna massaged the muscles on Jacob's neck and shoulders, pressing on a spot in his upper back until he winced. "Is this sore?"

"*Jah!*" It came out as a squeak. Jacob cleared his throat and tried again. "It's very sore."

"Your muscles are tied up in a knot right there. Just relax, I can loosen them up for you." She rubbed firmly but gently, rolling her thumbs on the spot.

About that time, Lizzie moved to the front of Jacob's chair, arms crossed tightly against her chest. "Anna, I think that's enough. It will be dark soon and you have a ways to go home. I imagine you're all worn out." She handed the empty pie plate to Anna. "You can take the dish back home with you."

Jacob tipped his neck from side to side. The kink was gone, but he was bewildered by Lizzie's shortness. "Yes, Anna, thank you for stopping by. You're welcome anytime, especially if you bring peach pie."

Later that night, Jacob crawled into bed with Lizzie, who was facing the opposite wall. He pulled up the covers. "It sure was nice of Anna to come tonight."

Silence.

"I said it was nice of Anna to come tonight."

Again, only silence.

"Is something wrong?"

"It wasn't necessary for her to spend so much time rubbing your back," Lizzie said.

"What was wrong with that? She gives massages to people all the time."

"You were enjoying it more than you should have." Lizzie's voice broke.

Jacob frowned. Was it true? They lay in silence for a long moment as he rehearsed the scene. He wasn't sure, but the fact that it had hurt Lizzie left a queasy feeling in his stomach. Sometimes Lizzie was so gruff that he forgot she could be hurt so easily.

"I'm not sure that I know what you mean," he said slowly. "But Lizzie, I'm sorry that it hurt you. I've loved you since the day I met you, back in Alsace. You are all I ever want or need." He put his hand on Lizzie's back and moved it lightly back and forth. "Lizzie, I'm so sorry."

Lizzie sniffed and turned toward him in the darkness. She said nothing but put a hand on his cheek. It was still there when he fell asleep.

-5-

Barbara and her children wove their way around several fallen branches on the way to her parents' house after the big storm. Magdalena made a game of it, ripping off leaves and tearing them into shreds as Barbara carried the two younger children in her arms.

Jacob and the boys were working near the barn, getting ready to go into the field. Barbara set Annie down and then rapped on the door of the house.

She opened the door and stepped inside. "I'm here," Barbara called, guiding Annie and Magdalena into the kitchen and setting Mary on the floor. Her shoulders ached from the weight of carrying her two children, along with the baby in her belly.

"Oh, look at her," Lizzie said after she saw Mary take a step for the first time. "She is really growing up!" She bent down and planted a kiss on Mary's cheek and then gave Magdalena and Annie a little squeeze. "How are you feeling, Barbara? You look a little worn-out."

"Pretty tired." Barbara rubbed her tummy, which was turning into a bump. "I have three more months before the baby comes. I hope I can hold out that long. I get so tired carrying the children."

Lizzie nodded. "You need a little wagon you can pull. Maybe *Dat* can make you one."

She turned to Barbara's little sister. "Franey, tell Christian I want him to start the fire in the bake oven."

"Okay, *Mam*." She stepped outside and skipped her way to the barn. In a few minutes, Christian burst into the house. He went to the fireplace, pulled a brand from the flames, and carefully carried it out the door.

Barbara sat down heavily and watched her mother take flour from a clay vessel and mix it with the other ingredients.

Her mother had baked bread every week for as long as she could remember. The morning sun shone through the window and warmed her face and arms. "I hope you don't mind if I sit a little. I'm tired from standing on my feet. And I need to feed Mary." Barbara picked up the little girl, who was clawing at her breast.

"Not at all. And Franey can help take care of the children."

Barbara helped Mary latch on and then settled back into the chair as the baby nursed. "I noticed that the sweet corn is almost knee-high."

"We're lucky the storm didn't hurt it much."

"Ours looks good too. But I saw the big tree in front of the house got torn up. And you have a broken window. How'd that happen?"

A branch fell against it." Lizzie sighed. "Anna Yoder had some branches down too. We helped her clean up, and then she brought us a peach pie."

"Was it good?"

"*Jah*, very good, but I wasn't so happy that she gave *Dat* a foot massage."

"I guess not! I don't even let Cristy rub my feet. It tickles too much."

Lizzie stopped kneading her dough for a moment "*Dat* enjoyed it. Too much, if you ask me."

"Oh?"

"Anna's a little too free with her hands when she does foot rubs. I know she's a healer, but there are limits."

Barbara leaned forward. Anna had always seemed a little different. "She's not afraid to get close to the men. They don't seem to mind."

Her mother nodded. "Now that Ulrich has passed away, Anna uses healing to get men to do things for her. She just mentioned to *Dat* that she needs to have her chimney cleaned, and he said he'd do it for her soon. Imagine that! I've been after him to get ours cleaned for the last year, and it's still not done."

"Well, I declare!" Barbara had never seen *Dat* flirt with a woman. And he always kept his promises. "Maybe he'll get into the mood and do both chimneys before long."

"But why did he promise to do hers so soon?"

Just then Franey burst into the house. "Christian and I got the fire going. Barbara, can the children come out to play?"

"If you're very careful, as soon as I'm done nursing Mary."

Lizzie wrinkled her brow and bent down to speak to Franey. "Don't go into the woods," she said.

Barbara nodded. "If you see any signs of Indians, come inside right away. We have to be extra careful these days."

"I will." With that, Franey took Mary from Barbara's arms into hers and led the other two children outside. Barbara grinned as she watched her sister carry Mary the way she had carried her little brother, Jakey, when she was Franey's age.

Lizzie watched them go and then turned to her daughter. "I worry a lot these days, not just about the children, but about all of us. It doesn't bother *Dat* in the same way. He just goes about his work and doesn't say much about it."

"Hasn't *Dat* always been that way? He gets along with everybody. How many times have I heard him say he never met a stranger, just friends he's not met?"

"*Jah*, it's one of the things that drew me to him. My father was just the opposite. Everybody had to earn his trust, and it didn't come cheap."

"I like that about *Dat*," Barbara said. "He even tries to get along with the Indians. At least he did before this war."

Lizzie rolled up a piece of dough and plopped it into a bread pan. "I don't think he realizes how much the war has changed things. The Indians used to be friendly, but now they're out for revenge. It's not safe here anymore. I feel it in my bones." She picked up several bread pans with lumps of rising dough in them and nodded at Barbara to help with the rest.

Barbara picked up the pans and followed her mother toward the outdoor bake oven. She glanced at the children, who were playing with no sign of care.

Lizzie yanked on the cast iron door of the oven, making the iron hinges creak in protest. She stirred the fire with a long stick, so that the embers blazed up into the unburned wood. And then she put the pans on the grid inside and slammed shut the door. She wrung her hands in her apron. "I keep thinking about what we would do if the Indians came here. *Dat* says we should offer them something to eat, since Indians are always hungry."

"Sounds like something *Dat* would say."

"If a war party comes to the house, they'll be looking for scalps, not just food."

Barbara's chest tightened. "What can you do but run away and hide? *Dat*'s certainly not going to shoot at them."

"Of course not," Lizzie said. "Now if he were like your Grandpa Detweiler, who fought in the Swiss army, things would be different. He'd shoot to kill. It's a matter of honor for him."

Barbara's lips parted and she opened her eyes wide. "How come you never told me that before?"

"*Dat* didn't want you children to know, especially the boys. It's one of the reasons we decided to come to America—to get away from my parents' influence. They belonged to the state church and didn't believe in nonresistance. *Dat* wanted to bring up the boys in the way of his father, who taught us that Jesus would never ask us to kill our fellow man."

Barbara sat down on a large stump near the oven. "What did your parents think when you left for America?"

"They were opposed to it. Truth is, I didn't want to come either. To leave my parents for good . . ." Her voice drizzled to a stop.

"That must have been hard. I couldn't bear to leave you and *Dat*, knowing I'd never see you again."

Lizzie took a deep breath. "That was the hardest thing I ever did. I was scared of the Indians right from the start. They remind me of the gypsies back in the old country."

"Did *Dat* make you come to America?" Barbara might have been pressing too hard, but she couldn't pass up the chance to ask.

"No, *Dat* never forced me to do anything, but he is very persuasive. He's always had high ideals and a wheelbarrow full of ambition." Lizzie twisted her covering string around her index finger. "He convinced me that God was calling us to come here, where we would have religious freedom. That's something our people never had in Alsace. Or before that, in Switzerland."

Barbara leaned forward on the stump. "I remember *Dat* telling me that everyone had to belong to the state church back there, or suffer the consequences." It wasn't just her father, however. Barbara had often sat up to listen when Bishop Hertzler told stories of persecution in the old country.

"That's right. My folks were members of the reformed church." Lizzie turned from the bake oven to head for the garden. "We might as well pull a few weeds while we wait for the bread to finish baking."

Barbara's thoughts whirled as she followed Lizzie to the garden. Had she ever been told that her grandparents were part of the state church? Or that her grandpa had been in the Swiss army? She couldn't imagine her father doing such a thing.

Lizzie said nothing until they had finished pulling all of the weeds in two long rows of cabbages. "We'd better check the bread," she said as she straightened up and rubbed her shoulders before heading back to the oven. She opened the oven door and checked the loaves. "Almost done," she said, breathing deeply of the warm fragrance.

And then she picked up the conversation she had dropped a little while earlier. "There were two reasons your *Dat* wanted to come to America. The most important thing, he said, was to bring up our children to follow God in the nonresistant way. The other reason was to get land of our own. He'd always wanted to farm his own land. That was hard to do in Alsace."

"You and *Dat* have certainly taught us nonresistance. And I love this farm."

Lizzie cleared her throat. "I'm glad to be married to a man with such deep convictions." She paused to blink back tears. "And I accept that it's God's will for us to stay on this farm."

"Your farm is one of the nicest in this area. And no one keeps a garden looking better than yours."

Lizzie looked down. "Maybe, but it's not good to be proud."

Barbara and Lizzie carried the newly baked loaves into the house. The children eagerly clustered around them, hoping for a snack. As usual, Lizzie cut a fresh loaf and slathered a few slices with butter and jam. For Barbara, the only thing better than fresh bread would have been to keep the conversation going about the way her *Mam* and *Dat* made sense of life. But her mother was finished talking about it, and the crumbs of conversation they'd had would have to suffice for now.

An hour later, as Barbara walked back to her house with her girls, her feet were tired and her head hurt. *If only I could be more like* Mam. *She always trusts* Dat *to make the right decision.* Or as carefree as Magdalena, who hopped and skipped along the path. The knot in Barbara's stomach told her that a different kind of storm was heading for the Northkill, likely much worse than the kind that had knocked branches into their path.

-6-

The Sunday after Anna came to their house, Jacob and Lizzie went to a church service at Hans Zimmerman's home. For years they had been meeting every other Sunday for worship, but because of the dangers of the war, they now met only about once a month. Bishop Jake Hertzler carried the spiritual duties for several different fellowships, which met in homes on different Sundays.

It was less than two miles to the Zimmerman home, and Jacob's family walked. Lizzie and Jacob walked alongside each other, with Franey trailing close behind. She insisted on carrying the *Ausbund*, the worship hymnbook. The boys all ran ahead, darting here and there off of the path and engaging in horseplay.

The Zimmermans' cabin was small, so it was somewhat crowded inside. A few of the older ones sat on chairs or beds, but many people sat on the floor. The memory of the Meyer family hovered in the air, yet people spoke about it only in whispers. It was the first Sunday their fellowship had met since the Meyer family was killed, and the mood was somber.

As Jacob often did, he started off the service by calling out a hymn number. "Number 15," he said, and then sang the words: "*Ich weiss wer Gottes Wort bekennt, das der sich viel musz leiden* (I know that whoever confesses God's Word must endure much suffering)." The congregation joined in, singing the beloved tune from memory.

And then, following long custom, they followed with the second hymn: "*O Gott Vater, wir loben Dich* (Our Father God, Thy Name We Praise)." They sang it more slowly than usual that morning. A few glances at the Zimmermans' mantle clock let Jacob know they had stretched the four stanzas to about twenty minutes. The news of the recent attacks cast a melancholy shadow on the song. Yet the last lines of the hymn spoke to the angst in Jacob's heart: "We praise you in the assembly, / Giving thanks to your name, / And beseech you from the depths of our hearts, / That you would be with us at this hour, / Through Jesus Christ. Amen." It was a comforting word from God. The assurance of God's love and protection in times of trouble was just what Jacob needed.

After the singing, Deacon Stephen Zug rose to read the Scripture from Psalm 91. Jacob had often heard these words before, but several phrases seized him anew as he pondered the Indian threat: "I will say of the Lord, He is my refuge and my fortress: my God; in him I will trust. . . . Thou shalt not be afraid for the terror by night; nor for the arrow that flieth by day."

Jacob glanced at Lizzie, sitting on the women's side of the room. Nothing terrified her more than the threat of attacks during the night. But now, she was distracted by their granddaughter Annie, who was playing on her lap. Jacob wondered whether she was still a little angry with him for enjoying Anna's massage. How often he had failed her as a husband, needing forgiveness and the comfort of God's promises. Was she hearing these words of assurance too? "For he shall give his angels charge over thee, to keep thee in all thy ways. They shall bear thee up in their hands, lest thou dash thy foot against a stone."

If ever Jacob's family needed the protection of angels over their lives and property, it was now. Jacob glanced around at the members of his family as the preacher expounded on the text. Franey was on the floor entertaining one of the babies. Joseph seemed absorbed by the new muscles he had made this spring, flexing them by squeezing his fists. Each time Jacob glanced at Jakey, he had his eye on Linda, the young woman Jacob expected to call a daughter-in-law before the first snow fell that autumn. That was Lizzie's intuition, and Jacob couldn't disagree.

Christian was thumbing through the *Ausbund*, probably practicing his reading. It was a plenty good thing to read if he couldn't pay attention to the meditation. Many of the hymns were written as testimonies by Anabaptist martyrs in the sixteenth century.

After the meditation was over and the congregation had prayed, Bishop Jake rose to speak. He was tall and thin, his dark brown hair showing only a few gray strands.

"These are trying times," he said. "We must rely on God for strength."

Jacob glanced at Lizzie, who nodded.

"During this time of war, we must remember the words of Jesus," he said, reciting familiar words from the gospel of Matthew:

> Ye have heard that it hath been said, An eye for an eye, and a tooth for a tooth: But I say unto you, That ye resist not evil: but whosoever shall smite thee on thy right cheek, turn to him the other also. And if any man will sue thee at the law, and take away thy coat, let him have thy cloak also. . . . Ye have heard that it hath been said, Thou shalt love thy neighbour, and hate thine enemy. But I say unto you, Love your enemies, bless them that curse you, do good to them that hate you, and pray for them which despitefully use you, and persecute you; That ye may be the children of your Father which is in heaven: for he maketh his sun to rise on the evil and on the good, and sendeth rain on the just and on the unjust.

Jacob glanced at Jakey and Joseph as the preacher repeated these familiar verses. Were they listening? The words of Scripture carried far more weight than any feeble explanation Jacob could offer of the church's conscientious objection to war.

Bishop Jake leaned into the implications of Jesus' words, declaring that allegiance to God meant that Christians must love their enemies, even the Indians who had attacked the neighborhood. "The red man is worthy of God's salvation."

Jake went on. "The Moravians are peace-loving people who have taken the gospel to several Indian nations. Some

Indians have become our brothers and sisters in Christ. If all of the settlers had treated the Indians as the Quakers and the Moravians did, they wouldn't be fighting this war."

Christian paused in his reading to look up at the preacher. Joseph too seemed to be listening. Perhaps it would strengthen their resolve to follow the way of Jesus. If only they would follow the counsel of the bishop rather than that of the soldiers at the fort.

"Let us consider the words of the apostle Paul in the book of Romans," Jake continued. As before, he drew the words from memory: "Recompense to no man evil for evil. Provide things honest in the sight of all men. If it be possible, as much as lieth in you, live peaceably with all men. Dearly beloved, avenge not yourselves, but rather give place unto wrath: for it is written, Vengeance is mine; I will repay, saith the Lord. Therefore if thine enemy hunger, feed him; if he thirst, give him drink: for in so doing thou shalt heap coals of fire on his head. Be not overcome of evil, but overcome evil with good."

Who could help but admire Jake for his ability to quote the Scriptures? Perhaps like Jacob's father, he rose early each day to memorize those passages before going to his work on the farm. Planted in his heart, the Scriptures took root for the benefit of the congregation.

Jake moved to conclude his sermon, "When I was in the old country, I heard stories of faith from a book called the *Martyrs Mirror*. It tells of Christians who were faithful in the face of threats like the ones we face today. I pray that we may be as faithful as they, even unto death."

Jacob's heart began to beat faster. That was the message he had come to hear. Whether or not anyone else in his family was paying attention to the preacher's words, they gripped him to the core. He didn't hear much of the final hymn or the benediction. The same was true during the simple meal afterwards, the usual bean soup and bread. He carried on bits of conversation, but his thoughts were occupied by the call of Jesus to love one's enemies. What would he do if French or Indian warriors came onto his farm? He didn't know. But Jesus' words held him fast.

The floor clock struck six o'clock on Sunday afternoon when Jake and Catharine Hertzler arrived at the Hochstetler home. Jacob welcomed Jake and Catharine into their house and bid them have seats.

After supper, Jake and Jacob went outside while the women chatted around the table. The sun was just touching the horizon as they strode toward the barn.

"I like these long days," Jake said. "The weather is perfect for making hay."

Jacob nodded in agreement. "*Jah*, we've gotten all of our hay mown, and were hoping to rake tomorrow. Ever since the Meyer family was killed while mowing grass, Lizzie is frightened of us even going to the meadow. We went to the fort that evening."

"Katie told me."

Jacob reached over the top of the fence to stroke Blitz's soft nose. "Lizzie never did want to come to America. Too dangerous."

"I see."

"So far, God has been good to us and we've all been safe. We have much more to show for our efforts here in America than if we had stayed in Alsace."

Jake reached out his hand to stroke the horse's mane. "We must be thankful for the freedom to work and worship as we please."

Jacob paused. "Did I ever tell you about the time when Indians left a mark on our door? That's one thing that makes Lizzie so afraid."

"I hadn't heard about that."

"A group of Indians came here one day, asking for food. Lizzie had just finished baking several loaves of bread. She was planning to take it over to the Stutzmans, where Barbara was sick in bed. The house smelled good and the Indians helped themselves to the loaves."

Jake nodded. "*Jah*, that's happened to us too."

"After they ate all the bread, they made motions to eat a peach pie, which she had baked for a neighbor. You know that Lizzie is very generous, but that was too much for her. She felt they were taking it away from our neighbor. When they insisted, she got upset and shooed them out the door. As they left, a man with a scar on his face took a charcoal stick from the bake oven and made a big mark on the door."

Jake scratched his head. "What do you think they meant by that?"

"Lizzie worries that they have marked our house for revenge."

Jake pursed his lips. "I hope that's not true."

"I tell her not to worry—that God will take care of us," Jacob said, fingering a splinter of wood on the top of the fence. "I wish there was a way to let the Indians know she meant no harm. But with the war—"

"*Jah*, that is most unfortunate."

"She's worried that the Indians will attack us or try to take our grandchildren. If the Indians come, what shall we do?"

"Jesus calls us to turn the other cheek, to love our enemies." Jake plucked a long stem of grass in the fence row and began to chew on it.

"That is what I tell my family, but my sons don't see it that way," Jacob said. "The soldiers at the fort convinced Joseph that it's part of our godly duty to defend our homes and this province."

"Perhaps he doesn't realize that the province has given our people a special exemption."

"I have never explained that to him. And I don't know the details."

The bishop shifted his weight to the other foot, apparently pleased for the chance to recount this part of their people's story. "In 1742, Emmanuel Zimmerman wrote a letter to the proprietors on behalf of our church, requesting that our people could follow the laws of God, rather than the laws of man. He made some specific requests."

"How did they respond?"

"The deputy governor sent a letter to the judicial officers asking them to release our peace sects from civil duties and taxes, and to be able to affirm rather than swear oaths."

Jacob took off his hat and scratched his head. "I must remind Joseph of that. He has not yet been baptized, so I pray he will come to see God's way. I told him about the time my father decided to join the Swiss Brethren, and his decision to forsake war."

"*Das iss gut, Jakob.* Hold tight to your convictions. God will give you strength to endure, just as he did our forefathers."

A lump rose in Jacob's throat. "In your sermon, you mentioned the *Martyrs Mirror*. Do you have a copy?"

"No, but I once saw it in Dutch. I wish I had the new German edition."

"Do you know where to get it?"

"I suppose Christopher Sauer of Philadelphia would have it for sale. Maybe I'll get a copy sometime."

"I think it would be good for my family to have a copy," Jacob said. "We need teaching about nonresistance. Please remember us in your prayers."

"I will." Jake's voice was gentle and low.

With that, the men turned and headed back toward the house.

That evening after their guests had gone, Jacob gathered the family for their daily evening devotions. After a short reading of Scripture, they knelt for the reading of a prayer from *Die ernsthafte Christenpflicht*, an Anabaptist prayer book.

After that, Jacob dismissed the children to dress for bed and then picked up his copy of *The Wandering Soul*, a devotional book given to him by his father. For years he had leafed through those pages, reading in snippets, learning about the history of God's salvation in the world. But that evening his eyes fixed on the final saying of the wandering soul, bidding farewell to Simon Cleophas, his aged guide who was about to die: "Your history shall be to me a comment upon the shadow of things, and lead me at once to the reality of the matter; and divert me from earthly things, and direct my attention to heavenly things—imperishable things, for which I shall always be under lasting obligations to you. Therefore, I wish that you may shine with Jesus Christ, in whom you trust; and although we part according to the flesh, that we may meet in eternal glory."

Jacob lingered at the table, pondering these words after Lizzie made her way upstairs to bed. Unlike Simon Cleophas, he surely wasn't ready for the life hereafter. The perishable things of life—his farm and the land on which it lay, his children, his wife—held him tightly. But what could he do to get ready? Maybe if he could get a copy of the *Martyrs Mirror*. But that would take some effort.

-7-

I'm planning to go to Philadelphia tomorrow," Jacob told the family at breakfast. "The wheat and the hay are in, so I can spare a few days."

Christian's face lit up. "Can I go along?"

Jacob shook his head. "You went along last time. I'll take *Mam* and Franey with me this time, since we have things to buy for them. And I need to replace the pane that was broken in the storm."

Franey bounced from the table and gave him a hug. "Oh *Daati*, I'm so excited."

Joseph mumbled something to Christian about Franey getting to do everything, so Jacob gave him a stern look. "There's work for you boys to do here at home. John needs help taking down a couple of walnut trees. Maybe you'll get to go next year."

After everyone scattered to the out-of-doors, Lizzie confronted Jacob. "*Jakob*, I can't believe you're going to Philadelphia in the middle of the summer. There are so many things to do in the field and the garden."

"I have some things that I need. Like a glass for the window."

"That could wait until the weather gets colder. And why would we leave here when there might be Indians—"

"The closer we get to Philadelphia, the safer we'll be. And the boys will be as safe by themselves as if I were here."

"Oh *Jakob*, how can you say that? Christian is too young to stay here with the others." Lizzie's eyes blazed.

"All right, let's take him along. Joseph and Jakey can take care of themselves. John will keep them busy on the farm."

"I still can't see why you're so determined to go."

Jacob sighed. Surely she wouldn't understand if he told her. "I want to buy a *Martyrs Mirror*."

"You're going to Philadelphia to buy a book?! You don't even enjoy reading." Lizzie shook her head. "I never thought I'd see the day."

"I talked to the bishop about it," Jacob said. "He thinks it's a good idea. It will help the boys to understand nonresistance."

Lizzie sighed. "If you must."

The next morning, Jacob hitched Blitz to the wagon and waited for Lizzie, Christian, and Franey to make their way toward the barn. After hoisting Franey over the side of the wagon, he assisted Lizzie as she strained to make the big step into the wagon box. Christian vaulted over the side. Jacob clucked "Giddup" to the horse and they were off.

"Why the jugs?" Lizzie asked when she spotted the two vessels under the seat.

"Whiskey for barter."

"That much?"

"We'll see."

The family arrived in Philadelphia shortly after noon on the second day. It was market day, and the streets were full of people. Franey hadn't been in the city for several years, so Jacob drove past the waterfront. Two large ships were docked at the harbor, and men scurried up and down the gangplanks carrying goods.

"This is where we landed when we came from the old country," Lizzie said, placing a finger against the base of her nose at the reek of dead fish.

"I want to see," Franey said as she hopped out of the wagon and marched to the water's edge. She stood with the toes of her bare feet hanging over the edge of the wooden dock. Christian stood alongside, scanning the busy waterfront.

Jacob handed the reins to Lizzie and joined the children on the dock. "These ships bring things to buy and people from other parts of the world. You'll see some of those things when we get to the market." He had come to the waterfront partly for the children's sake, but mostly to relive the moment when he arrived there in 1738. The pungent smells of the dock whisked him back to the time when the *Charming Nancy* bumped against the dock and the captain threw down the gangplank. Before he had stepped ashore on the continent, Jacob had been required to make his mark pledging loyalty to the king of England. And then he had applied for a land warrant at the Penns' proprietary office. Just standing at the dock reminded him of God's leading, and of his provision for them in the new land.

Franey broke into his reverie. "*Daati*, why did you come to Pennsylvania?"

"God made a way for us. Back home in Alsace where your grandpas live, they hated the beliefs of our people. This is a free country, so we can worship as we want. And we can farm our own land."

"Was the farmland free?" Christian said.

"We bought it from the Penns, who bought it from the Indians."

"Who did the Indians buy it from?"

"God gave it to them."

"Oh." Christian wrinkled his face the way he always did when he was thinking. "Did God want them to sell it?"

Jacob paused, not sure how to answer. "Children," he said, "you ask such hard questions."

They made their way from the dock to a hitching post not far from the market. From there, they strolled down the street next to two English couples dressed in their finery. Both of the English women wore jackets and skirts that were cut and sewed in one piece, opening in the front. Underneath they wore handsomely sewn petticoats trimmed with ribbon. Their outer skirts were made of blue cotton reaching down to their silver-buckled shoes. On top they wore fine white aprons.

"Don't stare," Jacob whispered to Franey, whose eyes were fixed on the women's jewelry. He tried to look without gawking, taking in the stark contrast between high society dress

and his family's humble attire. Fine strings of beads hung
on the women's necks, complementing embroidered neck-
erchiefs of pure silk and fine stones that hung on their ears.
The fine white bonnets on their heads were embroidered with
flowers and trimmed with lace and streamers. Their beauti-
fully embroidered gloves were made of velvet trimmed with
silver lace.

The finery was beautiful to look at, but could those women
work? Jacob had been told that the English men couldn't ask
their wives to do any household work except as they chose.
Their skin was milky white because they seldom exposed
themselves to the sun.

Lizzie was wearing a simple linen dress that only came
down to the knee, with heavy woolen stockings that she had
knitted for herself. Her cotton cap had no frills. But what a
helpmeet she was. Without her staunch labor in the farm and
garden, they could never have settled at the Northkill.

Jacob saw Lizzie glance at the two gentlemen who accompanied their wives. *Perhaps Lizzie is thinking the same thing
about me.* His knee-length woolen trousers and linen shirt
looked pitiful next to their fine cotton shirts and long, stiff
linen trousers reaching down to their shoes. Both wore light
jackets made of dimity. And both of them wore long wigs, the
custom among the English. Their beaver hats shaded them
from the hot July sun, a glaring contrast to Jacob's frayed
straw hat.

They soon arrived at the open market and wandered
among the crowded stalls. Hundreds of items were for sale.
First they purchased a bushel of salt, and Jacob carried it
to the wagon. That would help them get ready for butchering
in the late fall. Then Jacob found a glazier to cut a piece of
glass the size he needed, along with some pitch to hold it in.

Lizzie bought all of the items on her list, including several
tins of sugar and one of coffee. She hesitated about the coffee—what a luxury—but Jacob told her she need not worry
about the expense. It would be pleasant to have coffee on

special days. Besides, he liked to watch her bargain at the market. Those finely dressed English women almost certainly couldn't have gotten the bargains that Lizzie did that day.

From Market Street the family made their way toward Germantown. For some time, Jacob had hoped to visit Christopher Sauer's print shop, and now the moment had come. He tied Blitz to the hitching post, and the four of them went inside.

As they stepped through the door, the scent of fresh paper and ink rose to their nostrils. Reams of paper were stacked on several tables. A man looked up from the printing press.

Jacob doffed his hat. "I'd like to talk to Christopher Sauer."

"He's a busy man," the man at the press replied curtly.

"I have important questions." Was it too presumptuous to think that a man who practiced more than a dozen trades would have time for him?

"You can sit down," the man at the press said, pointing toward a backless bench nearby.

"I'll stand," Jacob said, but motioned for Lizzie to sit down. She said her feet were tired from walking at the market.

Franey held Jacob's hand as they watched the man operate the printing press. Christian stood close by. The operator turned a long wooden handle fastened to the heavy threaded screw that brought the press down on the paper. He went about his work with efficiency surely born of practice, squeezing the press onto the paper and then quickly raising it again.

Jacob leaned over the press. "I hear you printed a German Bible."

"Almost fifteen years ago. The first German Bible in America."

"Do you carry the *Martyrs Mirror* in German?"

"The Sabbatarians print it at the Ephrata *Gemeinschaft*. We keep a few copies here." The man grunted as he tugged at the long press handle.

"And the almanac?"

"On that stack over there." The press operator pointed to the wall behind him.

"What are you printing now?"

"*The High German Pennsylvania Historian,* our newspaper."

"It's a good paper." Although Jacob couldn't afford the subscription, Jake Hertzler sometimes shared his copy.

Mr. Sauer, the owner, soon arrived. He took off his hat and hung it on a hook beside the front door.

"I see you're printing the paper," Jacob said in German as Mr. Sauer headed toward him.

"Best German news in America," he said. "Much better than Ben Franklin's *Philadelphische Zeitung,* which didn't last long. What did Franklin expect, calling Pennsylvania Dutch 'boors' and 'dumb' and trying to start up a charity school mostly to teach Germans to read English? He hates us pacifists too."

"How can I help you?" Sauer appeared to be every bit as opinionated as Jacob had been told.

Jacob pointed to the shelf nearby. "I want to buy your latest almanac."

"Where are you from?" Sauer asked as he reached for a copy from the stack.

"Upper Bern Township in Berks County. I came from Alsace."

"You had Indian attacks a fortnight ago."

"*Jah,* they killed several members of our fellowship."

"That new string of forts along the frontier just stirs things up. Doesn't do much to stop the Indians." Sauer thumbed through a stack of papers as he spoke.

"Our family is worried that the Indians could come back at any time." Jacob hoped that Franey was watching the press operator rather than listening to the conversation. Christian was sitting beside Lizzie, absorbed by a copy of the almanac.

"There's always that chance. But you can't go wrong by treating the Indians fairly and trusting in the Lord."

Jacob glanced at Franey and Christian and then at Lizzie before he spoke. None of them seemed to pay attention to his conversation. "Some think it a sin not to defend one's family."

"We must not quarrel about our worldly goods, much less fight over them. If you can't escape the Indians, it is better to be killed than to kill another. Neither God nor the king has asked us to take up the sword."

"How can we live with peace in the middle of this war?"

"Don't take sides. Support the Quakers. Avoid politics, courts, and lawyers. Don't let the English take away our language, our customs, or our faith."

"The man here said you have the new German edition of the *Martyrs Mirror*?"

"In the other room. Only the embossed leather edition. It's more expensive."

"Fine. Might I barter some whiskey from my still? It's the easiest way to market my barley in Philadelphia."

"I'm sure we can work something out."

What a relief. It was the only way that Lizzie would approve the purchase. They had agreed that the cash they had buried in the orchard would help get Jakey started on a farm. As soon as he got married, he would want to farm his own place.

A few minutes later, they left with the *Martyrs Mirror* and the *Farmer's Almanac* in hand. In Jacob's mind, those two things alone made the trip worthwhile.

Franey and Christian leafed through the pages of the *Martyrs Mirror* as they bounced along in the wagon. "*Daati*," Franey said after a while, "this book has lots of pictures."

"*Jah*, Jake told me about them."

"Why did they burn people?" Christian looked up from his reading with a distraught look on his face.

Jacob sighed. "The authorities thought they were doing God's will as Christians. They killed our people because we practiced believers baptism and would not worship in the state church." By the time they got home, Franey had told

Jacob and Lizzie about every one of the pictures in the new book. Jacob was eager to see them for himself.

-8-

It was a quiet Sunday afternoon. After the noon meal, Jacob sat back in his chair and rested his eyes.

Franey tugged at his sleeve. "*Daati*, I want to sit on your lap."

"You're too big for that," Jacob said, with his eyes closed.

"No, *Daati*, I want to play with your beard." Franey crawled onto his lap and sat crossways, her right arm draped around his neck. She ran her fingers gently through the long strands of his beard, taking out a few tangles. Jacob was about to fall asleep when he felt something tickling his face. Franey giggled as he reached up to brush away the end of a long braid of her brown hair she had swished against his nose.

Jacob smiled and shook his head but kept his eyes closed. He drifted off to sleep soon afterward. When he awoke, the hands on the floor clock showed three o'clock. A good, long nap.

Jacob patted his face and tugged on his beard to chase away the dullness that daytime sleep sometimes leaves in its wake. First he felt something strange in his beard, and then he heard a little giggle from other side of the room.

"How do you like it, *Daati*?"

Jacob pinched his lips at first, and then laughed out loud at her nerve. Having just learned to braid her own hair, she had turned to practice on his beard. He felt four braids from one side of his chin to the other, each the length of his forefinger.

Lizzie was dozing in a nearby chair. She woke up to hear them laughing. "I wonder what you'll think of next," she said to Franey.

Franey ran out-of-doors, shouting for her brothers. "Come see what I did to *Daati*."

Christian popped in almost right away, followed a few minutes later by Jakey and Joseph. Franey was on stage now,

milking the four braids like the teats of a cow while imitat-
ing all of the barnyard sounds she could muster. And then
the braids turned to brushes in her hand, painting her father's
neck, nose, and cheeks. The boys laughed loud and hard, and
Lizzie smiled in mock exasperation. The lightheartedness was
a grace, a rare moment in the tenseness of those days.

"You'll have to take out those braids now," Jacob said after
things had quieted down. The boys went back outside and
Lizzie announced that she was going to visit Barbara for a
little while.

When Franey had finished taking out all the braids, Jacob
got up and went to the shelf that held the few books they
owned. Pulling the new copy of the *Martyrs Mirror* off the
shelf, Jacob laid the heavy volume on the table where the light
from the window would make it easier to read. He stroked the
embossed leather cover, glad that he had paid a little extra to
get such a good cover. He could pass it on to John when the
time came.

Leafing through the pages, Jacob paused to look at each of
several dozen woodcut illustrations. There were pictures of
the crucifixion of Jesus Christ and the execution of many of
his early followers. Eventually Jacob's eyes fell upon the picture of Dirk Willems, an Anabaptist martyr from Holland. He
recalled the mention of Willems from the time he was a child.
Because Willems had been rebaptized, he was sought by the
town council. When their deputy came to arrest him, Willems
fled, with the thief-catcher in hot pursuit. It was a cold morning, and Willems made his way across the ice on a pond with
some peril. The thief-catcher, however, broke through the ice.
Struggling to keep his head above the icy water, he called for
help. Willems turned back from his attempt at escape, held
out his hand to the man, and helped him get to safety. In return for Willems's good deed, the grateful thief-catcher wanted to let him go. But when the burgomaster sternly reminded
him of his duty, he seized Willems and put him in jail.

Jacob's eye drifted down the page to the copy of the town record by which Willems was sentenced to death. It said that Willems, "without torture and iron bonds," had confessed that he "permitted several persons to be rebaptized in his aforesaid house; all of which is contrary to our holy Christian faith; and to the decrees of his royal majesty, and ought not to be tolerated, but severely punished." The council then declared that Willems "shall be executed with fire, until death ensues" and "all his property confiscated, for the benefit of his royal majesty."

There was a strong wind blowing on the day Willems was executed, so the fire was driven away from his upper body, leaving him to suffer much longer than would otherwise have been the case. Witnesses testified that he exclaimed over seventy times: "Oh my Lord, my God." The bailiff was so moved by Willems's torment that he turned his back to the scene and told the executioner to dispatch the man with a quick death.

Jacob swallowed hard as he read the story. Similar things had happened to his own people in their beloved Switzerland. The town councils imprisoned them and took their property, so that Jacob's father's family fled the country with nothing except the things they could carry on their backs.

Jacob was haunted by the author's challenge: "There is no person who will not suffer for man's sake; why then should we hesitate or fear to suffer in the cause of God, who will recompense us with the purest love, and with joy and everlasting glory?"

Was he willing to suffer for the sake of God, even if it cost his life? What about his family? It seemed that he was standing on the brink of a precipice, and God was calling him to step over the edge in faith. The invitation weighed heavily on his chest, making it hard to breathe.

Several weeks went by with no further news of Indian attacks. But Jacob's mind was not at rest. One evening after supper he helped Lizzie pick peas in the garden, and then the children helped to shell them. When they were finished, everyone else went inside, and Jacob stood alone near the barn.

It was very quiet, and Jacob listened to the sounds of the barnyard—the hog snorting and snuffling in the dirt, the dog panting, the horse nibbling at some hay. He stood there in the clearing, the moonlight bathing his face. There was one more matter to get settled before he was fully prepared to face the future, and there was no better time than now.

Jacob knelt down on some wisps of hay left strewn by the side of the barn.

"*Herr Gott*," he prayed. "This farm belongs to you. My family belongs to you. And if people come to take them from me, I will not take up arms against them. I will be faithful to you as my Savior and Lord. You alone are my defense."

When Jacob stood up, the weight on his chest was gone. He breathed deeply of the warm night air. The fragrance of fresh hay mixed with the scent of freshly plowed earth. Gazing at the moon, Jacob felt a strange confidence and peace spreading over him. No matter what the future held, he was certain that he had made the right choice.

It was early September when Barbara helped her mother, Lizzie, pick sweet corn in her garden. They had done this for years—Lizzie planted loads of corn, and Barbara helped her pick and husk it in exchange for corn for her family. The two women made their way through the long rows, yanking off the succulent ears and tossing them into the basket.

Barbara glanced at her little sister, who was playing with her children near the edge of the woods. "Franey, please don't play so close to the woods. Bring the little ones over near the barn." Although the Indian threat seemed to have eased, Barbara couldn't relax when her children played so close to a place where warriors could slip in and be gone with her offspring in a matter of moments.

Franey led the girls closer to the barn. Barbara breathed more easily.

"I noticed that *Dat* is humming again," Lizzie said. Was she commenting on Barbara's fears?

"He's hummed for as long as I can remember. And talked to himself."

Lizzie straightened up to wipe her forehead. "No, he stopped humming for a while after our neighbors got killed by the Indians."

"Really? I suppose he was too worried to hum. That's like me."

"Maybe, but there's more. He says he got something straightened out in his mind. He's more confident to walk the path of Jesus and practice nonresistance."

Barbara stepped through the row of corn that separated them. "What? *Dat* has never been unsure about nonresistance."

Lizzie nodded. "He's always been steadfast about it. He's just more confident now of God's will, God's leading."

"How did that come about?"

"For one thing, he read some stories in the *Martyrs Mirror*. And he talked to Jake Hertzler."

"I don't think the boys feel the same way."

"No, especially not Joseph. He pushes *Dat* pretty hard."

"I don't blame him. He wants to keep our family safe."

"So does *Dat*. But he believes that if we show love to our enemies, God will help us be at peace with each other." Lizzie turned back to her row of corn.

Barbara was so taken by the conversation that she slowed her corn picking. "Cristy says the Indians don't care what we say or do. They want revenge on the white man for taking their land."

Lizzie turned to face Barbara. "It still makes a difference how we treat the Indians. *Dat* is planning what he'll do if the Indians come back here again."

"I'm praying that never happens." By this time Barbara had come to the end of the row and dumped the basket of ears onto a sheet lying on the ground. Flies swarmed over the milky whiteness where the ears were exposed.

Christian came running from the other end of the garden.

"Hey, *Mam*, can we have corn on the cob for supper?"

"If you husk it," Lizzie said.

She grinned as Christian's face fell.

It was the moment Barbara was looking for. "The Bible says whoever doesn't work doesn't eat." Barbara must have heard *Mam* say that a thousand times as a child. Now she could say it to her younger brother.

"Franey should help," Christian said. "All she does is play with the children."

"That's work," Barbara said. "If she didn't take care of the babies, I wouldn't be able to pick corn. Now sit down and start husking."

Lizzie stretched her back and arms. "Christian, if you start the fire in the bake oven, we'll have some roasting ears. And then you can help with the husking of the rest."

Christian dashed off. When it came to starting a fire, Lizzie never had to ask him twice.

The two women finished picking the corn and then took some of the unhusked ears to the bake oven. While those ears were roasting, they husked the rest. Christian carried the husks to the hogs. Barbara and Lizzie laughed as they heard them squeal, visualizing their jostling each other for their share of the goodness.

"*Mam*, did you say that *Dat* has a plan for dealing with the Indians if they return?" Barbara said.

"Yes. He says he's going to give them fruit from the orchard. Whenever we leave the house, he puts fruit on the table in case they show up."

"That's good, I guess."

"The Bible says, 'If your enemy is hungry, feed him. If he is thirsty, give him something to drink.'"

"I don't see how that's going to work."

Barbara grimaced when she saw the pained expression on her mother's face. *Why must I always say the first thing on my mind?* Barbara chided herself. She was glad that her father wanted to be faithful to God, but offering food to warriors hungry for revenge seemed naïve to her. What would be the cost of giving that trust to someone who didn't deserve it?

-9-

September 1757

It was Jacob's favorite time of the year—late summer when the days were getting cooler and the fruit in the orchard was ripening. During the second week in September, his whole family spent long days in the orchard, picking bushels of apples, peaches, and pears.

They usually packed the best apples in straw for the winter, where they shared space in the root cellar alongside other vegetables. They made the lesser apples into apple butter or pressed them for cider to be stored in two large wooden casks in the cellar. By this time, one of the casks was full.

The family pared and cut the apples into half-moons and then dried them in the sun. When Lizzie was ready to use them, she would soak them in spring water to plump and then use them as fillings for pies and tarts.

Lizzie dumped the apples she had just picked into a basket. "It's been awhile since we've had the neighbors over," she said. "It's so much more enjoyable to *schnitz* apples at a social."

"*Jah*," said Jakey. "Let's have a social." It was a good excuse to be with Linda, his sweetheart.

"I want to play games," Franey said.

"I suppose it's safe," Jacob said. There had been no reports of Indians in the neighborhood since the end of June. Many hands make work light, so they often invited the neighbors to help and to bring their own apples with them. Lizzie made plans for a *Schnitzing* to be held on Tuesday evening, the 20th.

Jacob's grown children arrived first that evening—Barbara with her family, John with his. Soon after that the Hertzlers arrived, followed by young people from other families—the Albrights, Mosers, Kurtzes, Graybills, the Detweilers, and a few others, both young and old.

Lizzie sent Jakey and Joseph to lug tubs of fresh water from the spring. A few older girls dumped apples into the cool water to rinse them off.

Several of the children gathered around the tubs in the dimming light, watching the apples bob in the water. "Watch me," Christian said as he tried to capture one of the larger apples with his teeth. Capturing an apple without the use of his hands turned out to be more difficult than he had imagined. Just as he was about to lift out an apple with his teeth, one of the older boys pushed his head under water and then stepped back as though innocent. Christian jerked his head up and shook the water off of his long hair, spraying a bevy of young girls nearby.

"Stop it," they said, their giggles betraying their enjoyment.

"I want to try it," another boy said. As soon as he got a hold of an apple, someone dunked his head as well. He came up snorting and waved his head wildly, swishing the water on the same group of girls.

Anna Yoder and Catharine Hertzler laughed aloud as they watched the boys' antics from where they were working. Standing at a temporary table made of several planks Jacob had laid on a pair of sawhorses, they used butcher knives to cut the apples into thin slices and tossed them onto a clean cloth. Barbara and others cut out the bruised or wormy sections with paring knives and threw them into a large bowl. Christian and Franey hovered nearby with switches made from small branches, chasing a few pesky flies away from the fruit.

Off to the side, Joseph and other teenage boys wrestled and chased each other in the gathering darkness.

"Let's race," Joseph said. "You have to touch the barn and come back past this line." He picked up a stick and drew a line in the dirt.

Jakey and four other boys joined Joseph at the line. Christian volunteered to start them off. "One, two, three, go!"

In a few moments, Joseph was out in front of the pack. Fritz barked and ran alongside, his tail bouncing. Joseph touched the barn first and headed back. He laughed as he crossed the line with his head thrown back. Jakey was three yards behind him.

Joseph grinned widely and stepped over to the tub with the bobbing apples. He pulled an apple from the tub and ate it with a few big bites. And then he put up the challenge again. "Anyone want to race?"

Jakey shook his head. A few others looked on but didn't move.

"Come on, let's race one more time," Joseph said.

"They say we need to get to work with the apples," Jakey said.

Joseph shrugged his shoulders and said, "Okay then. Just forget it." He winked at one of the young girls about his age. "They know I'm too fast."

Barbara pointed in the direction of the orchard. "Joseph, *Mam* thinks there's still one basket of apples left. Can you get it please? We need a strong man to carry it for us."

Joseph sidled up close to a young woman. "Want to help me find that basket?"

She hesitated and then invited a friend to accompany them. "Sure," she said. "We'll walk over there with you."

When the three of them arrived back where Barbara was standing, Joseph lifted the basket high above his head and then set it down in front of her.

"Thank you. Just put it here on the table," she said. Was that a twinkle in her eye? She clearly enjoyed her younger brother's attempts at romance.

Soon the apples were all cut up. "We can't have a *Schnitzing* without a little singing," Jacob said. "How about a song for Peter Graybill?"

Peter Graybill was one of the oldest men in the community. He had been born in Switzerland and often reminisced about the beauty of the homeland his folks were forced to abandon. Jacob started the song in the Swiss language.

Farewell ye Alps, ye fair and pleasant hill,
My native village in the quiet dell.
Your faithful fields another now will till.
My father's house no more I'll see at will.
May God be with you now, as I must bid farewell.

Lizzie stood close to Jacob, her mellow voice blending nicely with his. As the group finished the first verse, one of the young men began to yodel in the manner of the Swiss. His Adam's apple bobbed up and down as he ranged the scale from baritone to falsetto soprano. Jacob tapped his feet in rhythm with the tune. The group went back and forth from the yodeling to the other verses in the song. Peter swayed to the rhythm with the biggest smile of anyone.

With all the apples sliced and ready to dry, the neighbors loaded their apples onto their wagons or made their way home by foot. The boys helped Jacob clean up the tables. They worked in the dim light cast by the fire they had lit to stave off the coolness of the evening.

"Look at the Little Dipper tonight," Christian said, pointing to the familiar sign in the sky. "It's pouring apple cider into the Big Dipper."

Jacob gazed at the two constellations with his son. "Maybe it's a sign that we'll have all the apple cider we need."

Although the whole family was tired, Jacob shepherded them into the house for the evening ritual of prayer. It only seemed right to end each day with the familiar words of gratitude and petition from *Die ernsthafte Christenpflicht*. He read the first part of the daily evening prayer, and then after the family had prayed the Lord's Prayer together, he read the familiar closing: "O holy father, all of us together commit ourselves into your hands. Protect us as a body, O God. Surround us with your holy angels, and lead us with your holy and good Spirit through this vale of tears, until our blessed end and we are joyfully received into heaven."

Jacob placed the prayer book back on the shelf as the family prepared for the night. A few minutes later, Jacob climbed into bed beside Lizzie, who had just blown out the candle.

"That was a good evening," he said gently. "Did we get everything done that you had hoped?"

"Mostly. The young people had a good time."

"Joseph was showing off for the girls."

"He's outgrowing his shirts for the second time this year. I'll have to make new ones for him soon." She turned to face the wall and pulled the covers a little tighter.

Jacob reached over to put his hand on her shoulder. She was trembling. "Is everything all right?"

"Something didn't feel right tonight. Like someone was watching us."

"We had lots of people here."

"I mean outsiders, like Indians."

"Oh, Lizzie, nobody has seen Indians in these parts for months."

"Is the front door locked?"

Jacob swung his feet over the edge of the bed. "I'll make sure." He walked quietly down the stairs to the front door and stepped outside for a few moments. A cloud drifted slowly across the front of the first quarter moon. The crickets chirped their familiar chorus as he scanned the woods for any signs of trouble.

Fritz came trotting up from the barn. "How are you doing, old boy?" Jacob bent down to scratch his ears. "You be sure to let us know if anyone comes by."

Jacob locked the door and went back to bed. "It will be all right, dear. I didn't see anything to worry about."

"Thank you."

He leaned over and pressed a kiss to her cheek.

Jacob lay awake long after Lizzie's measured breathing told him she was asleep. What if she was right? What if the Indians had been spying on them?

He finally drifted off to sleep with the first verses of Psalm 91 in his mind: "He that dwelleth in the secret place of the most High shall abide under the shadow of the Almighty. I will say of the Lord, He is my refuge and my fortress: my God; in him will I trust."

It was still dark outside when Jacob heard Fritz's frantic barking. He sat up in bed, his heart thrumming in his chest. Slipping out of his night clothing and pulling on a pair of woolen trousers that were hanging on a chair, Jacob heard someone else downstairs reach the door first. Then the sound of a gunshot ripped through the quiet morning air, followed by a loud thump on the floor. "Help! I got hit in the leg!" It was Jakey.

Lizzie was out of bed and down the stairs in a few moments.

"Everyone get dressed," Jacob called to the household. "I'm afraid we've got Indians in the yard." He quickly pulled on his shirt and a pair of shoes and joined Lizzie downstairs.

Jakey had pulled himself off the floor onto a chair. He was moaning and holding onto his leg.

"Let me look at it," Lizzie said.

Blood dripped onto the wooden floor as Lizzie examined the injury in the dim light. "We'll need to get a bandage on that." She got some water from a wooden bucket near the fireplace, and then wet a piece of linen to bathe the wound.

"Does it feel like the bullet is still in there?" Jacob asked.

"I can't tell for sure," Jakey said through gritted teeth.

Lizzie wrapped the wound with a few strips of cloth.

"I can't see," Franey said. "Can't we light the lantern?"

"No!" Jacob said. "That would make it too easy for the Indians to see us."

Joseph went for the guns, which were hanging above the mantle. He handed one to Christian and then began to load the other.

Jacob looked out the window. The moonlight shone on the forms of a French officer and a dozen or more Indians standing near the bake oven. The natives were decked out with feathers and war paint. He turned to see Joseph crouching by the window with the barrel of his flintlock on the sill. "The rest of you stay back from the windows."

Jacob looked at Joseph and then at young Christian, their guns at the ready. A pain shot through Jacob's chest, and he closed his eyes for a moment. This was happening. It was happening now. This was the test he had hoped to avoid. It was the moment for which his prayer by the barn had prepared him.

Jacob opened his eyes and laid his hand on his son's shoulder. "Joseph, put your gun down."

Joseph wrenched his shoulder away from his father's grasp. "Why, *Dat*? I can get a good shot off from here."

"You know why."

"But *Dat*, we can't just let them shoot at us!"

"Joseph, that's enough. Christian, I mean that for you too." Jacob took the gun from Christian and hung it back on the wall.

Joseph put his gun on the floor close to him. His jaw twitched and his knees trembled as he crouched on the ground. He kept looking out the window. "But they're lighting a fire!"

A small flame was flickering near the bake oven. Soon it grew to light up several faces.

A warrior moved toward the end of the house with a pair of burning brands in his hand. That could only mean they were going to set the house on fire.

The pain returned to Jacob's chest, and he had the sudden urge to cover Franey and Christian with his own body, as if it could keep them from heat and flame. Lizzie rushed upstairs to get dressed while the others huddled by the door. Jacob tried to make a plan, but his thoughts felt thick and slow.

Soon, the crackling of a fire against the side of the house pushed any doubt from Jacob's mind about the warriors' plans. "They set fire to the house," Joseph said, his hand again clutching the gun beside him. "We'll never get out of here alive unless we shoot at them. I could shoot in the air, just to scare them into the woods."

Jacob held out his hand for the gun. "Joseph, you heard what I told you." For a moment the air was silent in the house except for the crackling of flames. Franey and Christian watched from the corner where they crouched, their eyes wide, and Lizzie froze as she came down the steps. "Joseph, give me the gun," said Jacob.

Joseph picked up the gun from where he had placed it on the floor and slowly handed it to his father. Their eyes locked for a moment, until Joseph dropped his gaze and released his grasp.

Jacob hung the gun on the wall and then moved toward Franey and Christian, who had begun whimpering. The smoke that was reaching his nostrils held all of the anxiety from the past few months in its hot breath. It smelled like his worst fear.

-10-

Barbara woke with the first hint of light shining through the bedroom window. Since the baby was coming soon, the press of nature often roused her before dawn.

On sudden impulse, she ignored the chamber pot to head for the outhouse instead. She slipped quietly out of bed and through the front door. All was silent except for the measured breathing of her family.

As she walked the short path back toward the house, a whiff of smoke from the north drifted into her consciousness. She paused for a moment. This was something beyond the smoke from a neighbor's chimneys. Where was it coming from? She looked around. Flames flickered against the sky above her parents' home.

Barbara let out a small cry as she rushed back into the house and up to the bed she had just left. "Cristy! I think *Mam* and *Dat's* house is on fire!"

Cristy was up in an instant. He yanked on his trousers and grabbed a shirt. "I'm going up there. It might be awhile before I get back."

Barbara watched from the window as Cristy hurried up the path toward the homestead. There was just enough light in the sky to show several plumes of smoke on her parents' farm. Barbara sat on the bed, rocking back and forth with her hands over her belly and closing her eyes. *God, please, please, please*, was the only prayer that came to her, and she said it in her mind over and over again.

Cristy returned in a short time with a strange, stunned look. His face was flushed and his voice tight. "We'd better hide in the woods. Indians are dancing around the house. It's on fire."

The two of them hurried the children out of bed. Barbara pulled dresses onto them and picked up Mary. "You carry

Annie," Barbara said to Cristy. "Magdalena, you come along."

The morning light was gray as they headed for the thicket west of their home. Barbara followed Christian to a spot where the floribunda was very thick. They walked around to the far side of it and nestled down in a bed of dead leaves.

"You stay here with the children," Cristy said. His voice had an urgency Barbara had seldom heard from him. "I'll go see what I can do for your folks. And warn the neighbors."

"Be careful! You never know where the Indians might have scouts."

Barbara watched Cristy hurry back through the woods toward the homestead. What did he think he could do? What was she going to do if the Indians came this way? Mother Stutzman's cellar would have been safer.

"I'm cold," Magdalena said.

"I'm sorry, I should have brought you a blanket." Annie started crying, so Barbara pulled the child onto her lap as she sat on the forest floor. The bulge in Barbara's middle didn't leave much room for her to sit. Barbara leaned back against a tree.

"I'm scared," Magdalena said. "What if the Indians find us?"

"God will take care of us." Could Magdalena detect the tremor in her voice that reflected the trembling in her soul? *Wasn't it just last night that we had such a good time at the* Schnitzing?

Magdalena clung to her wrist. "*Mam*, what are the Indians doing to Grandma and Grandpa?"

"I don't know. Maybe they found a place to hide, like us. We must be quiet. Now lie down and try to go back to sleep."

The smell of smoke grew stronger. Barbara couldn't stop shivering. This was worse than a nightmare. Was there anything she could do to help without endangering the children? Might one of the neighbors to the north alert the soldiers at the fort?

The sun was up when Christian returned with a grim expression on his face. "I didn't see anyone from our family. I'm afraid they're trapped inside the house. There are Indians all around the outside."

"Oh, Cristy. I must go and see." Barbara pushed Annie off of her lap and started to get up.

"Stay here. They may have scouts in the woods."

"But what if the folks need our help?" Barbara stood and started to move toward the clearing. "You wait here with the children. I'm going to see what's happening."

Cristy grabbed her arm. "No! You're not leaving here."

Of course he was right. As much as she wanted to make sure her parents were all right, it would have been foolish to endanger her children by putting herself in harm's way. Barbara sat down heavily as Cristy made his way back to the clearing for the third time. How could he possibly return with anything but very bad news?

Jacob watched with terror as the flames broke through the dry shingles of the roof into the upstairs rooms. Smoke came down the stairs and flames soon licked their way through the ceiling. Lizzie sopped several handkerchiefs in a bucket of water and handed them around for each of the family to hold over noses and mouths. When the ceiling began to sway, Jacob knew they couldn't stay in the house much longer.

"Follow me," Jacob said. "We can buy a little time by going into the cellar." On the way to the cellar door, he grabbed all four of their books off the shelf. He groped down the stairs in the smoky dimness. The cool and musky dampness was a temporary relief from the choking smoke. The family followed him down the steps, and Christian closed the door behind them. Jacob put the books on the dirt floor in the corner of the room.

Above the roaring of the fire, Jacob heard their fatted hog squealing in distress. Were the attackers butchering it for meat, or had they torched the barn with the hog trapped inside? Jacob shivered when Blitz's piteous scream mixed with that of the pig. Little could be worse than death by burning.

Jacob's nose and throat burned from the thickening smoke, and the water was gone so they couldn't keep the handkerchiefs wet any longer. Lizzie, Christian, and Franey huddled under the stairway, holding dry handkerchiefs over their noses. Jacob could hardly bear to look at them. The two older boys gazed out the small window to the back of the house.

The flames were gnawing their way through the floorboards, licking off the edges to expose the fire in the room above. The floor above them shook with a loud thump and then sagged as a shower of sparks fell into the cellar through several gaps in the boards. Franey screamed as a flying ember landed in her brown hair. Jacob flicked it off, but not before it had singed her. She burst into tears, and then wiped them with the sleeve of her dress, streaking the soot on her chéeks.

What was there left to do? Without water to quench the fire, the floorboards would soon give way. Jacob's eyes fell on the barrel of apple cider. That might do. He pried open the lid of the wooden barrel, and Lizzie found a wooden dipper lying nearby. Jacob took it from her and used it to throw cider onto the overhead boards where flames had pushed their way through the floor.

Joseph and Jakey joined Jacob to help, tossing handfuls of cider onto the ceiling until the barrel was empty. It made some difference, but the heat was suffocating.

Jacob tried to cough out the smoke in his lungs. "We can't hold on any longer. We'll have to crawl out that window." Better to be captured or killed than to be burned to death.

Lizzie's brown eyes were wild with fear. "I can't! I can't fit through there."

"You'll have to try. I'll help you."

Jacob rolled the empty barrel to the window and turned it upside down. He hoisted himself up and put his head out the window. No Indians. Maybe the sunlight sent them scrambling for cover. Maybe the family could find a place to hide.

He grabbed a handful of dried peaches from a basket in the corner. "Boys, I want you to put some peaches in your pockets. You might need them."

"Now it's time to go," he said. "Joseph, you go first. If the Indians are still nearby, maybe you can outrun them. Tell us what you see."

It didn't take long for Joseph to pull himself onto the barrel and out the window. He poked his head back inside. "I don't see them. They must have gone into the woods."

Jacob grabbed Christian's arm. "You go next." The boy scrambled onto the barrel and crawled out the window in a few moments.

"Jakey, you're next."

"My leg hurts. I can't swing it up that high."

"I'll help you." Jacob got a hold of the boy's good leg and hoisted him up. Joseph reached through the window and grabbed Jakey's hand. Before long, Jakey was outside.

"Come, Franey, you're next."

"I'm scared." Her face was streaked with tears.

"Come, I'll swing you up. If you see Indians, run to your hiding place." Jacob grabbed her and swung her up onto the barrel. Joseph reached in and helped her out.

Now it was Lizzie's turn. "I can't fit through that hole," she whimpered.

"You've got to. We can't stay in here." Jacob locked his fingers together, forming a step with his cupped hands. She gripped his shoulder as she stepped into his hands. Jacob grunted as he lifted her high enough so that she could put her other knee onto the barrel. She knelt on the wooden barrel and put her head out the window. Sparks hissed and sprayed onto their backs.

"*Mam*, take my hand." Joseph reached through the window, grasped her arms in a wrist lock with his and began to pull.

"I can't!" Lizzie said. "The window is too small." Her dress ripped against a nail that protruded from the side of the opening.

"Joseph, let go of me." Lizzie fought her way loose from the tightness of the frame.

A burning section of the floor fell into the cellar as Jacob helped Lizzie get off of the barrel. What more could he do to get Lizzie out of this fiery prison? He certainly wasn't going to leave without her. But time seemed to slow down, as if he were moving through a dream from which he could not wake up.

Jacob reached up to feel the edges of the window frame. "If we can get rid of that window stop, you'll have a little more room. But I'll need something to pry it off. Boys, find me a rock I can use for a hammer," he said to his sons. He tried to catch the panic as it rose in his throat. He held Lizzie tightly against his face as she knelt on the barrel, weeping.

The heat was becoming unbearable when Christian scurried to the window with a rock with a square edge. "That'll work." Jacob took the rock and pounded against the stop on all four sides of the opening. The wood splintered and flew off. Next he flattened the nails that protruded into the opening. "That'll give you another inch or more," he said to Lizzie. "Let's try again."

Jacob and Joseph went through the same motions as before. Joseph grasped Lizzie's arms and pulled. Jacob lifted up her legs from the back, his face drowning in the folds of her dress, and pushed. She wiggled and moaned, and soon lay panting on the ground outside the window.

Jacob quickly grabbed a small basket of peaches from the floor of the cellar and handed it to Joseph. Then he hoisted himself onto the barrel and was out the window in a few moments.

Jacob helped Lizzie to her feet and tried to get his bearings. Just then, Christian pointed toward the peach orchard and whispered, "Look, *Dat*, there's an Indian."

A young warrior stood by the peach trees, picking the ripe fruit. Jacob put his finger to his lips and beckoned the family to follow him around the corner of the house. Just then the warrior spied them and let out a loud whoop. In a few moments, other warriors came running from the woods, yelling and brandishing their weapons.

"Everyone run and hide!" Jacob didn't recognize his own voice. It came out strangled and muffled.

Franey headed for the woods beyond the spring house, on her way to her favorite hiding place in a hollow tree trunk. *Oh God*, Jacob prayed, *let her get there before the Indians see her.*

Joseph bolted off to the right and ran toward the woods with three braves in pursuit. *God*, Jacob prayed, *let him out-run them.*

Jakey started off to the left, hopping on one foot and drag-ging his injured leg. Christian started off toward the meadow on the right. Lizzie and Jacob headed for a thicket behind the house when four braves appeared in front of them. In a mat-ter of moments, Jakey, Christian, Lizzie, and Jacob were all hemmed in. A couple of braves grabbed hold of each of them. Joseph was nowhere to be seen.

The braves seemed determined to make Jacob watch the carnage. They dragged Jakey back toward the house. Pulling him within a few yards of where they were holding Jacob, they killed him with a tomahawk and took his scalp. Jacob heard the screams before he realized that they were his own.

Two other Indians dragged Christian back toward the house. Christian screamed in terror and threw back his head as a warrior raised his tomahawk and started to bring it down on his skull. But the warrior shouted something and stopped his strike in midair. He brought his arm back to his side. Another man helped the warrior bind Christian's hands and then they turned their fury toward Lizzie.

Lizzie shook with terror as two warriors pulled her arms behind her back. Another warrior stepped forward with a knife and waved it in front of her eyes. "You make hungry," he shouted in broken German. Jacob lunged forward to protect Lizzie but couldn't get free of the grasp of the man who held him. Again he screamed, the noise loud in his own ears and yet seeming to come from a distance.

"*Herr Yesus!*" Lizzie screamed as the young Indian thrust the knife into her chest. In a few moments, she went limp and fell onto her back. Her chest heaved several times before she lay silent. Jacob lunged for his wife, the loud roaring still in his ears, but the warriors held him back. They were laughing now, yelling taunts as they tied his arms in front of him with a hemp rope.

Jacob strained to look back over his shoulder, and he caught a glimpse of an older brave stepping forward with a scalping knife. In one smooth motion, he cut a circle around the crown of Lizzie's head. And then he grabbed her uncut hair, put his foot on her head, and yanked off her scalp. Her body sprawled on the ground, blood dripping from her wounds.

Jacob turned around and, sinking to his knees, vomited on the ground. A warrior jammed the barrel of his rifle into Jacob's ribs and forced him to stand up, and another yanked on the rope that bound his arms. The cords dug into Jacob's wrist as they led him back into the clearing.

Jacob watched, half-numb, as several warriors helped themselves to the fruit basket. Just then three warriors emerged from the woods with Joseph, bound in the same manner as Christian and Jacob. They yanked the three into a single line with Christian first, Joseph second, and then Jacob, with a warrior separating them from each other. A young Indian followed behind with a flintlock in hand. Jacob shivered at the fierce-looking paint on the man's face. His eyes were squinted and his jaws clenched.

Their captors began marching single file out of the farm lane, past the smoldering embers of the outbuildings. Jacob's throat tightened as he glanced around. The taste of vomit stung in his mouth. The barn was smoking in ruins. The fresh hay in the mow was like tinder, stoking the blaze like logs in the fireplace.

At the far end of the small corral, Blitz screamed. The log fence bulged out where the terrified horse pressed against it. As the braves marched past the corral gate, one of the braves yanked it open, then went inside and approached the horse. Blitz ran past the brave, dashed through the gate, and galloped up the lane toward John's place. A small mercy it was, as long as he didn't lead the war party to another farmstead.

As Jacob and his sons stumbled past the smoking remains of the barn, he spied the charred remains of the hog they had been fattening up to butcher was soon as the weather turned cold. The carcass lay half-exposed under a log that had served to hold up the hay mow. Why had the hog been inside the barn? Perhaps one of the boys had closed the door on it the night before. Or more likely, one of the warriors chased it inside before torching the building. The small distillery was half-burned as well. The roof had collapsed, bulging the side wall. The door hung suspended on the bottom hinge.

The war party stopped at Northkill Creek to get a drink. Jacob and his sons dipped their bound hands in the cold water and splashed it on their faces and in their mouths. "Let's try to stay together," Jacob whispered to his sons as they drank. Christian grimaced and nodded, his face smudged with dirt and tears. Joseph's face was like stone.

These sons of his were motherless now. Motherless. It was all that Jacob could do to raise himself to his feet.

The captain was a white soldier, dressed in the blue uniform of a French army officer. He gave an order, and the group of warriors and captives started marching briskly, heading mostly north and a little west toward what the Indians called the *keekachtanemin* (the endless mountains).

Jacob's head throbbed as he tried to take in what had happened. Lizzie was dead, as was Jakey. Only God knew what had happened to Franey. And what would happen to John's and Barbara's families? Only God knew how he could continue living.

Jacob stumbled along the rutted path, struggling to keep mind and body together. He was so numb that he barely heard a whimper in the woods to the right. There was Fritz, hardly visible in the underbrush, his nose pointed in Jacob's direction. A small gasp slipped from Jacob's mouth, and he spoke softly, "Stay!" Jacob slowed his steps to look back, but the warrior behind him poked him hard with his rifle.

Jacob walked on. Had his sons seen the dog too, and had it offered them any comfort? Would any of them ever return to the Northkill?

-11-

Cristy returned to the hiding place in the woods after what seemed to Barbara like an hour. He walked with his head down. Perhaps if she didn't ask him any questions, nothing he would tell her would be true. She waited until he knelt down beside her and the girls, who thankfully had fallen back to sleep.

"Are the Indians gone now?"

"*Jah*. John saw them leave. His family was hiding, like ours."

"Did *Dat* and *Mam* hide too? Is everyone all right?"

"The Indians took *Dat* and two of the boys as captives."

Barbara hunched forward and clutched her stomach, a sudden spasm tightening her skin. She pressed her hand against her mouth to keep a moan from escaping her lips. "Oh no. Oh no. Oh no!" she whispered, rocking back and forth, her breath coming in short clips.

Cristy put a hand on her shoulder and waited.

When Barbara could speak again, she looked at the ground. "And what happened to the rest?"

Barbara's breath caught when Cristy was silent. She looked up the pained expression on his face. He was slow to answer. And then she knew.

"They killed *Mam* and Jakey. We found their bodies not far from the house."

Barbara felt suddenly lightheaded. "Those savages killed my mother. And my brother." She clutched at her chest.

Cristy put his arm around her. "Let's go inside where we can sit down." He scooped up Mary in one arm and Annie in the other. Barbara roused Magdalena and they followed behind. It felt to Barbara like a funeral procession.

By the time they got inside, Barbara's head was pounding and her throat was dry, so she got a drink. They all sat down at the table, and she refilled the cup for everyone in turn.

"You didn't say anything about Franey." Barbara said, trying to piece everything together.

"We don't know what happened to her."

"I must go find out."

"What about our children?"

"Let's leave them at your mother's place."

Barbara followed Christy's lead as they walked the path toward his mother's home. She pushed herself along on wooden legs, relieved when they got to the front door. Mother Stutzman hugged the children tightly when Barbara told her the news. "We'll hide in the cellar if we see anything strange going on."

Soon Cristy and Barbara were on the way to witness the scene that her mother had always feared. Barbara held a handkerchief over her nose and mouth as they neared the smoking remains of the house. John was there, pacing the ground near the house.

Barbara's stomach wrenched when she spotted her mother, lying in a twisted heap. Jakey's body was not far away. Barbara's knees were suddenly weak, and she almost collapsed under the weight of the horror. She began to stumble toward the bloodied corpses, but Cristy stopped her. He took her forearm in his hand and led her away. "Let's try to find Franey," John said, and Cristy nodded.

Barbara consented. It had to be done, but what might they find? They called for her sister as they walked in the woods close to the smoldering house. "Franey, Franey."

Silence.

"Maybe she's in the springhouse," Barbara said. "She loves to hide in there."

They walked over to the small outbuilding, the only one on the farm that wasn't completely burned. Barbara struggled to breathe as she called into the little house.

"Franey, the Indians are gone now. You can come out."

Silence.

"Let's search near the creek," John said. "I know she has a hiding place in a hollow tree."

Barbara breathed a prayer as they walked toward the creek. *Oh God, please let her be there. Please let her be there.*

"Franey, Franey. You can come out now," Barbara called. "The Indians are gone."

John stopped and a groan escaped his lips. He pointed across the creek. There lay a small body in a blue dress, just a few feet from a large, hollow tree.

Cristy and Barbara followed John as he crossed the creek and knelt beside Franey's body. "They must have found her hiding place." A large gash marked the place where a tomahawk had smashed into her face. The blood was drying on her skull where she had been scalped. Barbara reached out for Cristy's arm. How could anyone kill a little six-year-old girl? How could they be so evil?

John bent down and picked up the lifeless body. Tears ran down his cheeks as he carried his little sister in his arms. Barbara and Cristy stumbled wordlessly behind him, through the creek bed and back toward the house.

Barbara's head throbbed. What if the Indians came to their house next? What would they do to her children, to her, or to the baby inside of her? She turned to look behind her, then all around. *They might be spying on us right now. I must get back to Mother Stutzman's house to be with my little ones.*

When John reached the clearing, he laid Franey on the ground next to the bodies of Jakey and Lizzie. "Cristy, why don't you get the bishop," he said.

Cristy nodded. "I will."

"Cristy, are you sure—" Barbara tugged on his arm.

"Take my horse. That will be safer," John interrupted.

Barbara breathed a prayer as Cristy rode out the lane. *God, deliver him in safety.*

"I'll go get Katie. She can help get the bodies ready for burial," John said. For once, Barbara was grateful for the way her older brother took charge.

"We should wash the blood off the bodies," Katie said when she arrived with a pail of water and a cloth from their house next door. "And we'll need to find burial clothes for each of them." Barbara nodded and reached down for a cloth.

"No," Katie told her gently. "Let me do it. Go sit down."

Barbara nodded again. She sank down to the ground a little way off from the bodies, her body shaking.

Less than an hour later, Cristy returned with Bishop Jake and his wife, Catharine. Jake was driving a wagon with Cristy's horse tied behind. The bishop climbed down from the wagon and helped his wife to step down. They walked toward Barbara and the others with somber faces.

"I am so sorry this has happened to your family," Jake said with trembling lips. His voice broke. "But we can be sure that God is with us." He and Catharine embraced each of them in turn.

They stood there for a few moments, gazing in silence at the three dead bodies. Barbara shuddered. It seemed disrespectful to leave the bodies lying there on the ground. They were cold and distant, so far from the living, breathing beings they had been at the apple *Schnitzing* the night before.

"What shall we do about a funeral?" John said.

"It will be too dangerous to plan for a church service," Jake said. "But we can call together a few neighbors for a burial this afternoon."

Barbara glanced at John, and they both nodded.

"Have you decided where you want to bury your loved ones?" the bishop asked.

"I'm sure *Dat* would want them buried right here on the farm," John said.

Barbara nodded.

"The two of you should pick the spot," the bishop said. "Catharine can help Katie prepare the bodies for burial."

"Let's bury them right next to the house," John said.

Barbara recoiled. They'd be reminded of their deaths every time they walked up to the house. "I think we should bury them close to the orchard," Barbara said. She walked toward the first row of fruit trees, and John followed after. "How about right here?" She pointed to a spot nearly shaded by a large apple tree.

"No, the roots will make it too hard to dig." John headed back toward the house.

"Wait. We could at least try. The shade is so nice around those trees."

John shook his head and then motioned to the bishop with his hand. "Let's dig it right here, next to the house. We'll make one hole big enough for all three bodies."

Barbara glared at him. What could she say? She didn't want to argue in front of the bishop.

Several neighbors arrived about the time they started digging. "I'll keep watch for Indians," one of them said. He paced from one side of the clearing to the other, glancing into the woods on all sides.

As the men dug the grave, Barbara walked around the foundation of the house, glancing into the smoldering ruins that had fallen into the basement. Something in the corner of the cellar caught her eye.

She waved to Cristy. "Come here."

He stood beside her as they gazed into the cellar. Barbara pointed to a lump on the cellar floor. "Can you see what that is?"

Cristy crawled into the cellar and made his way to the spot. "It's a book—partly burned." He handed it up to Barbara.

It was her father's copy of *Martyrs Mirror*. The book was charred on the edges, and stained with cider, but she could still turn the pages. She showed it to John. "Do you mind if I take this to my house?"

"No, you're more of a reader than I am."

Barbara set it aside to bring some cold water from the spring to the men who were digging the grave. They finished digging by about noon under the bright sun. They set up a table in the shade of the large oak tree where those who were hungry could eat food the neighbors had brought over. Barbara had no appetite at all.

When everyone was finished eating, Cristy brought the wagon to the burial spot and they gathered around. The men laid the three corpses not far from each other in the grave.

The bishop cleared his throat twice after he opened a little black book. After a few words of sympathy for the family, the bishop read several Scriptures. Barbara recognized snatches from the Psalms: "As for man, his days are as grass: as a flower of the field, so he flourisheth. For the wind passeth over it, and it is gone; and the place thereof shall know it no more. . . . So teach us to number our days, that we may apply our hearts unto wisdom."

Barbara scanned the nearby woods. What if the Indians were watching them, ready to descend on their gathering?

After a few more comments, the bishop read these words:

"Forasmuch as it has pleased Almighty God, in his wise providence, to take out of this world the soul of . . ." He paused to correct himself. ". . . souls of the departed, we commit the bodies to the ground; earth to earth, ashes to ashes, dust to dust, and commit the souls to God who gave them, looking for the general resurrection in the last day."

Barbara tried to listen, but her thoughts were jumbled. After the bishop prayed a benediction, they each took a turn with the shovel, heaving the soil back into the hole until it formed a small mound. She went through the motions in a dry grief, her tears spent.

The burial could only be the beginning of a long goodbye.

PART II

-12-

The war party walked single file, following the base of Blue Mountain. They walked along in silence, except for the times when the captain barked an order to the group. Jacob and his sons said nothing as they walked the path blazed in front of them.

Jacob heard the sound of an ax as they approached the clearing near John Miller's house. Jacob held his breath as the lead warrior raised his rifle. Should he shout a warning? The warrior fired as soon as he stepped into the clearing. Jacob got into the clearing just in time to see a settler running for cover. He breathed in a sigh of relief when no one gave pursuit.

After leading them along for several miles, the captain turned north toward the gap that would take them over the Kittatinny Ridge into Indian territory. The climb grew steeper, and Jacob was hampered by the ropes on his hands. The ground was stony, uneven, and he struggled to keep his balance. After hours of walking, the group paused to eat. The warriors sat cross-legged in a circle with the prisoners in the middle. They pulled dried corn from their pouches and ate it, and drank water from a small stream. The prisoners got no food but were allowed a drink.

The Indians exchanged few words as they ate. Their language was entirely foreign to Jacob, a world apart from the Swiss-German dialect he spoke at home. The Indians addressed the captain as Lou, who spoke mostly French. The musical sound of Lou's French evoked memories of Jacob's childhood home in Alsace, where he and a neighbor boy learned to speak each other's language. With effort, Jacob was able to catch the gist of Lou's meaning.

After they walked through the gap in the first range, Lou took them to the west, following the base of Blue Mountain until they came to Swatara Creek. Each time they came to a creek or river, one of the scouts told its name to Lou, who didn't seem to know the territory. The group stayed on the east side of the Swatara, following a path through a gap in the next mountain. Jacob hardly dared look down to the drop below as the group marched briskly over an eighteen-inch-wide shelf on the side of a cliff.

The trail rose again after that, passing through a second gap in the mountain chain. Jacob strained to keep up with the party. Whenever he lagged behind, a warrior poked him hard in the back with his flintlock. Each time, Jacob picked up his pace.

When the party came through the pass in the mountain, they turned left onto another trail that headed west. Since it seemed well worn, Jacob was sure it was the Great Shamokin Trail that led toward the Susquehanna River. He had heard reports about it from people traveling that way.

The path wound its way through the heavy forest. The trail varied in width from twelve to eighteen inches, so the group always marched in single file except at the times when they came to a clearing. Although Jacob walked only a few yards behind his sons, it might as well have been a mile. The guards who separated them made sure they did not talk to each other.

Lou led the way with the assistance of scouts that he sent ahead of him to check out the trail conditions and alert them to the presence of an enemy. At least Jacob could pray that the British would discover the party and rescue the prisoners. On the other hand, the chances that Jacob and his sons would be killed by their captors in a skirmish with their enemies seemed very high.

The group had marched for several hours when Jacob first noticed the scalp that dangled from the waist of the warrior who walked just behind the captain. There was no mistaking Franey's brown pigtails. *Those evil men killed my little Franey.* He had been holding on to the hope that she had escaped. Jacob slowed down as the knowledge slammed into his chest. A moment later, a blow to the back of his legs with a rifle butt forced him to pick up speed.

What had his little girl ever done to deserve such treatment? Their action was evil beyond anything Jacob could imagine. Didn't the Indians have little girls they loved? If only they had killed Jacob and let his little girl go free. What kind of spirit made it possible to carry out such evil? How could God allow it?

If only he had been the one to answer the door when the dog barked in the early morning. Perhaps he would have been the one who was wounded, and perhaps Jakey's life would have been spared. As it was, they had torn apart a romance that was about to bloom into marriage. Had Jakey's sweetheart found out by now that he had been killed?

If only he had moved his family farther south—even a few miles away—Lizzie might still be alive. Jakey and Franey too. Now Jacob was destined to see their scalps every day, to recall the terror of what had happened under his watch as a husband and father.

Joseph marched along in front of Jacob, never turning to look back. Had he seen Franey's scalp? *Maybe I should have let him have his way when the Indians first showed up.* Maybe Joseph should have shot a bullet over the tops of the Indians' heads at least once to let them know that they had firearms. Maybe Joseph had been right: that if they had stood their ground with weapons, the Indians would have left. Had Jacob yielded, perhaps the whole family would have been spared.

But no. Had they shot at the Indians, they would most likely have killed the whole family. They would have entered eternity together. But how could he have faced God at the judgment after breaking the promise he had made by the barn on that night that seemed so long ago?

This way, three of them were still alive, although only God knew what was still to happen. And if God ever allowed Jacob to return to the Northkill, he'd need to keep his bearings well enough to find his way back. The first part of the path would be simple enough, oriented as it was to the gap in Blue Mountain. But what about the places they had walked that day? Jacob recalled a few of the markers on the trail—the narrow pass high above the river, the rills at the mouth of a creek, the giant burl on the side of a chestnut tree, and the peculiar loop in the branch of another. Jacob would need to pay more attention if he hoped to ever retrace his steps. His sons needed to pay attention too.

But how was he to keep track of the number of days on the trail? The one day they had traveled already felt like two. Maybe he could collect something small to put in his pocket each day. The next time the group stopped at a creek for a drink, he picked up a small pebble from the creek bottom and slipped it into the pocket of his pants. One small pebble each day shouldn't be too burdensome, unless they were walking a long way.

After they had marched all day, the group set up camp at the edge of a thicket. A few warriors gathered broken branches and twigs onto a pile and set them ablaze for a campfire. Lou forced Jacob and his sons to sit a little ways apart with an Indian guard close by.

After the Indians had finished their supper, they pulled the four scalps from their belts and stretched them onto hoops. Jacob nearly retched as one of the men scraped bits of flesh off Franey's scalp. *My baby's head.* When he glanced at Jacob in triumph, Jacob quickly looked down.

After the warriors cleaned the blood and loose flesh off the scalps, they dried them over the fire, carefully holding back the hair to keep it from being singed. When the skin was dried out and clean, they carefully combed the hair and painted the edges of the scalp red.

Jacob's eyes narrowed to slits. What were they going to do with those scalps? Cash them in like fur pelts for a bounty?

When the warriors settled in for the night, they forced Joseph and Jacob to lie on their backs on the ground. With hemp ropes they tied their feet to saplings and their hands behind their backs.

Although the strength was drained from his body, Jacob couldn't go to sleep. He tried to recite his nightly prayer, but his thoughts were jerked back to the scene of the attack on his family. Tomahawks arced across his vision behind his closed eyelids. The smoke from the burning house seared his nostrils and Lizzie's screams rang in his ears. Had John and Barbara's families discovered the dead bodies next to the house? Were the neighbor families safe?

A small rock poked his right shoulder, so he shifted his weight to the other side. Not long after he drifted off to sleep, Jacob woke abruptly to discover that his left arm was numb. He opened his eyes and glanced at the fire. He managed to scrape together a few leaves with his elbow to make his resting place more comfortable. Jacob gazed upward. The moon showed through the leaves that swayed in the breeze. A warrior sat in the dimming glow of the firelight. When Jacob stirred and groaned a little, the warrior glanced in his direction.

Jacob had just fallen asleep, or so it seemed, when he heard shouts and the galloping of horses accented by gunfire and the whoops of Indian warriors waving their tomahawks in the light of a roaring fire. Dozens of Indians emerged from the woods all around, facing off against an enemy mounted on horses in a small clearing. A cannonball screamed above Jacob's head and crashed into a nearby tree. Bullets sang overhead, ripping through the low-hanging leaves.

The campfire flamed up into an inferno. Jacob shrank back in horror as Indian warriors dragged wounded enemy soldiers out of the darkness and tossed them into the fire, laughing with glee as their clothing burst into flames.

And then Lizzie appeared in front of Jacob, screaming in terror. Franey wailed as she clung to Lizzie's skirt. "*Daati*, help us! *Daati*, help us!" Jacob saw two warriors grab the two of them and throw them into the fire. He strained hard to rescue them but was held back by the fetters on his arms and legs.

Just then two braves cut Joseph and Christian loose from their ropes and dragged them toward the flames. "*Halten!*

Halten!" Jacob shouted. At that, three warriors ran toward him with painted faces, screaming with glee. They grabbed Jacob by the hair and jerked him upright.

Jacob woke up with his heart thumping in his chest. He looked around. All was quiet except for the brief stirring of the guard, who glanced in his direction. A gust of wind swept a few dry leaves against his skin, wet with sweat. His left arm was numb again. It took him a long time to go back to sleep.

He woke to the sound of a warrior stirring the fire. His wrists were sore and his hands were numb. He moved his arms a little, hoping to get some blood pumping into his hands. A warrior came to untie his ankles and his wrists. Jacob flashed him a grateful look but saw no emotion in the man's face in return.

After sharing a few bites of dried corn and beans with the prisoners for breakfast, the Indians led them back onto the trail. They crossed Lorberry Creek and headed up the side of Broad Mountain. It was a cool morning, which made the rapid march more tolerable. The group headed mostly north, soon to encounter the third ridge in the Blue Mountain chain.

Jacob searched for trail markers as they went along, but already he was so confused that he wasn't sure he could retrace his steps. The forest was so dense in places that he couldn't orient himself with a broad view of the area. The easiest thing, it seemed, was to remember the gaps where they had crossed the ridges.

Near the ridge at the top of Broad Mountain, the group stopped at a mountain spring. The warriors took long drinks out of their cupped hands and splashed the cool water against their skin. Jacob drank heartily as well. The cool water felt like a gift from God, a trickle of grace to counter a flood of evil.

After this cool refreshment, the group headed down the other side of Broad Mountain. The long descent was a refreshment too, a welcome break from the uphill climb to the top. By evening, the group reached Mahantango Creek at the foot of Mahantango Mountain. The captain pointed to a small clearing, and they got ready to eat. When the warriors un-bound Jacob's hands to eat, he found a second pebble to put into his pocket to remind him that it was the end of the second day on the trail. Day two.

As his captors huddled around the fire that evening, the warrior who had cleaned Franey's scalp the night before took a pair of brass tweezers out of his tobacco pouch. Jacob re-strained a smile as he plucked the hair out of his beard. He worked across his chin, grasping each fine hair by the root and yanking it quickly, like Lizzie used to pluck fowls with her fingers. Why not let that hair grow? What vanity, plucking the hair on one's face. Whatever God had put there might as well stay there. He would never pluck out this symbol of his faith and his manhood.

The warriors appeared somewhat different from one an-other now, not all alike as they had the first day. Why should he have expected them to look any more like each other than his friends looked like him? If I he was going to survive the time with the Indians, Jacob thought, he had better learn to know them individually.

The tall man with the tweezers wore a dangling silver ear-ring on the lobe of each ear and a matching silver ring in his nose. A large scar ran from the top of his Roman nose across his left cheek. Was this the man who had made the mark on the door after Lizzie turned him away? Jacob's eyes narrowed. In his mind he dubbed him Scar Face.

The man's hair was shaved except for a scalp lock, a four-inch circle on the crown of his head. His long black hair was gathered up in a cloth band and hung down onto his shoul-ders. A wide strip of black paint spanned from the middle of his nose to the top of his eyebrows, and ran around the sides of his head to where it was lost to sight behind his ponytail. Blotches of black paint decorated the crown of his head like giant teardrops.

The man wore a small pouch on a leather thong that hung around his neck and a cow's horn on a leather strap filled with

gunpowder. He also wore a heavily embroidered bag, decorated with tassels, that hung by a wide strap, in which he carried his food.

The warriors tied Jacob up for the night as they had before.
He lay there straining at the ropes on his hands and legs, a
foolish thing that only made them tighter. There was no slipping away to relieve himself or to talk to his sons, his own
flesh and blood. After all of the years he had given to rear-
ing his boys, he was now forced to watch someone else take
charge of their destiny.

-13-

The sky was overcast when the group started out the next morning. The war party led the prisoners through the Mahantango Creek and headed for the far end of a long ridge. It soon began to drizzle, wetting the grass along the sides of the path as the group skirted the slope of a second ridge. Lou headed mostly west, following the valley of a small creek that ran between the ridges.

As the war party moved along, they acted with much greater caution, moving quietly under the cover of trees. They lit no fire that night. Perhaps they were getting close to a fort. Most likely Fort Augusta, where there would be British soldiers.

Jacob lay bound under the stars not far from the boys. In the absence of the prayer book he had used each evening at home, he simply recited the Lord's Prayer.

Before dawn the next morning, the captain sent out several scouts, who returned in less than an hour to say that all was clear to cross the river. Jacob waded in and shivered as the water became deeper and deeper. Eventually he was wet all the way up to his armpits, and was sure that he was going to drown. The rocks on the bottom were somewhat slippery, making it hard to keep his footing. Christian struggled too, since it was all he could do to keep his head above water. Fortunately, the Indians untied their wrists for the crossing, but neither Jacob nor his boys could swim. He heaved a great sigh of relief when they made it to the other side.

The group hadn't hiked long before they met a group of Delawares who brought another prisoner for the war party, a settler named Bryce Hayes. He might have been about thirty years old. Bryce said nothing to Jacob or his sons. He kept his head down as the Indians forced him to walk in line just ahead of them.

That day on the trail, the heel of Jacob's left shoe came off. It threw off his gait to walk with a heel on one shoe and not the other, but what could he do? There were no tools to mend the shoe, and it would soon be too cold to go barefoot. He stooped to pick it up, but the guard behind him jabbed him with his gun. With his nose in the air, he told Jacob his name was Tom Lions. He was the warrior who had first spotted Jacob and his family after they got out of the cellar on the day of the attack.

Tom took obvious pride in his role as rear guard, taunting and poking Jacob whenever he stumbled or slowed down. But the more Jacob tried to ignore him, the more he provoked him. "Lord," Jacob prayed under his breath, "help me make peace with this man." Although the Indians had him bound in the flesh, they could never bind his spirit. God helping him, they could not direct his thoughts or make him a prisoner of hate. He could always choose his attitude, even toward his enemies.

The group was pushing its way through a dense thicket when they came upon a large tree that had fallen across the path. Likely uprooted by high winds, the huge chestnut thrust its upper trunk across the path, blocking it more than four feet high in the air. The force of the fall had broken several substantial branches, which now lay crushed under the trunk, blocking the way to crawl underneath the trunk.

Lou stopped to look it over. To the left of the path was a steep slope. To the right was underbrush dotted by flori-bunda, wild rose bushes so thick that it was nearly impossible to push through.

Lou turned and pointed back to the path they had just walked. The group retraced its steps and then plunged into the undergrowth. Jacob pushed forward with the others, weaving his head and body through the thicket with his hands tied be-hind him. He fought his way around the end of the tree and headed back to the path. Although the group skirted the main body of floribunda, the rose thorns scratched deeply through the skin on Jacob's forehead. Blood tricked down over his left eyebrow and into his eye. He shook his head, trying to clear his vision by blinking. He tried to rub his eye against the sleeve on his left shoulder, but he couldn't scrunch it up high enough. When he stopped briefly to stoop down and rub his eye against the leg of his trousers, Tom gave him a sharp kick in the rear. Heat flushed through his body as he jumped to his feet and stumbled on.

When the flow of blood dried up on his forehead, Jacob's skin tightened like stitches in the late morning sun. Blood co-agulated around his eye. If only he had a cool spring and his hands were free so he could splash cold water onto his face. What could he do but plod on under the glare of his captors?

When they forded the Chillisquaque Creek near its mouth at the Susquehanna, Jacob managed to splash enough water onto his face to wash off the dried blood. As before, the cool water was a touch of God's grace.

On the north bank of the creek lay the Shawnee town of Chillisquaque. The sun was high in the sky, so the four Shawnee warriors urged the group to stop there. The villagers offered them dried venison, the best food they'd eaten so far.

After Jacob finished eating, he sat on a rock and felt for the pebbles in his pockets. There were only two of them. He must have forgotten to pick up a pebble the night before. It seemed as though the evening before had been the third night on the trail, so he put another pebble in his pocket and chided himself for having forgotten. If he didn't remember to do it each evening, he'd soon lose track of the days.

The group walked through rugged landscapes that after-noon, scrambling over loose rocks on the side of a hill and wading through deep water. It was almost more than Jacob could endure to watch Christian struggle over the terrain only a few paces in front of him with his hands tied. *He's still a child. How can they treat him this way?* Joseph was as stoic as his Indian guards, hiding his anger behind an expressionless face.

For the rest of the afternoon, the group followed the course of the river in a direction that seemed like north. When they came to a creek that angled into the river, a scout told Lou it was the Delaware Run. As they bedded down for the night, Jacob made sure to put another pebble in his pocket. Now there were four of them.

Several times during the night, Jacob woke up shivering. One of the warriors finally fed the fire in the morning, and Jacob rubbed his hands together above the flames. After the usual breakfast of dried corn and beans, the group followed the east side of the Delaware Run all the way to its mouth.

In the late afternoon, the war party came to a slate quarry. One of the warriors put a small amount of the crumbly slate into his pocket. He could mix it with water to make black war paint.

Down the hill from the quarry, near the bank of the river, they found a spring with crystal clear water. Jacob got to drink until he was satisfied. Not far from there, the group stayed at a Delaware Indian village named Muncy. The villagers brought out food enough for all to eat and to replenish the supply in the warriors' bags. They brought out blankets too, since the nights were growing colder. Even Jacob and his boys got blankets, a welcome relief from the night before.

Back home, they'd always had enough to eat, although the boys had grown so fast they sometimes complained about being hungry. Lizzie had commented that they both outgrew their shirts and trousers twice in the last year. How would they fare on limited food?

Jacob didn't have a full stomach that night, but it wasn't growling either. He put another pebble in his pocket. Each of the five days had taken them farther from home. If only he knew how much farther it would be.

The next morning, the warriors led the way up from the mouth of Muncy Creek for some three-quarters of a mile before they found a suitable place to cross. Not long after, the group came to Mingo Run. As they crossed the run, they came to the site of an ancient fort, likely built by the Indians. It stood on the crown of a hill with a good view of the area. It was surrounded by a deep ditch, which must have served as a moat. The earth around it was thrown up in the shape of a wall, some eight feet high and perhaps as broad. But the place was in decay, deserted years before. The Indians must have been there long before the white man.

That evening the warriors set up camp near Lycoming Creek. It was one of the few times that Jacob had a chance to speak with Joseph and Christian without interference from a warrior.

"I hate that guard named Tom," Joseph said through clenched jaw. "I'd like to put him in his place."

"Me too," Christian said. "He's evil."

"*Naw geb auchdt* (Be careful), boys, he has weapons and you don't."

"I could lay him out with my fists," Joseph said.

"That's what he wants," Jacob said. "If you hit him, he'll kill you with his gun."

"If I show him what I can do, maybe he'll respect me."

"If you hit him, you'll be acting just like him. Show him a better way."

"If you'd have let me shoot back at the house, we wouldn't be in this trouble." Joseph glanced briefly at Jacob as he spoke and then dropped his eyes.

"Joseph, I—" Just then Tom swaggered up to them, glowering and threatening them with his flintlock. If only Joseph could keep his temper under control. Didn't he realize that any trouble from a prisoner meant a death sentence?

Jacob prayed with fervor as he lay down that night. He had just fallen asleep when he heard Christian screaming and thrashing in his sleep. *He must be having a night terror.* The first time it had happened two years ago, it put the whole family in a panic. Christian bolted out of his bed and ran screaming down the stairs. The whole household awakened at once, and Jacob ran after the boy, hoping he would not harm himself.

"Christian, Christian, we're right here. Everything is going to be all right." Jacob caught the boy just as he was about to go out the door. He could feel his son's heart pounding as he hugged him to his chest. Christian's breath came in short gasps. Jacob picked him up in his arms and carried him back to bed. The boy mumbled to himself and soon went back to sleep. The next morning, he could not recall what had happened.

Now, as the boy screamed and thrashed against the ropes that held him, Jacob shouted to his son, "You'll be all right; we're right here." But Christian kept screaming. Jacob struggled to get loose from the ropes that held him to the saplings, but they only dug deeper into his skin.

A warrior kicked him in the ribs. "*Stillen.*" He headed for the place where Christian yanked on his ropes.

"Don't hurt him," Jacob said firmly. "He's just having a bad dream."

By now, everyone was awake from the commotion. "What's going on?" Lou said. He got up and went over to the boy. Christian was quiet now. He must have been terrified at the sight of soldiers leering at him.

"He's just having a bad dream," Jacob said. "Please don't punish him. Just let him go back to sleep."

"I'll teach him not to yell that way," Lou said. He whacked Christian hard with a stick he had picked up from the ground.

"But he can't help it," Jacob said. "He doesn't even know what happened."

"You shut up and go back to sleep," Lou said. "We'll deal with you in the morning."

Jacob lay awake, trembling, as Christian sobbed softly. He longed to go to his child and wrap him in his arms. How could Lou and the Indians be so cruel? What did these Indians and French have against them except that they lived next to the English? War is a jealous neighbor, bribing people to hate others whom they've never even met.

-14-

A week after the attack, Cristy asked Barbara whether she ought to write a letter to her grandparents in the old country. "We should let them know what happened. It's been a week."

"I don't have any ink. Or paper."

"*Mam* might have some. She writes a letter every once in a while." Cristy's voice was gentle, as though he knew how painful this would be. Although Barbara hadn't cried at the burial, she could hardly control her tears in the days that followed.

Barbara wiped tears from her eyes. "Maybe Mother Stutzman can write it for me. Or we could wait until the baby comes, so we'd have some good news to share as well."

"I think it's better to let them know right away," Cristy said. "I'd want to know if my daughter had been killed—"

"Okay, I'll do it today," Barbara said, with enough firmness to show him she wasn't looking for more suggestions. "I'll see if I can get it done today."

Cristy nodded and headed for his work outside. Barbara turned to clean up after breakfast.

Magdalena had been sucking her thumb lately and clinging to Barbara as she tried to work. Barbara couldn't blame her, but it made it hard to get anything done in the house. The days were long and slow and flat with her mother gone. Twice, by long habit, she had started out for the folks' house to see Lizzie and then caught herself when she realized what she was doing.

After she finished cleaning up the dishes, Barbara walked to Mother Stutzman's house. It wasn't far, and she was glad to let her take care of the children. On the way, she carried Mary and Annie in her arms while Magdalena followed behind. They walked past Cristy, who was cutting a little patch of meadow grass for hay, leaving the aroma of fresh-cut grass in his wake. A meadowlark flashed across the path as they went by. Barbara admired the way Cristy swished the scythe in a graceful arc, laying the grass to rest. It was harder than it looked; *Dat* had let her try her hand at it when she was Joseph's age.

Barbara and the girls watched Cristy for a few minutes and then went on to Mother Stutzman's house. She welcomed them in and agreed to help Barbara with a letter. "Magdalena," she said, "would you like to help Grandma make some ink?"

Magdalena nodded eagerly, making her blond pigtails dance.

"We'll need to gather some raspberries," Mother Stutzman said. Barbara and the girls followed her to the row of canes not far from the house. It was late in the season, but they found a few berries still clinging to the canes.

Annie and Magdalena helped to pick the ripe fruit, eating a few berries and staining their hands the way Barbara had as a young girl.

Soon afterward, Magdalena helped Mother Stutzman press the berries through a strainer. They added a little vinegar and a pinch of salt. Magdalena stirred it and Mother Stutzman poured it into a glass ink well.

"Magdalena, don't wipe your hands on your dress," Barbara said. Taking care of three young children while she still felt such raw grief was draining her patience.

"Will you write the letter for me?" Barbara asked Mother Stutzman.

"No, you should do it. I'll watch the children." Mother Stutzman pulled a blank piece of paper from a shelf in the living room and laid it on the table along with a gray quill pen. And then she took the children outside.

Barbara dipped the quill into the inkwell and began to write: "Dear Grandpa and Grandma Detweiler." She stared at the paper, distracted by the drift of her daughters' childish voices through the open door. The late September sun shone through the east window, casting a shaft of light onto her work. It was an oddly pleasant morning for a horrible task.

A few minutes later, Mother Stutzman poked her head inside. "How's it coming?"

Barbara lifted the nearly blank paper. "I don't know how to get started."

"Just think of talking to them as if they were here, and write down what you would say."

That was the problem. She didn't know what she would say to them if they were there. She hadn't seen them since she was four years old. How could she describe the awful murders of her mother and two of her siblings, or the burning of all their buildings, or the panic that made it too dangerous to give the three loved ones a decent funeral? What should she say about her father and her two brothers—carried off to who knew where—and her fear that she would never see them again? What should she say about how depressed she felt, about the sleepless nights she spent worrying about the children, or about the terror that gripped her whenever she heard an unfamiliar noise outside?

Barbara covered her face with her hands. If only her brother John would write this letter; he would just write the facts and get it over with.

Maybe that was the answer she was looking for. She wrote down a few basic facts she thought they should know about the recent attack—who, what, where, and how. It would be a long time before she could write about the why. She closed the letter with "Love, Barbara."

Mother Stutzman sealed the letter in an envelope. "One of our neighbors is going to Reading in a few days," she said. "I'm sure he wouldn't mind taking this along. From there, someone can get it to Philadelphia and onto a ship."

"Grandma, can we go to the creek to play?" Magdalena asked. The children often begged to go to the creek.

"*Jah*," Mother Stutzman said.

Barbara was shocked. "Isn't it too dangerous?"

Mother Stutzman shook her head. "I think it will be all right. We'll all go. It will do us all good."

And she was right. There was nothing like the ripple of the water over the rocks at the creek to calm Barbara's spirit. If Mother Stutzman wasn't going to let the Indians frighten her away from that simple moment of enjoyment, neither was she.

Barbara and her mother-in-law found a comfortable place to sit on the creek bank. They watched the three children closely as they played in the water. The sun threw splotches of light that danced on the ground as the wind stirred through the trees. The creek ran clear and cold, yet the air was warm enough that she didn't mind if the children got wet.

It was a peaceful scene until Magdalena made a chance discovery. "Look at this, Mama." She held up a flat stone with sharp edges. "What is it?"

As Barbara turned the flinty stone in her hand, an invisible hand clutched her heart. "That's an Indian arrowhead, honey." A perfect one, except for a broken edge where it was once fastened to the shaft.

She hadn't found an arrowhead in twenty years—not since the time she had first played in this creek as a child. She was about Magdalena's age, and her parents were choosing a plot in the virgin forest on which to settle and set up a farm. Next to the ocean voyage on the *Charming Nancy*, it was the most exciting time she could remember from childhood.

Jacob carried a small map drawn by the land agent in Philadelphia. They explored a tract called Ipswich, named by William Penn after an English town. The agent told her father that if no one was living on the land and he was the first one to claim it, the land could be his.

Barbara and her brother John held the map while their father had set up the boundary stones. Jacob said it was a map of Lancaster County, Pennsylvania. Later, the government split off the eastern part and called it Berks County.

Jacob and Lizzie walked around the woods, marking trees and setting up stones to mark boundaries. Lizzie let Jacob do most of the choosing, but they decided together about the place to build the house. "I'd like to build it close to the spring," Lizzie said. "I don't want to carry water farther than I have to."

They agreed on a spot near two large oaks that looked to be well over a hundred years old. Most of the nearby trees looked much younger and smaller, which would make them easier to cut down. And this creek was close by; a place where they could trap game in the wintertime and the cattle could stay cool in hot weather.

Barbara had never seen her father so excited. He moved eagerly from one part of the woods to another. As they moved toward the west end of the plot he had chosen, they came upon Northkill Creek. Her father showed it to her on the map.

Barbara was so fascinated by the creek that she let her brother John hold the map by himself and took to playing with stones. That was the moment she found the arrowhead, nearly buried in the bank just next to the creek. It was as thick as her thumb and cut into the shape of an arrow. She took it to her father. "What's this?"

Jacob turned it over in his hand. "Maybe it belonged to the Indians. They might have fished in the creek and hunted here."

"Are there Indians here now?"

"No, the Indians sold this land to William Penn and moved farther west," Jacob said. "Penn called this land Pennsylvania and invited our people to come live on it. Penn is a Quaker and believes in peace, like we do. He believed that you should never harm or kill your fellow man, and you should get land only by paying for it. That's why we moved here." His gaze swept over this land, their new home. "I can't wait to write to my father and brothers back home about this place."

Jacob walked here and there, poking at the soft, black dirt lying under the cover of leaves on the forest floor. He tested the soil in a half dozen places, admiring its makeup and moisture. "Smell this," he said, holding out his palm filled with topsoil. He could tell how well the crops would grow just by smelling the musky odor of the loam in his hand. He pointed out the places for an orchard here, a garden plot there, and fields of flax, wheat, and barley. And now—

"Barbara?" Mother Stutzman interrupted her thoughts. "It's about time for dinner."

"*Jah*," Barbara said. "I'm ready."

It wasn't true. She wanted to stay there at the creek, remembering the good times from the past. If only life at the Northkill were as safe and simple as it had been when she was Magdalena's age.

-15-

Lou glared at Jacob and Christian when he got up the next morning. Was he still angry about the events of the night before? Christian was rubbing the heavy streaks on his wrists where he had yanked against the ropes during his night terrors. Did he even realize what had happened? As soon as the guard untied Jacob's hands for breakfast, he tried to get close enough to Christian to assure him of his love, but the guard stepped between them and shoved him away. Jacob clenched his teeth, struggling to remain calm while Christian's eye was on him. It would do no good to show anger.

The hills were draped with morning fog as the group broke up camp and started out onto the path. The sun gradually burned off the fog, and the air was clear by the time they forded the shallows of the river onto an island. Lou and the warriors huddled around a painted post standing near the path. There were several symbols on it. Bryce mumbled that it had to do with the war, telling the number of people killed or captured.

The island looked larger than Jacob's farm back home. It lay in the middle of the Susquehanna, a stretch of sandy soil with tall trees and a large clearing. A field of ripening corn stood close to a group of huts. The warriors entered the village, firing their guns and shouting scalp halloos, a yell that tied a knot in Jacob's chest. "Aw-oh! Aw-oh!" they yelled, in a repeated chorus of triumph. The yell sounded like a distant cousin to yodeling; they hammered on the "Aw" and then leaped an octave to the "oh," holding it as long as they had breath.

The warriors who had taken scalps marched out front with their trophies on hoops, each fastened to the ends of a thin, short pole. The prisoners followed at the end of the procession. Jacob marched along with his eyes downcast, glancing up just enough to see where he was going. How could he look up when three of the scalps on display had been robbed from people who once sat around his dinner table?

The village appeared to be small, but a crowd of men, women, and children soon gathered around them. The children clapped and danced at the sight. The village chief came out and spoke to the guide, who took his cues from Lou. The warriors showed off Jacob's family's scalps, carrying on in their language.

Jacob responded like an Indian. Instead of weeping or shouting at them, he guarded his face. Perhaps with practice, he could learn to keep a sober expression regardless of what he was feeling inside. He wouldn't give them the pleasure of seeing him upset.

The chief led the war party to the west end of the village where there was a large tent at the edge of a clearing. There they lit a fire, likely a sign that they would stay for a while. The guards took the ropes off the prisoners' hands and let all four of them walk freely within the open space. Two guards—one at each end of the clearing—sat cross-legged with their guns lying across their legs.

It was the moment Jacob had been praying for. He stepped up to the chief and offered him two dried peaches from his pocket. Although the peaches had been squeezed in his pocket for nearly a week, they were still recognizable.

"For you, the chief," Jacob said, and bowed slightly as he held out the fruit.

The chief took one and put it into his mouth. His face brightened as he sucked on the morsel. Finally, he chewed and swallowed it. "*Wanishi* (Thank you)," he said.

He took the second slice and called for a little boy who stood in the clearing. He said something to the lad, who scampered toward the group of huts. A few minutes later, the boy returned with a woman decked in ornaments. Jacob took her to be the chief's wife.

When the woman came to him, the chief offered her the peach, motioning toward Jacob and telling her something. She ate the peach as Jacob watched, showing the same signs of appreciation that the chief had shown.

Joseph saw what was happening and came up to the chief with the one peach slice he had left. What discipline, to have kept from eating it while he was hungry on the journey. Joseph held it out to the chief, who took it and paused, as though deciding what to do with it. Just then Christian came with a peach slice he had saved too and gave it to the chief.

The chief smiled and handed the peaches to two other villagers. Both ate them with gusto. Surely they had done the right thing, Jacob thought, by feeding the enemy.

The villagers crowded around the warriors. Apparently something important was about to happen. The chief gave an order, and the people began to line up in two rows about ten feet apart. Within minutes, some fifty men, women, and children stood in the two lines. In their hands they carried axes, clubs, switches, brooms, and heavy sticks. So this was what the gauntlet looked like.

The villagers looked at the prisoners and brandished their weapons. Some laughed, apparently enjoying the discomfort on the prisoner's faces. Their eagerness to inflict pain only added to the fright inspired by the hideous paint on their faces.

The chief motioned for Bryce, the newest prisoner, to go first. Bryce cursed and started off running between the two rows of people toward a pole perhaps thirty yards away. No one blocked the way, but an elderly woman threw sand into his face and a young brave tried to trip him by thrusting a stick between his legs. Bryce tripped and fell down about halfway to the pole. Three Indians rained extra blows on him. Jacob turned away his eyes, not willing to bear the sight.

When Jacob looked up, Bryce was back on his feet, pushing his way with his arms in front of his face. He staggered to the end of the line and fell onto his knees, grasping the end post with both hands as though they were the horns on Aaron's altar.

After he caught his breath, he staggered to his feet and held his hands over the lower ribs on his right side, a pained expression on his face. Blood ran down his cheek from a wound just above his left eyebrow. He limped away from the crowd, favoring his right leg. He sat down on the ground and rubbed the blood off of his face with his tattered shirt.

The chief looked at Jacob as though to say he was the next in line. Jacob began walking toward the line. It was time to show his sons the importance of bravery. *Oh, God, help me.* As Jacob stepped toward the line, the chief's wife whispered in his ear. And then the chief stepped forward and stopped Jacob with his hand. He shook his head and said, "You gave peaches. No run gauntlet." *Thank God!*

The people in line scowled and brandished their weapons when the chief spared Jacob's sons as well. How could Jacob and his sons face Bryce, who would surely resent such unequal treatment?

The humiliation was not over, however. The chief stood by as a number of women made him sit cross-legged on the ground and started shaving Jacob's head. Two women chopped at his thick hair with a dull razor. Soon his scalp was bare except for a three- or four-inch circle on the crown of his head.

Although it was painful to have them jerk at his hair with a razor, it was nothing compared to what followed. Several women begin to pull the hair out of his beard, yanking it out a few strands at a time. Each time they pulled out a tuft of hair, they dipped their fingers into a pile of ash heaped on a piece of bark. Jacob's head soon throbbed from the searing sensation on his face. It was as much a test of endurance as running the gauntlet would have been.

Jacob's chin throbbed with pain, but he resisted the urge to cry out. Mindful of the Scripture that the bishop had read from the prophet Isaiah last Easter, Jacob recalled the words:

"I gave my back to the smiters, and my cheeks to them that plucked off the hair: I hid not my face from shame and spitting." The bishop had said it spoke of Christ. Having his beard plucked was but little, Jacob thought, compared to what his Lord endured.

It had been so long since he'd shaved his beard that he'd forgotten the smoothness of his bare chin, the square feel of his jaw. What would Lizzie say if she saw him now? Would the people back home recognize him as being Amish? That is, if he ever saw them again.

After the ordeal of losing his beard, a woman handed Jacob a new pair of moccasins. "I make," she said with a smile, pointing at herself and then the beaded footwear. She motioned him to take off his shoes, which he was glad to do. He tried on his new moccasins. The soles didn't offer much support, but if the Indians fared well with them, so could he. It was better than walking barefoot through the woods.

The chief nodded with approval. "Fruit Grower," he said to Jacob. "You are Fruit Grower." And then he repeated it more loudly for the group to hear. "New name for white man—Fruit Grower." It was the first time the Indians had called him by name. A name of their choosing.

Bryce cursed and swore as they cut his hair. When he flailed his arms to stop them from tying a feather into his scalp lock, they bound his hands behind his back. When they were finished shaving him, a woman gave him new moccasins as well and the chief dubbed him Broken Stone. The people laughed with glee and a boy beat his drum.

The women went even further with Jacob's sons, Joseph and Christian, painting their faces and chests. They called Joseph "Swift Foot," since he had outdistanced the warriors during the attack. They called Christian "Stargazer," for they had seen him pointing at the stars in the evening. The new names fit them well, but they were far removed from the biblical names he and Lizzie had chosen for them with care.

Lou sauntered up to Jacob. "Stargazer's blue eyes make him a real prize for the Indians," he said. "That's why they spared his life."

Jacob jerked his head to look at Christian. So that's why the warrior had arrested the strike of his tomahawk in midair over Christian's head on that fateful morning.

Just then a woman pulled a small brass mirror from her bag and held it in front of Christian's face. At first the boy studied his reflection with a somber face, and then he began to smile. The woman smiled with him, and then put the mirror back into her bag.

Jacob fought back tears. His beloved son was painted in the likeness of the warriors who had wreaked violence on his family.

It was late afternoon when the captain led the war party back onto the Great Shamokin Path. When they came to a wide creek, they paused for a minute while Lou talked with the scouts. Although Lou was the captain, he depended on the natives for direction. They spoke enough French that when Jacob strained his ears, he could make out what they were saying. Perhaps if he got free from his captors, he could retrace their steps toward home.

That evening when they stopped for the night, a warrior pulled a rabbit carcass, which he had shot an hour before, out of his bag. He skinned it while one of the other warriors kindled a fire. When the fire was hot enough, the warrior cooked the meat over the open flame, suspending it with a sharp stick he used as a skewer. Afterward, he cut up the rabbit and handed out the pieces. Jacob's stomach growled as several of the men roasted their pieces over the fire with sharpened sticks. But Christian was the only prisoner who got a piece for himself.

The next morning, the war party followed a path along several creeks. From there they walked up to the crest of a ridge.

The ascent was long and tiring. At the bottom of the descent from the ridge, they came to a deer lick where they stopped to rest for a few minutes. The warriors dug at the mineral deposit with knives and sharp sticks, and a few of the warriors put salt into their bags. It raised the happy prospect for Jacob that they would salt their provisions, since everything they had eaten on the trip would have tasted better that way.

Lou decided to stay the night at a camp, a wide open place where another river flowed into the Susquehanna. No one lived there, but there were several small wooden huts to be used by travelers who came by. The guards would not allow Jacob and the boys to sleep together in a shelter. They forced them to use different ones, laying them bound on the dirt floor.

The temperature must have dropped close to freezing that night, so the shelter was a welcome place. But when Jacob woke up the next morning, fleas were hopping on his skin. He picked at them after a warrior untied his hands, but soon gave up.

The next evening, the group came to another sleeping place, with small shelters for travelers. While the others were tending a fire, Jacob pulled the pebbles out of his pocket. With the one for that day's journey, the number came to eleven. This time, before he bedded down for the night, he looked for fleas. Seeing none, he gladly slept under a roof. It was better than sleeping on the frost-covered ground.

The maple leaves along the trail the next day were beginning to take on their fall colors. Like the cool water in the springs, they stood as signs of God's grace. Jacob needed it that day, with all of the river crossings they had made. They had followed the Susquehanna, first on one side and then the other, trying to avoid the dense mountain laurel. But the laurel grew on both sides of the river, so they had crossed the river five times in one day. It was impossible to keep his moccasins dry.

That day, Jacob found a few fleeting minutes to speak with his sons. "It looks like Tom hasn't been as mean," he said to Joseph. "I haven't seen him poke you with his gun lately. Or hit you."

"Not since they shaved our heads back at the island," Joseph said, "and gave us new names."

Christian showed his wrists. "And they're not tying my hands so tight."

It wasn't true for Bryce. He was still resisting. When would he learn that he'd be better off by cooperating with his captors? Or would he rather be beaten?

That night, the sky was clear and heavily speckled with stars. Christian sat close to Jacob as they warmed themselves by the fire. The boy pointed to the sky. "Is Mother up there with God?"

It was the first time he had mentioned Lizzie. He must have missed her terribly. Jacob winced. "Her soul is alive."

"Does she see this paint?" He touched the broad band of red paint on his temple.

"*Mam* always liked red strawberries and bright red cardinals, especially when it snowed."

The tension in Christian's face relaxed a little.

Their stargazing ended abruptly when a guard motioned them to a place where they would be bound for the night. They lay down in the open air, but at least there was a bed of pine needles.

Christian's questions about Lizzie stirred up Jacob's own. Where had they buried his loved ones? Had there been a funeral? Were his married children's families safe?

-16-

Jacob and his sons had been on the trail for more than two weeks when the war party arrived at a fort that sported a French flag. "Fort Machault," he heard Lou say. The encampment lay close to the Venango path, adjacent to an Indian settlement, nearby a fork where a creek fed into the river. As they approached the fort, they passed by some thirty log houses off to their left, between the Path and the river. A half dozen Indian children ran up to watch as they approached and then trailed them after they went by.

The fort looked quite new, surely built by the French during the war. Was this the place where they would be held?

As they approached, the warriors let out the usual scalp halloo. The soldiers at the fort echoed the shouts with their guns, firing them off faster than Jacob could count. The warriors came back with another loud chorus of joyful shouts. It made his skin crawl.

The fort was built in the shape of a rectangle, with odd-shaped bastions in each corner. The outside walls were made of saplings planted in the ground. The logs were about eight inches thick and stood some thirteen feet high. The gate of the fort faced the river, approximately sixty yards up the slope from the river's edge. Between the river and the fort lay barracks that housed French soldiers.

As they came to the gate, a French officer stepped out to welcome the warriors. He looked pleased as the captain reported on the raid and the warriors held up their scalps. Jacob felt sick to his stomach.

The officer ordered the prisoners delivered to the inside of the fort, and they were led through the gate. Rifles and ammunition stood inside the magazine in one of the corners. A small cannon mounted on wheels stood nearby.

After looking over the captives with care, the captain wrote something down in a ledger. What kind of records was he keeping?

Jacob woke up to the sound of a rooster crowing outside a small window in the room where he had slept. The cock was perched on top of one of the upright logs that formed the wall surrounding the fort.

Sleeping with Indian warriors for a fortnight on the trail had been difficult enough. But being locked up inside the French fort hammered home a truth Jacob was just beginning to see. The Indians were hostages of the same struggle that he and his sons, as prisoners, were. The real battle was between the French and the British, who had stretched their wars of empire into the Ohio territories. The Indians had chosen to fight on the side of the French, but in the end it was not likely to make much difference. Their native lands hung in the balance between the two foreign powers.

Jacob got up when he heard the reveille that summoned the soldiers to rise. The French flag flapped in the morning breeze. By the time he had eaten a few bites of breakfast, he had counted some fifty men in uniform in the large clearing. Most of the soldiers nearby wore dark blue uniforms with black shoulder belts, matching that of Lou, the captain of the war party. Like him, they spoke French.

After giving the prisoners a few bites of breakfast, the guard opened the gate and directed them down to the creek, where several Indians were readying several batteaux at the water's edge. Jacob had never seen boats constructed this way. They were made of wood—more than twenty feet long and over three feet wide. The flat bottoms met the sides to form a point at each end. The captain gave Joseph and Jacob each an oar and told them to sit in the middle of the first boat in the convoy. Another oarsman sat in the back, using an oar as a rudder. They sent Christian and several other prisoners from the fort to a boat farther back.

When everything was loaded, several natives stepped into the water and pushed them away from shore before climbing in. The captain of the party called instructions from his seat at the helm. One of the soldiers showed Jacob and Joseph how to row and called out the rhythm for them to get started.

Having to row was better than having his hands tied. But the two weeks of being bound had weakened Jacob's muscles. Or was it that he was paired with his son Joseph, who showed off his strength with long and hearty strokes?

French Creek was only about twelve yards wide and shallow enough at places that Jacob poled with his paddle rather than rowing. The creek wound lazily around many bends, so the man with the rudder in the back earned his keep. Had the creek run in a straight line, it would have cut their travel time in half. The use of batteaux made sense as they went through the shallows. Had the boats had a regular keel, they would have scraped bottom.

As they floated along on the creek, the warriors entertained themselves by spearing fish. When they stopped for the night, several of the warriors gathered clams. They crouched in the shallow water to harvest them, gathering them up in a basket. The men baked the clams over heated rocks, so everyone ate well that night.

On the morning of their second day on French Creek, the captain banked the convoy at the mouth of another creek. It was the site of an Indian village named Custaloga's Town. Custaloga was a Delaware chief of the Wolf clan, in charge of the treaties for his nation under Chief Shingas.

Because of Custaloga's status as a chief, the war party called out the usual scalp halloos and fired their guns. The village turned out in force to celebrate—drumming, dancing, and kindling a huge fire. After the victory procession, a number of the villagers convinced the captain to stay for games, including a race. They freed the prisoners of their ropes and allowed them to watch from the clearing. Because the war party referred to Joseph as Swift Foot, they asked him to race with the young men. The steel in Joseph's eye told Jacob that he was intending to win.

All of the young Delawares were wearing deerskin, a contrast to Joseph's linen pants and shirt. The chief pointed to a painted post perhaps fifty yards away, motioning to show that the racers were to run to the post and back to the starting line.

Joseph got off last, but he leaned into the race and got to the painted post at the same time as the lead runner, and headed back in the front of the pack. He ran with long, easy strides born of practice on the farm; he had seldom walked when he could run.

When Joseph finished the race a stride in front of anyone else, the villagers cheered. Joseph swaggered up to his father. "I knew I could outrun them, 'cause that's what I did on the day they attacked our house. The only reason they caught me was because they found where I was hiding."

Jacob's eyes widened. So Joseph had come that close to escaping the attack.

After the captain urged the war party to get back to the batteaux, the chief bargained to have one of the villagers accompany them. The emissary traveled in the first boat with Jacob and Joseph, staying close to Joseph. Were they hoping to bring him back to the village?

As they rowed along, the emissary spotted a deer standing at the edge of the wood. He motioned to Joseph and pointed to the deer. "*Achtu.* You say—*Achtu.*"

"*Achtu*, Joseph said.

The emissary dipped his hand into the water. "*Mbi.*"

"*Mbi.*"

The emissary pointed at the warriors in the boat. "*Ndopaluwinuwak.*"

"*Ndopaluwinuwak.*" Jacob tried to repeat the words under his breath, but they were hard to pronounce. Joseph made it look too easy. What if he forgot the German language? Or worse yet, the German ways?

After the third day of travel on the creek, the group moved back to land. Yet the path was so marshy that someone had laid down logs to form a wide path for portage. The bumpy wooden surface stretched for miles. The prisoners and most of the warriors walked, but the captain rode in a wagon piled high with supplies.

By the time the sun dropped low in the sky that day, seagulls circled overhead and the marshy meadow gave way to a shallow bay. Beyond the bay was a body of water as far as one could see.

The captors quickened their pace as the group neared the water. "Presque Isle," Jacob heard the captain say. A narrow strip of land arched into the immense body of water, which Jacob took to be Lake Erie.

A fort stood close to the water's edge with a ragged French flag flapping in the stiff breeze. A small creek wound its way around the southern and eastern edges of the fort and then emptied into the shallow bay. Off to the right, a block house stood next to a pond.

The warriors marched briskly toward the fort, which was surrounded by an abatis, a wall of defense made of branches stacked on their sides with sharpened ends pointing outward. Unlike the fort they'd just left, the walls of this garrison were made of heavy squared timbers laid upon one another in the manner of a log cabin. The wall must have been at least twelve feet high and perhaps 120 feet long on each side of the square enclosure. Bastions jutted from each corner of the enclosure to enable soldiers to fire at the flanks of an enemy storming the walls.

The war party marched through the wide gate that opened toward the path. An officer stood to greet the captain. The tone of their voices showed that the officer was happy with what Lou had brought with him.

The officer ordered the ropes removed from the prisoners' arms. Here the walls of the fort would serve as security. A soldier stood guard at the gate with a gun.

The officer led Jacob and the other prisoners into a large structure made of rough-hewn logs and a roof of cedar shakes. A young soldier with a French uniform led them toward a room at the end of the building. The soldier directed them inside and then stepped in behind them. Several other prisoners shared the room with them.

Jacob woke up sweating several times during the night, even though the room wasn't heated and the October air was rather chilly outside. What was amiss? Might this be the place where the French were rumored to sell prisoners as slaves? Or where they released them to Indians for adoption? What was to happen to him and his sons?

After breakfast the next morning, the captain separated the dozen or more prisoners into three different groups. A sense of dread grew in Jacob like a chill, starting in his chest and spreading out to his limbs. This might be the last time to speak to his sons.

Jacob motioned to Joseph and Christian, who stood unbound but were being closely watched by a French guard. He ignored the scowl of the guard and spoke to them in the Swiss dialect. "Boys, if you are taken so far away and are kept so long that you forget the German language, do not forget your names. And say the Lord's Prayer each day."

Christian's eyes widened. "Where are they taking us?"

Jacob fought back the chill in his soul as he put his hand on Christian's shoulder. "It's hard to tell. As far as your conscience allows it, always treat them with respect and do what they ask. God will give you wisdom."

Just then a warrior stepped between them. "Come, Stargazer," he said to Christian. He motioned for the boy to follow him. Christian looked at his father with panic and longing in his eyes. Jacob reached out and took his hand just before they led him away.

Jacob pressed his fist to his mouth as Christian glanced back over his shoulder, fear etched on his small face. Would they ever see each other again?

Next it was Joseph. "Swift Foot, we go now," the emissary from Custaloga's village said to him. Jacob nodded toward his son and raised his hand slightly in a parting wave. But it was as if Joseph was becoming an Indian; he showed no emotion in his face and didn't wave back. He turned and fell in the back of the line of prisoners. Tom Lions marched in his favored place at the back with a twisted grin on his face. If only Joseph would keep his tongue, he could stay out of trouble.

Ever since that first day on the trail, Jacob had steeled himself for that moment of parting, but he was far from ready. There were too many things he should have said, too many things left to teach the boys before they were on their own. Now there was nothing to do but commit them into God's hands.

The boys were only a few rods away when Captain Lou tied Jacob's wrists and pushed him toward a small knot of prisoners and Indians. "You're going with the Senecas."

Why the Senecas? Had he just been traded by the Delawares as a prisoner of war? Jacob walked slowly toward the place where Bryce stood sullen-faced with two other white prisoners, his hands tied behind his back. He glared at Jacob.

Just then a Seneca warrior gave a command and took the lead on the path. Jacob fell into the line of prisoners, followed by a guard eager to wield his power. Even though Jacob was keeping up with the group, the warrior poked him hard in the ribs with his rifle. Jacob had no idea where they were headed, but he knew that every step meant more distance from his beloved sons.

-17-

It was one of those October days when Barbara didn't need a coat to work outside. If the frost hadn't killed the tomatoes a week earlier, they would've been getting plump and ripe in the balmy fall weather.

After supper, Cristy cut grass for hay, trying to get as much work done as possible before winter set in. As soon as he came in for the night, Barbara cornered him. "Can you watch the children for a while?"

Cristy wrinkled his eyebrows. "Where are you—"

"I need time to be by myself."

Cristy shrugged his shoulders. "It's dark—"

"There's a full moon." Barbara slipped out the door before he could stop her. *Mam* used to say, "A man works from sun to sun, but a woman's work is never done." Barbara hoped Cristy could understand that and wouldn't mind putting the girls to bed.

The sun had set and the first stars were twinkling in the sky. She took several deep breaths and then started up the path toward the old homestead. She came to the charred remains of the house where the awful killing took place. The burnt logs cast spooky shadows in the moonlight where pieces of the structure lay scattered in the cellar.

Barbara stared at the ruins. How much warning had her family been given? Had they tried to escape? Did *Dat* try to defend the family?

Barbara took the familiar path to the bake oven, the place where she had spent countless hours with her mother. The iron door was hanging open so she slammed it shut. So many memories tumbled inside her head. Here is where *Mam* taught her to bake, a duty that had taken up many of their days.

"The fastest way to a man's heart is through his stomach," *Mam* had often said. She proved that actions spoke louder than words. Week in and week out, her fresh-baked bread and pies drew *Dat* to the table regardless of how much work he had to do, even at harvest time. *Mam* dimpled the edges of her pies and pricked patterns into the crust. They looked delicious before you even took a bite. And Barbara's brothers would scramble to get the first taste of the jam she made from the berries each fall.

When Cristy and Barbara had started courting, she had set herself to learn *Mam*'s cooking skills in earnest. "You can't learn this by talking," *Mam* would say. "Watch me and I'll show you." Talking came easier for *Mam* when her hands were busy. Barbara had learned to ask the hardest questions when *Mam* was in the middle of something. She'd say the most honest things about herself when she was sweating at the stove.

Barbara could almost feel her presence as she leaned against the cold stones that formed the oven. If only she could ask *Mam* a few questions about those last minutes, when the house was on fire. Was she terrified? Did she know she was dying?

Barbara tore herself away and walked over to the barn. She stood by the corral where *Dat* raised the calf he had given to them as a wedding present some years later. She had seen that calf being born—one of the few times she had watched a cow deliver.

It was springtime and the snow was melting. *Dat* tried to coax the laboring cow into the barn, but she wouldn't budge from the corral. The birth was taking so long that *Dat* intervened. He tied a rope to the unborn calf and tugged on it. The calf came out so suddenly that *Dat* lost his footing and slipped in the mud. *Dat* sent Barbara to the creek to fetch a couple of buckets of water. It was past midnight by the time they got *Dat* and the calf cleaned up. *Dat* let Barbara name the calf. Since it had a white spot on its head that looked like the new moon, Barbara called her Moonface.

Moonface started giving milk about the time that Cristy and Barbara got married. Since then, she'd kept them supplied. Since *Mam* taught Barbara how to make cheese, they depended on Moonface for curds and whey.

A sharp pain in Barbara's ribs jolted her into the present. The baby was kicking, pushing hard against her right side. She rubbed her round abdomen. This baby was due in less than three months. *Mam* had predicted she would have a boy. With her mother gone, who would assist with the birth?

The moon had risen to the tops of the trees so that Barbara could easily see where she was going. She walked over to the still, which had burned to the ground. Barbara had often watched her father heat up the still, making whiskey out of corn or rye.

"It's the easiest way to store and sell my crops," *Dat* would say when anyone asked why he made strong drink. Whiskey always brought a good price and was easy to store. Not that *Dat* kept much around the house. He made sure that when the Indians came by to visit, he didn't have anything within reach. He'd heard too many stories of trouble when the Indians got ahold of strong drink. Or other people, for that matter.

Dat had kept it from Barbara and her siblings too, except when they were sick. Once when she was about ten years old, she had a bad cold. She had coughed so hard one night that it had kept the family awake, so *Dat* had poured a bit of whiskey in a cup and told her to drink it slowly. *Mam* knew it would burn, so she had added a little bit of honey and peppermint to make it taste better. It had cleared out her sinuses and helped her cough up the phlegm. No wonder they called it fire water. The boys begged to try some the next day but *Dat* wouldn't let them. "We only use it when we're sick."

Cristy was like *Dat* in that way. He built a still not long after they got married and was careful with it, like *Dat*. Barbara wasn't worried about strong drink ruining their house, although Cristy had reminded her twice since *Mam* died that it was meant only for times of illness.

From the still, Barbara walked over to the orchard. *Dat* had planted those trees soon after they had moved onto the land. He taught the children a proverb as they helped plant the trees: "In smallest space, a fruit tree place. Attend it well, have fruit to sell." When those trees grew up, they paid back many times the hard work it took to get them started.

Barbara had been about Franey's age when *Dat* had first sent her up the branches with a little bucket to pick fruit. How many hours had she spent picking peaches and apples in those trees? She had loved to reach for the highest apples. Whenever she could barely touch an apple with her fingertips, she would inch out just a little farther.

"Be careful," *Dat* would say. But when she handed him the full bucket, his eyes always twinkled. "I could never reach those." The memory swelled up inside her chest, making it hard to breathe for a moment.

Her father pruned the branches in his orchard every year. It seemed like cruel punishment; the trees looked forlorn and naked after he'd chopped them back so far. "Aren't you ruining them?" she would ask.

Dat chuckled at her worries. "Don't you know what Jesus told the twelve? 'Every branch in me that beareth not fruit he taketh away: and every branch that beareth fruit, he purgeth it, that it may bring forth more fruit.'" He was right. She was always amazed at how the pruned branches grew back thicker than ever.

Barbara now stood among the trees in silence. Would *Dat* ever trim these trees again? Or eat their fruit?

On sudden impulse, she lifted her hands like the branches around her and prayed a simple prayer. "God, if it is possible, bring my *Dat* and my brothers back home to this farm."

Barbara turned to make her way back home but stopped for a moment at the springhouse when she realized how dry her mouth felt. The roof and walls of the building were mostly burnt, but the door of the small house still hung on the lower hinge. She yanked on the door and stared inside. The moon shown through the open roof and glinted off the small metal cup that sat on the ledge beside the spring. How many hundreds of times had she drunk out of that cup?

Barbara knelt by the spring and dipped the cup into the cool water. She rinsed out the cup and then filled it with water again. She took a sip. It had never tasted better. The freshness of the water quenched her thirst, and she filled the cup again and stepped into the moonlight.

Her eyes fell on the mounds that marked the place where she and John had buried their loved ones a few weeks earlier. She strode over to her mother's grave, the cup of water still in her hand. There she recalled the story *Mam* had once told her about David the psalmist. When he was fleeing from his enemy Saul, several of David's mighty men sneaked through enemy lines to bring him a cup of water from the well at Bethlehem. But when they handed it to David, he poured it out on the ground as an offering to God. He declared it holy because the men had risked their lives to bring the water from his beloved well.

On impulse, Barbara poured the water from her cup onto the head of the grave where her mother lay. She too was standing on holy ground. When she looked up at the moon, she sensed God's assurance in its light. Barbara lingered for a moment in its white warmth. Should she return the cup to the springhouse or take it back to the house with her? It would be a comfort in her home, a reminder of her better days as a child. But if she left it at the spring, perhaps someone passing by would find comfort there.

Barbara wavered for a minute and then returned the cup to the springhouse. Her father had always said it is more blessed to give than to receive.

With a final glance back at the farm of her childhood, Barbara started down the well-worn path toward her home. The moon lit the path ahead like grace itself, or hope, pushing away the darkness.

-18-

Jacob shivered in the chilly fall weather as they marched back down the wooden portage road from Presque Isle and then followed a large creek to the east. The rolling hills were alive with red, orange, yellow, and green, mixed with shades of brown. Back home, he would have basked in the beauty of God's creation, but the guard's ill mood brought to mind the way that Tom Lions had treated his sons. Where were Joseph and Christian by now? Was Tom still harassing one of them?

After marching for three days, they came to an Indian village. The late afternoon sun shone bright on fields of corn and squash that lay outside a tall palisade that surrounded the village. Jacob heard one of the warriors say, "Buckaloons."

The palisade was made of logs at least twelve to twenty inches in diameter, buried in the ground next to each other. The poles stood shoulder-to-shoulder like sentries, much taller than he could reach. The fence stretched around all four sides of the village, announcing that this was no temporary settlement.

The warriors led Jacob through a gate in the wall along with the other prisoners from Presque Isle. Three longhouses stood inside the fortress walls. By now, Jacob was getting used to the fuss that the villagers would make when they came through, but this time it was different. The warriors had left the scalps behind at Presque Isle, so there were no scalp halloos, and no one marched in a victory parade. Instead the prisoners were forced to sit on the ground in a clearing near one of the longhouses. A few villagers tossed wood on the campfire as men, women, and children came from all directions to join the event. As usual, the villagers spoke in a language Jacob could not understand.

One of the other prisoners sat next to him as the sun was setting. His full name, he told Jacob, was John Henry Specht, but he went by Hank. He was from the area near Fort Augusta and had been captured in a raid several months earlier, so he knew the camp well. He spoke German and knew a lot about the Indians and the war. "They're telling the people who you are, where you got captured, and why you were chosen to come here."

Jacob wrinkled his brow. "Good question. Why are we here?"

"This a secure place to keep prisoners. They probably chose you as a replacement for family members they lost to sickness or war."

Jacob's mind flew to Christian and Joseph. Was that why they had been taken to different places? Was that why some-one had accompanied them from Custaloga's town? "I can see why they want children. But why an older man like me?"

"You'll be good for ransom, unless they decide to kill you instead."

Jacob shivered. Why would they have marched him through the woods for three weeks only to kill him?

The drumming, dancing, and speech-making at the camp-fire ended after the sun had gone down. One of the guards led the prisoners into a longhouse and loosened the hemp ropes that bound their wrists. Jacob sat down on a ledge that was fastened to the wall about three feet from the floor. It looked as if it was meant to serve as a bed. Several men sat on the edge of the beds, watching them get settled. A warrior stood guard at the door with his rifle.

It was the first time Jacob had seen a longhouse, so he squinted to make out the way the building was constructed. The round-topped structure was three times as long as it was wide. It was made of tall saplings pushed into the ground along the two side walls and bent to meet in the middle. Horizontal poles ran in parallel rows across the uprights at several dif-ferent heights along the whole length of the walls. Sheets of wooden bark were fastened onto these poles to form a cover for the outside. A door opened into each of the two ends of the building, which rose straight from the ground and were covered with the same material.

Three fires burned along a line through the center of the longhouse, so the house smelled strongly of smoke. The smoke curled upward and out of openings at the peak of the roof.

A large bear hide lay on the rough wooden platform that was to serve as his bed. As usual, Jacob lay down to sleep without taking off his clothing. He ran his hand across the fur of the bear. It was much better than sleeping on the frosty ground outside. Yet the musty smell of the wooden sheeting on the walls pressed in on Jacob, as did the dusty smell of the earthen floor. Had it not been for the autumn chill, he would much rather have slept with the smell of the freshly fallen leaves under the night sky.

Jacob slipped his hand into his pocket and pulled out the pebbles he'd been saving. He counted twenty-four of the little stones in the light of the flames that cast their wavy shadows on the walls and ceiling. If they had marched twelve to fifteen miles a day, how many miles would that be? Maybe Hank could help him figure it out.

There were perhaps two dozen men in the lodge that night—mostly white prisoners along with a few native villagers. The sound of snoring from several places in the room broke the silence of the night. A soft murmur rose from the place where several warriors talked around one of the fires. Perhaps they were plotting Jacob's future. Would he be sold for ransom, put to death, or adopted into the tribe?

The next morning, Jacob woke to the sound of two roosters in a crowing contest. He sat on the edge of his bed and rubbed the sleep out of his eyes. He signaled to the guard that he needed to relieve himself, so he was led out of the longhouse and pointed toward a small grove of trees inside the palisade. When Jacob returned, he stood at the edge of the grove for a few moments, breathing the fresh morning air and looking toward the west. The fall foliage that painted the western hills brought a Scripture to mind. "I will lift up mine

eyes unto the hills, from whence cometh my help." Nothing—
not even confinement—could take away his commitment to
the One who had made those hills.

Later that day Hank told him that Buckaloons was a well-
known Seneca Indian village. The Senecas were known as
"The Keepers of the Western Door" for the Iroquois League.
Unlike the other nations in the league, they aligned with the
French during the war.

Jacob shrugged his shoulders. "I know nothing about that."

Hank was an eager teacher. "Captain Celoron came close
by here on the Le Belle River in '49." He claimed all of the
Ohio Indian territories for the French king. He planted lead
plates in the villages along the riverbanks—there's one close
by here. The British were upset by the French claim. That's
why we're in this war."

Jacob nodded. The reasons for war often involved land.

"The French army lets the Senecas keep prisoners here.
They're strict for the first several months but when they come
to trust you, they give you more freedom. They've let me go
hunting and fishing sometimes."

"Aren't they afraid you'll try to escape?"

"Maybe. But if they caught me, they'd kill me. If you cooperate, they'll likely let you live."

Bryce and one of the other prisoners weren't about to cooperate. "I'm going to kill that guard the minute I get hold
of a knife," Bryce had said, after he was forced to go into the
longhouse.

"Cut his throat for both of us," said the other. "And good
riddance." He looked a bit younger than Jacob, maybe thirty-
five years of age.

Jacob slept with his hands unbound at night, but not these
two. Their hands were tied at all times except to eat and do
their private duties. The guards hovered over them like a
hawk with a mouse in its talons.

"They're going to kill those prisoners," Hank said. "The Indians won't put up with them."

It wasn't long before the Indians proved him right. Early that afternoon the village elders lit a council fire. The chief sat at the inside edge of the circle, surrounded by the village elders. Men and women joined in the conversation from the perimeter of the circle.

Jacob sat with his hands bound at the edge of the crowd, trying to make out what was going on. The Seneca language was every bit as difficult to comprehend as the Delaware, but their faces and gestures told him something serious was about to happen. They glanced often at the two rebellious prisoners, the obvious focus of the conversation. Hank slipped up beside Jacob and sat down. "You watch. They're deciding which of the prisoners are going to die."

Jacob swallowed hard. "I try to cooperate but—"

"Don't worry. Both of us have been behaving."

At the end of the council session, the chief singled out Bryce and the other restless captive. Four warriors stripped the two men naked and led them to the place where the creek emptied into the river. The warriors dragged the prisoners into the water to about knee height. There they scrubbed the prisoners' bodies with the stones from the river bottom, rubbing their white skin until it was laced with red scratches.

When the captors dragged the prisoners back inside the village, two men smeared them with black paint. They dabbed it on with brushes made of turkey feathers, dipping them into a small kettle and stroking out the color with artful flourishes.

"I hope they never touch me with that stuff," Hank said. "Black is a sure sign of death."

Jacob shuddered. The warriors led the blackened prisoners to the place where a group of women were stacking a rim of firewood about waist high in a circle around a tall post. They tied the prisoners to the post with ropes that gave some leeway to move around.

Jacob tried to walk away, but a guard blocked his way. Several women carried flaming torches from the council fire and ignited the stack of firewood in several places, so that the fire soon burned on all sides. The chief stood next to the burning circle while men, women, and children stood around the perimeter.

The crowd whooped as the fire cackled and roared in a hot circle around the prisoners. The captives coughed and retched as the smoke blew into their faces and then yelled in protest as the fire burned their skin. The only freedom they gained from the slack in the ropes was to move from one fiery part of the circle to another. The smell of burning hair wafted in Jacob's direction. Then, everything was black.

Jacob opened his eyes to see Hank's hand, reaching down to help him up from the ground. "Here, let me help you up." No one else seemed to notice that he had fainted in the midst of the spectacle. All eyes were fixed on the scene around the pole.

"Kill me, kill me. For mercy's sake, kill me," Bryce said between groans of agony. Jacob's head pounded as several women took up long poles with sharpened ends, gouging and ripping open the blisters that had sprung up from the heat. The crowd was in a frenzy, whooping and yelling encouragement to the women.

Jacob stepped to the edge of the crowd and walked back to the lodge on unsteady legs. Why had they bothered to bring Bryce all the way from the settlements, only to kill him here? How much kinder to have tomahawked him at home.

That night Jacob lay in bed thinking of Lizzie. He tried to shake off the picture of her last moments at the hands of her attackers. At least her death had been mercifully short, not the prolonged torture of death by fire. Where was Lizzie now? Somewhere beyond the stars in heaven? Could she see him here in the village? Did she know that he was thinking of her?

Jacob reflected on the twenty-seven years they had enjoyed together. He saw her at the bake oven in the summer, wiping the sweat from her face with her apron. He watched her grinning at the antics of the boys, and teaching Barbara how to embroider. He sensed her warm touch as they bid each other good night in their rope bed. What a good life they had enjoyed together.

Before Jacob drifted off to sleep, he repeated the Lord's Prayer. When he came to the words, "Forgive us our debts, as we forgive our debtors," he recalled the horror of the deaths he had witnessed that day. Did Jesus truly mean that if his followers didn't forgive others who had wronged them, they wouldn't be forgiven by God?

Surely he didn't need to forgive the Indians for what they had done to his family. The warriors showed no signs of remorse for having murdered Lizzie and his children. How could God expect him to forgive them for that awful deed?

Jacob's father had taught him that he must always forgive, just like Dirk Willems, who had turned to rescue his pursuer who had fallen through the ice. As a reward for his kindness, Willems was burned at the stake in a lingering fire, much like the men Jacob had witnessed being burned by the Indians.

Maybe God expected heroes in the faith, like Willems, to forgive their enemies, but surely not ordinary people like Jacob. He wanted to get as far away from them as possible. The Indians had robbed him of his farm, his family, and his freedom. They would have to wait for another day—maybe forever and a day—for Jacob to forgive them.

As he stared at the walls of the longhouse in the dim light, Jacob could almost hear his father opening the door of his childhood home in Alsace. He had just returned from a trip to Switzerland.

Mam rushed to the door to embrace him. "What took so long? It's been weeks."

"Got caught by the Anabaptist hunters when I tried to help a couple of Anabaptist women get out of the country. They threw me in the jail at Bern."

"You look starved."

"They kept me on bread and water. My friends were afraid to bring food, lest they get labeled as Anabaptist sympathizers and lose their land, like we did."

Mother scurried to the larder and back. "Here, have a piece of cheese and some bread. How did you get away?"

"They let me go after I promised I'd never come back to Switzerland again."

"Oh *Jakob*, Switzerland is our home." Mother gave a heavy sigh.

"They treated me like a criminal. What else could I do?"

As a young boy growing up in Markirch, Alsace, Jacob had wrestled with many questions. Why had his father risked imprisonment to assist a couple of Anabaptist women? What made the Swiss hate the Anabaptists so much? Why had his father consented to be a fellow minister with Jacob Amman, after whom the persecuted Amish were named?

Coming to America had seemed like the perfect way to get away from those questions—to live in the freedom and joy of a country open to all. But as Jacob lay awake that night at Buckaloons, his mind was flooded, like the Northkill Creek after a big rain, with similar questions. There was no escaping them.

-19-

It was a gray Sunday morning in late November. Several inches of snow covered the ground. Cristy did his usual Sunday morning chores, and then he and Barbara gathered their little brood for church. The service would be at the Jake Hertzler home. With Cristy's help, Barbara got the children into *Dat*'s wagon and they were off. Although the church discouraged its members from hitching up a horse on Sunday, Christy thought they had good reason on this occasion to ride in the wagon. The horse's breath was frosty in the cold air, and Barbara drew the horsehair blanket tightly against the children on both sides of her. Even so, cold air seeped in around the edges.

As they bounced along the rutted road, Barbara's mind rolled over the events of the past week. They had butchered a hog with John's help. It reminded Barbara that she had never quite learned all the details of butchering. Several times during that day, she wished for *Mam* to show her what to do next.

What bothered her most was that butchering reminded her of the way *Mam* had died. The sights and sounds of the butchering process took on a different feel than before her death. The scream of the hog as John had stuck it for bleeding, the metallic ring of the butcher knife as he scraped the hog's hide, and the sight of its entrails all reminded her of the gruesome scene of the attacks.

When they arrived at the Hertzler home, Cristy tied the horse and helped Barbara and the children down from the wagon. Catharine Hertzler greeted her at the door with a gentle kiss. The whole family stood near the fireplace where the warmth of the blazing logs soon drove the chill out of their faces and heated up their clothing. By the time everyone arrived, there were twenty in the room, on chairs or on the floor.

The church service started as usual, with the singing from the *Ausbund* and silent prayer, but it was Jake's sermon that caught Barbara's attention that day. He recounted the story of Stephen, the first Christian martyr, from the book of Acts. He told how Stephen, a devout Greek believer, was condemned to death for blasphemy after a run-in with the Jewish leaders. Just before he died a cruel death by stoning, he asked God to forgive his accusers.

Bishop Hertzler likened Stephen's prayer to the one that Jesus prayed on the cross: "Father, forgive them, for they know not what they do." He urged the congregation to forgive the people who had wronged them, even the Indians.

How was that possible? Barbara knew Jesus taught his followers to love their enemies, but she had never thought about forgiving the warriors who had murdered her mother. Not once. It was far worse than the trifling wrongs done to her by family or friends. It was hard enough to forgive the occasional gossip and backstabbing that took place in the church circle. It would be immeasurably harder to forgive the French and Indians for what they had done.

As Jake finished speaking about Jesus and Stephen, he said, "Jesus and Stephen both forgave their enemies before they asked to be forgiven. God calls us to do the same. And remember, Jesus said that if we don't forgive others who sin against us, our heavenly Father will not forgive our sins."

Barbara looked around the room as the bishop wound up his sermon. Several of the men sat and listened with expressionless faces. She glanced over at Cristy, who was staring at the floor, and John, who was resting his chin in his hands. What was going through their minds?

Barbara hoped she would never meet the warriors who had attacked her family. If she did, she doubted that they would be asking her for forgiveness. Besides, what difference would it make if she did forgive them? Wouldn't God punish them for their wrongdoing regardless of what she had to say?

As soon as the service ended, they ate lunch, beginning with the men. When she wasn't watching her little ones, Barbara helped to serve. She stood near Fanny Mast, who told her that her husband was considering moving a little ways to the south, where it was supposed to be safer. Barbara's heart sank. She hated to see any neighbors or church members move away.

The men talked the same way. Hans Zook spoke vehemently, his voice trembling with emotion. "It's not safe to stay here. You see what happened to several families this year. Our family is going to move."

Several heads nodded in agreement.

"We always treated the Indians right," Hans went on. "Always fed them when they came begging. Never said an unkind word. Now they turn on us. Who knows what will happen next?"

"There's no doubt about it, things have changed since we first came here," Eli Renno said. "It feels like our kindness has come to naught. Now our lives are in danger, just like our worldly neighbors who take up arms."

"But where would we go?" Benedict Miller said. "How can we know it's safer anywhere else? We hear news of Indian raids from all around us."

"Well," said another, "I'm not about to move farther east. I wouldn't want to live in Germantown."

Bishop Jake cleared his throat, and all eyes turned toward him.

"We must seek the Lord," he said quietly. "Let's not be hasty in making decisions during a time of trial."

"But we shouldn't wait until—" Hans stopped when Jake raised his forefinger.

"As I was saying, we must call on the Lord. Our ancestors faced worse times than these, and the Lord brought them safely through."

"I'm not moving," Benedict said. "The Lord gave me this land, and I'm not going to move off of it."

"This world is not our home," Eli said. "We are pilgrims and strangers. Like Abraham, we may be called to move to another place. We must be willing to go where God tells us."

"But what shall we do if the Indians come?" Hans said. "Must we let them kill our families or drag them off as prisoners like they did to the Hochstetler family? Wouldn't it be better to move to a safer place?" He looked directly at Jake as he spoke.

The bishop stroked his long beard for a few moments before speaking. "I understand why some of you want to move away. But I have decided I will stay here to shepherd the flock. The Indians have often been mistreated by the white man and they are seeking revenge. If they harm us, we must not take revenge, but leave any vengeance in the hands of God."

Barbara glanced up quickly as Cristy spoke. "It's been hard for Barbara and me—losing her mother and a brother and a sister. Our children are afraid to go to sleep at night. But Barbara and I have decided to stay here at the Northkill. We are praying that her father and brothers return home again."

Barbara's face felt warm. Several of the men and women gazed at her. What was going through their minds?

After putting the children down for a nap that afternoon, Barbara looked through the *Martyrs Mirror* for the first time. Turning its large, thin pages, she didn't linger for long on any of them. Too many stories of evil done to innocent Christian people. Too many disturbing questions about suffering. How could it possibly have been God's permissive will that her family had gone through such a trial?

If Jake was right that God required them to forgive the Indians, Barbara needed to find someone to talk to. She would have liked to talk to Cristy but wasn't sure how to get started. He hardly flinched at pain and seldom spoke of his feelings. How could he understand hers? With *Mam* gone, who could help her make sense of the turmoil inside, especially when her thoughts were too shameful to share even with God?

It was getting dark when Cristy came in from doing the chores. "It's definitely getting colder out there," he said as he stirred up the fire in the chimney. "We don't need to worry about the fresh meat hanging in the shed. It'll soon freeze in this weather."

"Good. And I suppose you'll soon be finished smoking the other part."

"*Jah*, I checked the smoke before I came in. I can't wait to taste that pork."

The wind grew stronger that night, whistling through the chimney and rattling the window sash. The children joined Barbara by the fire so they all stayed warm. At least the Indians weren't likely to be out on a night like this, Barbara thought.

Despite the warmth, she shivered to think of her mother, buried in the woods just west of the garden. Her body must be chilled to the bone in that shallow grave. It gave her goose bumps to imagine her mother lying under the frozen earth, covered with several inches of snow.

Were *Dat* and the boys still alive, or were they buried in a place she would never know? If they were in an Indian camp, were they keeping warm? Did they have enough to eat? If only she could take them a blanket and some of the pork they had butchered. And tell them how much they were loved.

It was well after dark when Barbara pulled in the latch-string on their front door. In days gone by, they had always left it hanging out as a sign of hospitality. Now Barbara pulled it in every night, if Cristy hadn't already done it. They didn't talk about it; they just knew that it was the right thing to do.

-20-

One day in late November, Jacob asked Hank what he missed the most about home. "The food," he said. I'm so sick of parched corn I could vomit. How about you?"

"I hate the food too. And not having a schedule to eat. At home, we always had three meals a day. Even more, I miss my farm. If I was home, I'd be plowing or doing something worthwhile." He paced the floor in the smoky longhouse. "I'm going outside."

The air was clear and crisp, though the sun was hidden behind clouds that blew in from Lake Erie. The guard let Jacob walk outside the longhouse and watch the activities in the village. The women and girls carried in the last of the corn and squash from the fields and heaped them in a pile.

Jacob sauntered over to watch the women at work. Two young mothers with babies bundled on their backs pulled the ears off of the cornstalks. Others took the ears and hung them up to dry on horizontal poles stretched from one side of the longhouse to the other. Some of the older children carried the cornstalks and leaves off to a different pile.

An elderly woman with leathery skin sat cross-legged on the ground at the edge of the longhouse, weaving the dried cornhusks into a round disk, forming a face. A mask. Jacob had seen warriors wear such masks during a celebration.

At home he would have fed the stalks and leaves to the livestock, but the Senecas didn't keep farm animals. If only he could have a taste of cream and butter from a cow, like back home. Were John or Barbara milking Bessie now?

"The women work really hard to bring in the harvest," Jacob observed to Hank, who had walked up beside him.

Hank nodded. "You won't catch a man working in the field around here."

Jacob wrinkled his brow. "How come the men take the easy work and leave the hard work to the women? I can't imagine Lizzie and me doing it that way."

"Finding game is harder than it looks. Last winter they ran out of food."

Jacob's eye turned to a red-haired young mother who was cutting up squash. Two children played nearby. They looked about the same age, although one had black hair and the other had red hair. Both had dark brown eyes and skin that was darker than their mother's.

Although this young mother was deeply tanned from the sun, Jacob was sure she was white. Real Indians had dark skin and black hair. Jacob took her to be a "white Indian." As Hank said, "They have white skin but a red heart." The red-haired woman must have been taken in a raid on one of the white settlements.

Two of the children who helped carry squash from the field were white as well. One of them looked just a little older than Franey, with blondish hair, blue eyes, and a dimple in her chin. She looked so much like the daughter of their fallen neighbor, Fred Meyer, that Jacob took in a sharp breath.

"Sarah," Jacob said. "Can you speak German?" That would be a good test.

She stopped and looked at him with wide eyes but said nothing.

Jacob bent down to look into the girl's face. "I'm Jacob Hochstetler, from the Northkill. Was your father Fred Meyer?"

The lass stood there with a squash in her hands, her eyes cast downward. She remained silent. At that moment, the red-headed woman stepped between them and whisked the girl away, her eyes flashing fire.

Why would white people want to become Indians? Of course little children had no choice, but what about the woman? Had she ever run the gauntlet or gone through torture?

"Torture breaks their spirit," Hank said. "Makes them willing to join the tribe."

Jacob shrugged. "Makes no sense to me. But something makes people stay. They seem proud to be part of the tribe now."

Hank shook his head. "I'll never become an Indian. I'm just biding my time to escape."

But what if there was no way to escape? What if Jacob was held as a prisoner for several years? Maybe he could adjust to life in the village if he had to. That is, if he put his mind to it. Being a prisoner was partly a matter of the mind. His father would say that it is possible to be free even if one is bound, or to be bound even though one is free. The Indians might bind his body, but he would not let them bind his spirit. He could decide whether he was bound or free.

In his bones, Jacob knew that even if he decided to adapt to Indian ways, it would take years. His habits were like the rutted road that ran through the north end of his Northkill property. The spring rains turned the sod into a quagmire, and when it dried, the wagon tracks were so deep you couldn't get out of them.

Jacob smiled to recall the story of his neighbor, Moritz, back in the Northkill. Moritz was riding home from the blacksmith shop with his son beside him when another neighbor came toward him in his wagon. The road was so narrow and the ruts so deep that the only choice was for one of them to back up, something they were loath to do.

Moritz called out to the other man, "Back up."

"No, you back up."

It went on that way until Moritz said, "If you don't back up, I'm going to have to do something I don't want to do."

So the neighbor had backed up his wagon to a place where Moritz could pass him, and he made his way on home. "*Dat*," his son said to Moritz after their neighbor had passed. "What would you have done if that man hadn't backed up?"

"I would have backed up," Moritz said, and then they both laughed.

Here at Buckaloons, it was no laughing matter. Jacob was the one being forced to back up, to get out of the rut he'd been in for his whole life. He was being forced to do something he'd rather not do. Surely if he learned to live like a native, he'd be given more freedom, which would increase his chances of escape.

Could he ever enjoy eating like a native? There'd be no milk, butter, or cheese, and no homemade bread and pies. No smoked pork, no fresh beef after butchering each fall, no chickens or eggs.

It was bad enough to get used to a new diet, but it was even worse to be forced out of the routine of a Swiss schedule. How was he to govern his life without a clock, a calendar, or an almanac? How could he ever enjoy life without the rhythm of daily chores, the weekly Sabbath, or the church fellowship each fortnight?

Jacob looked at Hank through the mist in his eyes. "How am I supposed to live without knowing what month it is? I won't even know when it's time for my daughter Barbara to have her baby."

"These natives look at the same moon we do. They seem to know how many moons they've lived."

Of all the rhythms of daily life, farmwork was the most difficult to leave behind. At Buckaloons they wouldn't let him trade his sweat for the fruit of the earth—to plant, to prune, to harvest, to store up goods for the winter.

Jacob came to his senses when the Wandering Soul, the narrator in his devotional book, whispered in his ear that these were all earthly things, of no eternal worth. It was true—being away from the church fellowship was even worse than being away from the farm. How could he forsake his Christian faith for the pagan life of a native?

Jacob looked at Hank. "Actually, the thing I miss most here at Buckaloons is that there is no church fellowship. The Indians don't believe in God."

"They worship the Creator," Hank said. "And there are some native Christians."

"Here in the village?"

"Maybe. The Moravians traveled up this way, making converts."

"I miss my prayer book. And the church services."

"Does anybody keep you from praying?"

Hank was right. God would give him the strength he needed, either to get away from Buckaloons or to get used to Indian life.

Jacob's hands were bound for the last time in late December, the Month of the Big Moon. That day they moved him from the prison house into a longhouse with several families living in it. For the first time, he had the freedom to move about without the guard's constant eye on him.

In the evening, he sat near the fire in the center of the longhouse. The time dragged on as the wind howled outside. What might he do with his hands? Back in the Northkill, he might have been cracking walnuts with his sons as the snow blew outside. The sharp pain of his separation from them had settled into a dull ache. What might they be doing in the cold of winter? Was there a chance that he'd see them in the spring when Indians begin moving about?

The next day, after his daily chores of carrying water from the creek and chopping wood for the longhouse fires, he gathered up walnuts under a large tree that grew just outside the palisade. The squirrels had claimed the bulk of them, but he collected a kettleful. That evening, he broke open the walnuts with a rock, and then took up the tedious work of digging out the bits of meat with the tip of a dull hunting knife.

Several women gathered around as Jacob worked. They watched with curiosity as his little pile of pieces grew. He could almost read their minds—*This is women's work!*—but he didn't care. It felt good to do something worthwhile.

A slender old woman with a wrinkled face flashed him a smile. "Fruit Grower. Good."

Jacob smiled back. "Do you want to taste it?" He held out a few pieces of walnut to her. Her face brightened after a bite, so he offered several more.

Each evening, the Indians watched him work. As the level of shelled walnuts rose in the clay jar, so did the Indians' trust in Jacob. To be able to use the knife as a tool was a great freedom, but the Indians' trust was even more important.

As Jacob finished the last of the walnuts, a little girl sat cross-legged on the dirt floor nearby, playing with wooden sticks. That was what Franey had done as a four-year-old, until Jacob carved her some wooden animals.

His mind flew to a cold night in late January two years earlier. Franey was watching him form a cow out of a scrap of chestnut wood. "I love you, *Daati*," she had told him.

"I love you too." Jacob said it a little self-consciously, since he didn't often use such affectionate words. Jacob's parents had said that kind of talk could spoil children and make them proud.

Franey was so happy with her cow that she danced around the room, waving it and saying, "I love my cow and I love my *Daati*." Jacob's heart had welled with pride. Love was always a good thing.

The wind howled against the longhouse as Jacob picked out a piece of chestnut from the stack of firewood and started whittling it into the shape of a horse. Jacob sharpened the knife he had used to clean walnuts by whetting it against a stone. He needed a sharp edge to carve. As he whittled the piece of firewood, the little girl with the stick toys moved her head in rhythm with the strokes of his knife. Could he make this little Indian girl as happy as his Franey?

When Jacob looked her in the eye, the little girl dropped her gaze. "That's okay," he said. "You may watch." She seemed to catch the drift of his halting Seneca despite his German accent. Soon two other children came to watch alongside her, their dark eyes beaming with expectation.

The little girl's father came over and stood next to her. When he saw what Jacob was making, he flashed him a broad smile. Jacob made a few more cuts on the horse's mane and declared it complete. He held out the wooden horse to the little girl. "Here, you may have it."

She looked at it with longing eyes, but didn't reach for the toy.

Jacob glanced at her father. "I made this for your little girl." He nodded and spoke to his daughter, and then she took the toy.

Jacob looked into her dark shiny eyes. "What is your name?"

She dropped her gaze toward the floor.

Her father turned to answer for her. He spoke slowly enough in Seneca that Jacob could understand him. "Snow Owl."

Snow Owl played with the horse on the dirt floor, making it neigh and gallop around the room. Jacob's chest swelled inside to see faces light up all around the room as she went by.

That night he went to bed with new lightness in my heart and looseness in his limbs. For the first time, Jacob sensed the pull of friendship from an Indian, young and innocent as she was. Nothing was better on a cold night than to keep his hands busy doing something worthwhile, especially if it brought happiness to a little girl who reminded him of Franey.

The next two evenings Jacob carved a wooden dog and a wooden owl for Snow Owl, just in time for the midwinter festival. Hank said it was the most sacred event of the year, a time to thank the Great Spirit for the harvest of the past year and to offer prayers for the needs of the one to come.

Anticipation hung in the air for several days prior to the event, especially as the woman prepared food for the event. They used a large kettle to heat up the kernels of popping corn that the children had helped to husk a few months earlier, and everyone had a chance to enjoy the popped corn. It was a pleasure Jacob had never had in the Alsace.

Snow Owl shared her wooden toys with the other children, who ran around the room with them. They played many games, shrieking with delight as they competed with one another. Their favorite game was a race in which they pushed a hoop in front of them with a stick. That was a game Christian would love. And he'd be good at it too. Maybe he was playing it somewhere. The thought brought Jacob comfort.

"You'll like the feather dance," Hank said. "There's nothing like it. Feathers are sacred to the Indians." They made their way to the council house, where the elders had cleared out everything on the inside to make room for the crowd.

The celebration began with two singers seated in the middle of the room, each with a turtle-shell rattle in hand. They set a rapid pace, striking the rattles on the seats and chanting words to a sacred song. At the signal, twenty dancers entered the council house in full costume. All were men, bare down to the waist except for the colorful ornaments on their necks and arms. Their copper-colored skin was rubbed with oil to a shine. Their leggings and moccasins were strung with ornamental beads, and they wore bells and rattles on their ankles. They danced with enthusiasm, following the dance leader in a slow-moving line that made its way around the inside of the building.

The crowd observing from the middle of the room clapped and cheered in rhythm with the music. Snow Owl waved the wooden owl in her hand. Her eyes were fixed on each dancer as he went by. She turned her head back and forth to catch a full view of each performer.

The dancers had circled the room twice when the crowd broke into applause. The spectators were transfixed by a spirited young dancer who moved with extraordinary speed and grace. Sweat ran in rivulets down the performer's face and steamed from his back, rising like vapor to join the smoke of the fire. "To the front, to the front," the crowd shouted in chorus, so the young man moved to the head of the column. He led the column for several rounds before one of his comrades earned the same privilege.

On the fourth round, a woman dancer in ordinary apparel stepped out to join the men. She took her place at the end of the line, moving sideways in the column while facing the crowd. She danced in slow step to the music, raising herself from heel to toe, first with one foot and then the other. Soon other women came and went in the line, stepping to the music for a time and then taking their place back in the crowd.

The dance went on until the performers were exhausted. Even the most energetic Swiss dancers of Jacob's youth could not have matched what he had just seen. The Indian way of worshiping the Great Spirit stood worlds apart from the way the Amish praised the Creator in their fellowship back at the Northkill. For Jacob to cross over from the Amish way to theirs would be like crossing the Atlantic in a canoe.

-21-

January 1758

As winter came in earnest, Barbara took time in the long evenings to read more stories in *Martyrs Mirror*. She found a few places where *Dat* had made a note in the side columns. Beside the picture of Dirk Willems rescuing his captor from drowning, he had penned: "A true follower of Jesus. Someone to imitate."

Barbara's eyes grew misty as she gazed at the picture of Anneken Heyndricks, an Anabaptist woman from Holland who faced the town lords with courage, even when they tortured her and threatened her with death. She was burned alive after her tormentors stuffed her mouth full of gunpowder. She gave up her life as a martyr, even though she had a chance to recant.

How could so-called Christian authorities treat a woman this way? Surely we must be willing to die for our faith, Barbara thought, but it is evil to kill others for it.

Barbara lingered over the drawing of Catharina Mulerin's arrest in the Swiss district of Knonow, gripped by the scene of a child tugging at the brave woman's waist as the bailiff dragged her out of the house. She was troubled by the accounts of several Swiss women who gave birth while being held in prison for no crime but belief in the Anabaptist way, rejected by both Catholics and Protestants. No wonder her parents had wanted to come to this new land.

It was the first Friday in January, time for Barbara's own baby to arrive. This time, without her mother's help. She'd been by Barbara's side with the birth of her three girls. This time she would have to rely on Mother Stutzman to help. Barbara must have sniffled as she thought about it, because Cristy asked, "Are you all right?"

"*Jah*, I'm fine," Barbara said. I'm just thinking about the baby. I'm so tired of waiting."

"I'm sure it will be born in 1758."

"What? I want it to be born this week."

"This week is 1758. Remember, the new year now starts in January." He had a twinkle in his eye.

Barbara rolled her eyes at Cristy's attempt at humor. "I never paid much attention to the calendar until I married you. I just saw it hanging on the wall at home." She had forgotten that the province had changed the calendar to begin the calendar year in January rather than March. They had also taken eleven days out of September, which moved Christmas from January into December for the high churches, like the Reformed church at Muddy Creek. Barbara's people kept celebrating the holy day on January 6 and called it Old Christmas. They celebrated it like a Sunday, with no work except daily chores.

"Maybe if we have a little boy, he'll grow up to understand these things," Cristy said with sideways grin.

Barbara grinned back. "I hope he will." After three girls in a row, they were both hoping to have a boy to help on the farm. She and Cristy had decided that if the new baby was a boy, they would call him Christian, after him. If it was another girl they would name her Lizzie, after her mother.

Early on Sunday morning, the birth pangs began, gently at first and then with increasing persistence. Barbara sent Magdalena out to the barn to tell Cristy that she needed him. He hurried to fetch Mother Stutzman, who came in a rush. She helped get the girls dressed and bundled, and then Cristy took them over to John and Katie's house to stay for a while.

While he was gone, Mother Stutzman stirred up the fire in the fireplace and got some water boiling. "I brought along an old bed sheet," she said, "and a clean blanket for the little one."

Barbara watched her mother-in-law as she worked. She didn't have Lizzie's experience of midwifery, but there was no doubt she knew what she was doing.

Cristy was back before long. "Katie says she can keep the children for two days," he said. "We don't need to worry about picking them up this evening."

"Good," Mother Stutzman said. "Cristy, you go get water from the spring. It's always good to have plenty of water on hand." She handed him the large wooden bucket.

"If it wasn't so cold outside I'd get you walking," Mother Stutzman said to Barbara. "I always found that things moved along faster if I stayed busy. Lying around waiting for the baby to come just makes it seem longer. When Cristy was born, I worked in the garden until I could hardly stand up straight, and then I went inside and lay down. He came about an hour later."

Cristy was back with the bucket in a few minutes. "Do you want me to stay in the house?"

"No," Mother Stutzman answered. "Men aren't much help when it comes to babies. You just go outside and work until I call you."

"I won't be far away if you need anything." His eyes were wide and his cheeks a bit flushed.

Cristy peeked in about every hour or so; each time the women assured him that everything was all right. Mother Stutzman threw some dried vegetables and a few chunks of smoked ham into boiling water and made Cristy some soup at noon.

She turned to Barbara. "Do you want some?"

"No." The thought of food made Barbara's stomach turn.

The pains were coming regularly now, so Barbara lay down on the bed. What had her mother told her for her first three? "Let your body do the work for you until the baby is ready to come." That was hard to do.

Mother Stutzman swabbed Barbara's forehead with a wet washcloth. "You're doing really well. I think the baby will come soon."

The pains came in waves, gripping her womb with fists of iron. How could she have forgotten how painful it was to give birth?

The baby came late in the afternoon. Mother Stutzman caught the baby and washed it with water she had kept warm by the fire. "It's a boy," she said with excitement as the baby gasped and filled his lungs for the first time. She wiped him off, wrapped him in a blanket, and laid him at Barbara's breast.

Spent from labor, Barbara held the infant and stroked his tiny ears. She counted his fingers and toes; everything seemed normal.

Mother Stutzman stepped to the door. "Cristy! Come and see the new baby."

Cristy came running to the house, threw his gloves onto the table, and headed for the bed.

"What have we got, a boy or a girl?"

"Be sure to wash your hands and warm them up before you hold the baby," Mother Stutzman said sharply. "You can use some of the warm water in that basin."

Cristy stepped over to the basin and splashed water on his hands.

"You can dry your hands with this towel," Mother Stutzman said.

"We've got a little boy," Barbara said. She pulled back the blanket to introduce Cristy to his son.

Cristy picked up his newborn son and gently held him to his chest. It might have been Barbara's imagination, but she thought his eyes sparkled more than they had when the girls were born. He had been looking forward to having a boy.

It didn't matter to Barbara if it was a boy or a girl. Bringing forth new life after so much death: that was more than enough. If only her mother and father could have been there to celebrate it.

-22-

The weeks following the winter festival disappeared into a blur for Jacob, one that only got grayer as the winter wore on. The damp and overcast weather brought such biting cold that the warmth from the fire hardly reached the ends of the lodge. The bearskins staved off the cold in bed, but Jacob could hardly stop shivering when he worked outside.

The weather stayed cold into the spring season. Game was so hard to find that the whole village ran short on food. They ate only two small meals a day—mostly dried corn. As the weeks wore on, Jacob's body used up the last of the reserves he'd stored from Lizzie's good cooking. If only he could have some of the meat from the smokehouse back home. Why didn't the Indians butcher a deer or a hog and cure the meat with the smoke from hickory embers?

The hungry village turned somber as the elders prayed for the Great Spirit to show them where to find game. The people took the shortage of food in stride, their pleasant expressions masking the gnawing in their stomachs. Hank said they were used to being hungry and saw little use for laying up food in store the way the Swiss did.

Surely this is not what Jesus meant when he told his disciples not to be anxious about what to eat, or to drink, or to wear, Jacob thought. What could be wrong about building a barn to store up goods for a time they were needed most?

Sickness stalked not far behind the hunger that ravaged the village. Early one morning, Jacob woke to the sound of a rasping cough. People often coughed from the smoke of the fire, but this was different. The man coughing was Swift Arrow, an elder in the village, loved by all.

That afternoon, the village healer came to the longhouse. He wore a large mask carved from basswood and painted red and black. The mask was another half the size of a grown man's face, with an exaggerated nose and eyes. The nose was bent and wrinkled and a large tongue dangled from the twisted mouth, filled with crooked and poorly-spaced teeth. Bright pieces of metal in the center of the large, round eyes reflected the light of the flame from the fire. A mop of black hair hung from the top of the mask, covering both of its ears. The surface of the wrinkled face shone with an oily finish.

Hank whispered to Jacob that the Indians talked of the mask as though it were alive. "I've heard them call it 'Grandfather.' The mask stands for the Bad Twin. They say it scares away witches and disease."

The healer walked to the bed of the sick man and began to dance, gesturing toward him with his right hand while shaking the turtle rattle in his left. Several of the village elders gathered around, their eyes fixed on the healer as they tapped their feet to the rhythm of the rattle. The healer chanted incantations and offered prayers to the Great Spirit. The sick prisoner kept right on coughing after they left.

That evening, Jacob began coughing too, along with several others in the longhouse. His throat swelled to that point that he didn't feel like eating even the little food offered to him. The healer came back again with his rattle and his incantations, but Jacob turned his head away.

The next morning, Jacob's head began to pound. Although he was sweating, it was hard for him to stay warm. When he sat close to the fire in the center of the room, the smoke aggravated his raw throat.

That afternoon, Swift Arrow died in his bed. This was no ordinary cold or fever. Jacob watched as two guards wrapped the dead man in a sheet and carried him outside.

Not long after that, an Indian woman came into the longhouse carrying a jar in her hand. She made her way through the longhouse, pouring steaming hot tea from her jar into a small gourd to offer them a drink. When she came to Jacob, he grasped the drink and savored it to the last drop. His heart welled. "Thank you."

The woman returned the next day. Again Jacob sipped her tea, which soothed his throat and warmed his stomach. This time, she motioned with her hands, offering to put something on his chest. After a time, he realized that she wanted to apply a poultice.

Jacob lay quietly as she gently rubbed the medicine onto his chest. Her tender touch brought a measure of healing. The poultice smelled of menthol, a fragrance from childhood days. When the woman finished applying the poultice, she covered it with a cloth and motioned for Jacob to put his jacket back on. The poultice prickled his skin.

The woman came into the longhouse twice a day to bring tea and change the poultice. After three days, Jacob's cough had lessened. Within a few more days, it was gone.

Jacob's heart welled with gratitude for the woman and her remedies. She was as kind as any white woman he knew. She reminded him of Anna Yoder.

The thought of Anna sang itself through his brain. How was she faring during her second winter as a widow? Had she remarried by now?

The maple trees were sprouting leaves when five Dutch prisoners were brought up from Fort Duquesne. To Jacob's surprise, one of them spoke enough German that they could talk to each other.

"They have three hundred men garrisoned at the fort," the man said, "but provisions are scarce."

"We've been short of food here too," Jacob said.

"The Indians were forced to take their women and children from the fort. They usually leave them there when they're out raiding."

That evening, Jacob's hunch about new raids was confirmed. Most of the adults in the village gathered around a council fire. A few men made impassioned speeches. Although he could not understand all their words, Jacob could feel emotion rising in the group. There were dances accompanied by drums and war whoops.

The emotion from the council fire carried over to the lodge that night. Jacob saw it in the worried looks on the faces of the women as they carried their children to bed. He read it in the faces of excited young men, eager to prove their worth as warriors.

The next morning a group of men formed a war party. Jacob watched with dread as they painted each other's faces and braided feathers into their hair. Two young warriors beat out a menacing rhythm on their war drums.

Jacob shivered as warriors whooped in chorus and danced around a circle. Which of the frontier families were they planning to attack now? If only he could issue a warning, especially if they were headed for the Northkill.

The chief took up a stick and drew a crude map on the ground. Jacob tried to observe without appearing too interested. It was hard to make sense of the drawing, but it looked as though they were planning to head southeast toward Fort Augusta, the same direction Jacob would head if he made an escape. The Dutch prisoner told him that the French were conniving with the Indians to attack there.

By midday the war party made its way into the woods, leaving mostly old men and young boys to tend the village with the women. Perhaps the time had come to attempt an escape; it would never be any easier.

With many of the warriors gone, the village was desperate for food. "Fruit Grower," one of the old men said to Jacob, "you must help us find food. I am giving you this gun to hunt."

Jacob nodded and took the flintlock into his hands. It was a big step toward freedom.

"We'll give you three bullets each day," the man said, "so we expect three pieces of game. You must give account of your bullets. Here is a butcher knife as well."

It was a thrill to walk out of the village with weapons. For a fleeting moment, Jacob was tempted to escape that day. He quickly dismissed the thought. Bad timing.

Within a few minutes, Jacob spied a cottontail rabbit some three rods away. He took careful aim, fired, and shot, glad to see he hadn't lost his touch in the months of captivity. He picked up the rabbit and laid it in the crotch of a tree to keep it out of a fox's reach. Although Jacob hunted several hours longer, he got nothing more. He went back to the place where he had left the rabbit and carried it to the village.

The old man smiled when he saw Jacob coming with the game in hand. He handed back his gun and the two unused bullets. His shoulders straightened a little as he watched them butcher the rabbit and cook it over the fire.

Jacob didn't spot any game worth shooting the next day, or the day after that. He would have to go deeper into the woods to find something. By now, most of the snow had melted and the creeks were swollen with runoff. He took care as he crossed the creek, lest he slip into the chilly water with his moccasins.

Over the next week, as the sun warmed the earth, game moved about more freely. He was able to bring in several rabbits and a beaver, along with a few fish from the stream. At the same time, Jacob missed several shots and tried to explain, in halting Seneca words, why he had less game than missing bullets.

"The rabbits run very fast," he explained to the old man when he came back.

The man frowned. "Bad shot, you waste bullets."

The truth was that he had begun to stash away a few bullets and a little powder in a hollow tree, in preparation for an escape. Jacob's stomach turned to a knot, reminding him that his father had taught him to be fully truthful. But how else was he to get bullets for his trip back to the Northkill? God would have to forgive him as he had forgiven his biblical namesake, the patriarch Jacob who deceived his brother, Esau, and his father, Isaac.

As Jacob walked away from the old man, he headed for the grove of trees. A wave of nostalgia washed over him as he smelled the warming earth. Jacob strode to the edge of the woods, pushed aside a layer of leaves, and scooped up a handful of soil. Two earthworms wiggled on the clump in his hand. He lifted the moist clod to his nose and breathed deeply of the earthy fragrance. It made him tingle inside.

The length of the days and the leaves on the oaks told him it must be early May. If it hadn't been for the attack last fall, he'd be helping Lizzie plant radishes and peas in the garden. Not at Buckaloons, where they thought of gardening and farming as women's work.

It would soon be time to head for the Northkill or to look for his sons, if there was half a chance of finding them. What could he do but pray? Trying to escape was risky, perhaps even foolhardy. With the warming of spring, the woods would be full of Indians. The villagers were more suspicious too. They watched him every time he left the camp and hardly let the captives talk to one another.

God would have to show him the right time, he thought, as he tossed the clump of soil back onto the forest floor and walked back toward the longhouse.

-23-

One morning as Jacob set out to fish in the nearby creek, he had a moment alone with Hank, so he told him about his plans. "The next time they send me out to hunt, I'm going to head for home. Will you go with me? You know the Indian paths better than I do."

Hank looked serious. "Are you sure? I'm not nonresistant like you. If we run into Indians on the way, I'll shoot to kill."

"The war party should be a ways off by now."

"Okay, let's go tomorrow." Hank glanced anxiously at an old man who was looking their way. "We mustn't leave at the same time."

Jacob nodded. That would rouse suspicions. "We'll have to meet somewhere."

Hank looked up at the old man who was walking toward them with a bucket. "How about meeting at that large oak at the fork of the trail south of here? The place where they shot a bear out of the tree."

"*Jah.* By the time the sun sets on the mountain."

Hank nodded at Jacob and then took the bucket from the old man and headed toward the creek for water. Jacob walked to the river with his net. It would be a lot safer with Hank along. He knew the Indian customs and the lay of the land better than Jacob did. He'd be less likely to get lost.

The next morning dawned clear and bright. After a few bites of breakfast, Jacob was issued a gun with three bullets and told to go hunt. He was given a butcher knife as well, the alternative to a tomahawk. He caught Hank's eye for a brief moment. How could he stash a little extra food without arousing suspicion?

Jacob's heart pounded as he crossed the creek and headed down the path toward the hollow tree where he'd been saving bullets. He reached into the hole at the base of the red oak but found nothing. His heart stopped for a moment. Had someone taken them? He stepped back and looked at the tree. Surely this was the right tree. It had a large burl on the side.

Jacob reached in again and closed his eyes in relief when he felt the smooth shape of a bullet. They had been scattered to the edges, probably by some animal. Jacob put the seven bullets in his pouch with the other three. He also rescued a little powder he'd left on a piece of bark and put it into his bag. It would have to do until he got home.

Jacob jerked his head to follow a movement in the dense woods to his right. Was someone watching? A twig snapped and then the white tail of a deer flashed from the other side of a magnolia. The deer bounded away as Jacob knelt to prime his gun.

Jacob followed the deer, but with only half a heart. He lost its trail where it crossed a little creek near some big rocks. It was the last game he saw all day. Hungry as usual, Jacob would have welcomed a meal of fresh game, but his mind was consumed by what might be in store on the way home.

By late afternoon, Jacob found his way to the oak tree and waited for Hank to arrive. The sun dropped low in the sky. If only he hadn't told Hank he'd wait for him, Jacob could have put more miles between him and the camp. How long should he wait? What if Hank didn't show up?

The sun had dropped below the hills when Hank came striding down the path with a rifle as well as a tomahawk. "Any game today?"

Jacob shook his head. "No. Was it hard for you to get away?"

"They asked more questions than usual."

Jacob took a quick breath. "Will they send someone after us?"

"Not sure. But we better stay off the main trail or else hide our tracks." Hank set off to the left of the trail, so Jacob followed his long strides.

The woods had turned to shades of gray when Hank slowed for the first time. "Let's stop here for the night. We can make a little fire under that overhang."

"Won't the fire give us away?"

"Not likely, so close to that big rock. I hate to sleep in the woods with no light or fire."

Jacob set his rifle against a tree. "Me too. It's a little too cool at night."

Jacob gathered a few sticks in the near darkness while Hank kindled a fire with leaves and twigs. They sat listening to the bubbling of the nearby brook as the warmth of the fire took the chill out of the cool night air. Jacob ate the little corn-meal left in his pouch.

Suddenly a voice cut the dark silence. "Hello."

Jacob whirled around to face an Indian in war paint. He was carrying a flintlock at the ready and had a tomahawk and a knife hanging from his waist. He stepped between the campfire and the rifle Jacob had leaned against a tree.

"Hello." Jacob tried not appear startled at the stealthy intrusion.

"There are more," the warrior said without changing his expression. Did he mean a group of warriors nearby? Where was he from? Did he know they were from Buckaloons?

"Hello," Jacob said and then turned and spoke to Hank in Seneca. "We need more wood." And then, in German, "Pretend you're gathering wood and then meet me a little ways up this stream."

Hank nodded and began gathering wood.

Jacob gathered a few sticks nearby and threw them onto the fire. The Indian stood near the fire with his eye on Jacob and his gun at the ready. Jacob went farther for sticks the second this time, beyond the light of the fire. From behind a tree, he watched as Hank gathered a few sticks too. And then Jacob walked away as quickly as he could without making too much noise. He stayed near the stream, looking for any sign that the Indian was trailing him.

Jacob was waiting for Hank in the darkness when he heard him shout. A gunshot rang out. More shouts and then all was quiet. Not a good sign. Jacob started running for the river but an invisible hand drew him back. He could never live with himself not knowing what had happened to his friend.

Jacob waited for a time and then turned to go back. In the dim light of the crescent moon through the trees, he slowly circled around to the top of the outcrop of rock that hung over the campsite. Jacob peered over the edge. The fire was dim and no one was in sight. An owl hooted. Was Hank signaling him? Jacob heard the signal again, off to his left. But it wasn't Hank, he realized, when he spotted an owl perched on a branch in the moonlight.

Jacob crept forward on the ledge as far as he dared, straining to see in the glow of the embers that remained of the fire. Where did that fresh blood on the ground come from? Neither Hank nor Jacob had shot any game. Fear shot through Jacob's chest when he realized that the Indian had killed Hank and that he was now likely out looking for him.

Jacob strained to see more, but didn't dare lean any farther forward on the crumbly rock of the small cliff. Who knew where that Indian might be or how many others were nearby?

Easing back from the edge of the outcrop, Jacob took a deep breath and silently crept toward the creek. He followed the creek downstream, guided by a few wisps of light from the moon that filtered through the leaves on the trees. It would likely take him to the river, where he could cross without leaving tracks.

When Jacob reached the river, he recognized the place where the village kept a canoe in the underbrush. He dug it out and launched it. Paddling a little ways upstream, Jacob landed the canoe on the other side. He dragged it into the undergrowth and followed the river a little ways east.

When he was too tired to go any farther, he scraped together some leaves for a bed and lay down. He faded in and out of sleep. What if the Indian was on his trail? The trip that had started out in the bright sunshine of hope had suddenly turned to utter darkness.

It was still dark when Jacob got up and started walking, stumbling over fallen logs and slipping on moist rocks. The sun was coming up when he came upon a path. He followed it for a little while until he came to a painted tree. The bark had been stripped off not long before; the wood was still somewhat damp. It exposed a spot about two feet high and more than a foot wide. On the trunk in red ochre and charcoal paint were a number of symbols—crude pictures of guns, some parallel lines, and other markings Jacob couldn't understand. He shivered as he took it in. Indian warriors could be very close by.

It was too dangerous to travel the woods by day, even if he stayed off the beaten path. Better to sleep during the day and travel at night. So he found a place to lie down and soon fell into the welcome forgetfulness of sleep.

That night, as Jacob pushed his way through the woods, it started to rain. He looked for shelter, either a hollow tree or an overhang. He was thoroughly soaked before he found a giant cottonwood with a hollow large enough for him to get completely out of the rain. He curled up with his back to the opening, thankful for the grace of a dry spot.

Jacob shivered for a while in his wet clothing, but eventually warmed up enough that he could sleep. He woke up the next morning feeling comfortably warm.

Despite his resolve to travel at night, Jacob walked most of that day, eager to put as much distance between the Indian village and himself as possible. It was cloudy all day, and he relied on the moss on the north side of trees to show him direction.

The dried corn was gone, and Jacob had no way to capture game, so he was hungry all day. As he went through clearings, he chewed on stems of grass. They put a sweet taste in his mouth that at least dulled the hunger pangs.

After several days of walking in the woods with no food, Jacob was drawn to the odor of dead meat that wafted toward him. He followed the smell toward a thicket. As he approached, a crow flapped out of the thicket and landed in a branch overhead.

Jacob headed into the thicket and found a dead opossum. He pushed through the rancid smell as he bent down to look at it more closely. Maggots swarmed over the surface of the half-eaten flesh. A question surfaced in his mind that a year ago never would have occurred to him. *Dare I eat it?*

Jacob gingerly scraped off the maggots with his butcher knife and carved a chunk out of the graying flesh. The crow scolded him from a few yards away. Jacob closed his eyes and put the meat to his lips briefly before gagging. It was too much. He would have to cook it.

Jacob picked up the dead animal by the tail and pushed his way through the thicket to the small clearing around a walnut tree. There he gathered up some twigs and started a fire with the flint and gunpowder he carried in his bag. As the fire gathered strength, he added wood until he was confident that he had enough flame to cook this flesh. The fire had not even settled into embers when he cut up the remains of the mammal into several small pieces. Having sharpened the end of a stick, Jacob poked it into one of the chunks of meat and held it over the fire. He heated up the meat one piece at a time, pulled it off the bones, and ate it. He nearly retched as he swallowed each piece of the foul meat. Surely it was better than an empty stomach

That night as he slept, Jacob dreamed of Lizzie. She walked toward him with a loaf of freshly baked bread in her hand. "*Yacob*, you look very thin," Lizzie said, her voice clear and strong.

"I'm starved. I want to go home, but I'm not sure of the way."

"God will be with you. Just keep going the same direction, and then follow the next river you come to."

Jacob reached out for the loaf of bread and tried to clasp her hand in his. "Thank you, my love." Just then, he woke up.

The moon was all but hidden behind a small cloud drifting across the night sky.

Jacob closed his eyes, hoping to feel the comfort of Lizzie's presence again. Perhaps from her vantage point in the heavens, she could give him further direction. But she was gone. Jacob's stomach gurgled as he lay awake, wishing for even the smallest bite of fresh bread. How was he going to keep that meat down?

When he awoke, the sun's rays lit up the tops of the trees. Seeing Lizzie had only been a dream, he reminded himself. How could he possibly trust it for direction?

Why not?

Yes, why not? It was as good a sign as anything else he had to go by.

Jacob got up and washed his face in a nearby stream, gathered up his things, and started walking. All day he searched for signs of nuts or berries but came up empty.

That evening, Jacob came to a river. Had he made it to west branch of the Susquehanna? If so, it would take him toward home. Was this the river Lizzie had spoken about in his dream?

Jacob closed his eyes for a moment, afraid to trust his dream but afraid not to. When he opened his eyes again, he raised his face toward the sky. He breathed a prayer for Christian and Joseph, wherever they were, that they might somehow, through the grace of God, also be led home.

Then he set out to follow the river toward the east.

-24-

After four days along the river, Jacob was sure that he was on the right course. He was so hungry and so eager to get home that he decided to build a raft. It would surely float twice as fast as he could walk. He didn't have an ax or a tomahawk, so he would have to make do with fallen logs lying on the ground.

Jacob scoured the woods near the river and found a log about six inches in diameter to serve as the base for the bed of the raft. Despite the risk, Jacob started a fire and tended it until it was big enough to start several smaller fires at intervals to burn the log into sections. Each piece was just a little longer than he could reach with his arms stretched out. Jacob tended each of the small fires, turning the log often enough to burn it somewhat evenly all around. Where the pieces were not burned through, he used his knife to chop at the cuts. Whenever the blade got dull, he sharpened it on the edge of a rock.

The next morning, Jacob rolled the larger logs to a smooth place at the edge of the river and then rolled the smaller ones on top of them. He made several trips into the woods, cutting vines with his knife and carrying them to the water's edge. He used the vines to bind the top layer of logs onto the two larger ones below. By the time the sun reached its peak, Jacob was satisfied that the raft would hold together and carry his weight in the water. But by that time he was so weak that he couldn't even move the raft into the water. He hobbled back into the shadow of the woods to rest with his back against a tree. His strength was waning, and he had begun to despair of finding food.

After he had gotten his breath back, Jacob walked down to the river to wash the perspiration from his hands and face. The surface was calm in a small pool at the edge of the current. When he bent down to splash water onto his face, he could hardly recognize himself in his reflection. His beard hairs were growing out thick now, covering his gaunt cheek bones. He couldn't remember ever seeing his face so thin. And his brown hair was now flecked with gray.

I look like a scarecrow. Jacob laughed, maybe to keep from crying.

As he tugged the raft into the river, Jacob paused several times to get his breath and gather up his strength. He climbed onto the raft and pushed it away from the shore, using a long, thin pole to push the raft toward the center of the river where the current was the strongest. Soon the makeshift craft moved at a pace faster than he could have walked. And with far less effort.

As long as he stayed in the center of the raft, Jacob learned, he could sit or lie down without tipping it. As he floated down the river, he busied himself by scraping the rough bark off the top of the logs with his knife. He let the chips fill up the cracks between the logs on the surface. It made a smoother surface for him to lie down on.

By the end of the day, the vines holding together the logs were coming loose, so Jacob poled his raft to the edge of the water. He tightened up all of the vines and gathered a few leafy boughs to make a softer surface on the platform. After a brief night of rest, he would be ready to launch the raft for a full day.

Jacob woke up to the damp feeling of rain on his skin. It started as a drizzle, but soon it was falling steadily. He would have to float down the river fully exposed to the elements. Although the blooming flowers and the length of the days announced that it was late spring, the rain felt cold on his skin. Before long, he was sniffling and his nose was running.

The rain was falling in sheets when the current jammed his raft onto the skirt of a small island. Even though he pushed with all his strength, Jacob couldn't dislodge the raft from its hold.

Jacob crawled off the raft and onto the small island, pushing his way through a tangle of vines toward the cover of a large maple tree. Along the way he pulled off the ends of some sweet-tasting grass and chewed on them. The cool sap soothed his throat and the grassy stems calmed the growling of his stomach.

Jacob sat down to rest against the trunk of the tree. The rain dripped from the leaves overheard, but it was better than being on the river. When he woke up from a nap, the rain was falling as fast as ever.

Jacob determined to keep going despite the rain. He headed back to the raft, then took off his ragged, old moccasins and tossed them onto the raft. By wading into the water, Jacob was able to push the raft back onto the river. It tipped as he mounted but then leveled off as it floated into the current. At least he'd have a better chance of getting to safety before he starved to death.

By the fourth day on the river, Jacob was so famished that he no longer had the strength to move the raft with his pole. Jacob prayed as he drifted along, straining his eyes for signs of human life along either bank of the river. It took much of his strength just to cough out the phlegm that had begun clogging his lungs.

Jacob was lying on his side on the raft, scanning the east bank, when he saw a soldier watering his horse at the edge of the river. Jacob tried to sit up and get his attention, but he only managed to raise his hand. Thank God, the man happened to look toward him. The soldier tied his horse and ran toward a boat that was moored not far away.

Oh God, Jacob prayed, *please let him be British and not French.*

The man paddled furiously, and caught up with his raft a few minutes later. "Looks like you're in trouble. Want to come with me?" He tossed a rope toward Jacob.

Jacob nodded and reached for the rope. He was too weak to hold it, so the man tied the rope to the raft. And then, with one leg in the boat and the other on the raft, the soldier put his arms under Jacob's arms and pulled him into his boat. Jacob slumped onto the bottom and everything went black.

When he came to, he was lying on a small cot in a house that smelled of hot broth. Was it another dream? He opened his eyes to see a woman, a portly soul about Lizzie's size.

"Are you ready for a bite to eat?"

Jacob nodded.

She helped him sit up in the cot and then brought a bowl of soup to spoon into his mouth. She fed him with small amounts, like his mother used to feed Grandpa when he was old and could hardly swallow. The steaming gruel settled into Jacob's stomach and followed a path to his tired bones.

Jacob's rescuer stood watching, dressed in a uniform like that worn by soldiers at Fort Northkill. Jacob took him to be British. He looked up at the soldier, who seemed concerned for his condition. "Thank you. If you hadn't seen me on the river, I'm not sure I would have lasted another day."

"Thank God I happened to look up at the right time." He turned to put a couple of logs on the fire.

"Where am I?"

"Fort Augusta. The Indians called it Shamokin."

Jacob's lips parted and he closed his eyes. So it was a British fort. And only a few days walk from home.

The woman had just finished spooning his soup when a man in an officer's uniform opened the door and strode in. "I'm Colonel James Burd, the captain here. I had you brought in from the river. What is your name?"

Jacob tried to prop himself up higher on the cot. "Jacob Hochstetler from Berks County. I was taken by the Indians last fall. They killed my wife and two children."

The colonel's face twisted into rage. "Savages! Where did they take you?"

"Up to Presque Isle and then to Buckaloons. I escaped two weeks ago. I want to get back to my family as soon as possible, if they're still alive."

"I hope they are."

"If I hurry home, I might still be able to plant some crops this spring."

"Not so fast. It will take time for you to get your strength back. Today I'm taking you to Colonel Bouquet at Carlisle. He is trying to learn the whereabouts of the enemy in the parts where you just came from."

Jacob grimaced. "I'm obliged to you, sir, if you think it's necessary. But I want to get home as soon as I can."

"I was just ready to lead a garrison to Carlisle when I saw you on the river. We've been held up for days by rain, and we must go now. I'll let you ride in the wagon while we march."

Jacob stood up and walked out the door on wobbly legs. The man who had rescued him steadied his arm as he went and then helped him onto a supply wagon.

The captain gave an order and the men began to march. There must have been two hundred of them, marching in step on a wide path that ran along the river. The horse's hooves made a sucking sound in the mud as they plodded along in the rear. Jacob bounced along with only a thin blanket between him and the hard boards of the wagon bottom. It was worse than the raft.

With the gruel afforded by Colonel Burd, Jacob gained a little strength each day. Still, he disliked the trip. Not only was it taking him out of his way, it pained his pacifist conscience to be traveling with the army. Besides, his meeting with the officer might be used to bring harm to others. That was worse than going to a fort overnight.

It took several days for them to get to the military head-quarters in Carlisle. The sun was settling behind the tops of the tallest trees when the driver pulled up to the hitching post. The gatekeeper took Jacob inside and explained his situation to the host. He assigned Jacob a room and promised that

Colonel Henry Bouquet, an officer from Switzerland, would plan to see him the next day.

The next morning, Jacob was brought before Bouquet for examination. He was dressed in the manner of a commanding officer, wearing a blue uniform with brass buttons.

He leaned forward in his chair and plied Jacob with questions. "How many Indians attacked your farm? And from which tribes?"

"By the Delaware and Shawnees, led by a French captain. Fifteen in the whole."

He frowned at Jacob's response. Was it the way he mixed his Swiss and German? If he was indeed from Switzerland, he could surely understand either language.

"Which way did you pass before you came into the enemy's country?"

Jacob told him about the long march, and the way his sons had been separated from him.

After further questions about his captivity, the colonel asked, "Did you ever hear anything of Fort Duquesne?"

Jacob coughed, the phlegm catching briefly in his throat. "Ten days before I escaped, five Dutch prisoners were brought up by the Indians from there. They said there were three hundred men garrisoned in the fort, and that provisions were scarce. The Indians were forced to take their wives and families from there. It was a hardship for the Indians, seeing as they depend on the French for supplies, and had little time to hunt when they were on the war trail."

"Did you hear of any works about, besides at the fort?"

"The Dutchman said that if the British struck from the hill on the other side of the Monongahela, they could take the fort with two hundred men."

The colonel glanced at his secretary, who was taking notes, and then back to Jacob. "Did you hear of any French orders for Indians to march against us?"

"Most of the warriors in our village were on the warpath when I left. Five days before I escaped, an old Indian told me about Indians coming and going in various parts. He showed where they were planning to attack the English to the south and east, which I took to be Shamokin."

The colonel arched his eyebrows. "Where do you suppose they got intelligence of the English?"

Jacob paused to cough several times before he spoke. What was the colonel going to do with the knowledge he was going to share? "Six weeks before my departing, two Delawares came to Buckaloons from Shamokin. Their arms had been taken from them by the British, for want of trust. They said the English were drawing together in Conestoga, or Lancaster, paying up with cattle, and planning to attack the great fort at Duquesne as soon as the grass was green."

The colonel's head jerked back. "Savages." He motioned to the note-taker to make sure that what Jacob had said was included in the notes. A few more questions, and he released him to go.

"Stupid peasant," Jacob heard the colonel say to his secretary just as he stepped out of the office. His ears felt hot as he walked away.

"Don't go without some provisions," the gatekeeper said, holding out a bag filled with beef jerky, some crusty bread, and a few nuts.

"Thank you." It was the least they could do, after stretching out Jacob's trip to at least five extra days. The officer told him it would be about sixty-five miles from Carlisle to the Northkill.

Jacob struck out on the same trail that had brought the battalion and him to Carlisle the day before. If he kept gaining strength, he would be able to make the trip to the Northkill in four days. The Allegheny path would take him across the Susquehanna River just south of Fort Hunter. From there he could follow the path down to Paxtang and then east to Weiser's, just a day from home.

Home! He could hardly allow himself to think about it. He worried that he would wake from a dream and find himself far away again, in captivity in Buckaloons or half-dead on the raft.

Jacob got so wet and chilled on his way home from Carlisle that his cough stayed with him. By the afternoon of the fourth day, he was so tired that he almost stopped for the night. But he wanted to get home so badly that he pushed his legs to keep moving regardless of how he felt. He stumbled over roots and rocks, but he kept up his pace, even speeding up a little as the landmarks became more familiar.

The sun had dropped just below the horizon when he walked the last little stretch toward his farm. The sweet scent of blooming honeysuckle wafted toward him when he reached the edge of the farm. He pulled off a few blossoms and carried them with him. Lizzie had often cut the blossoms and put them in a vase on the table, a sign that it was time to plant corn.

Jacob's knees buckled. The place where the house had stood was ahead of him. A few charred logs still lay on the ground. Jacob knelt on the ground, his gaze sweeping the yard as he relived the moments when the warriors had rushed toward them on that fateful day in September the year before. There was the spot that Lizzie had been killed. There was the spot where Jakey had been. He looked toward the woods where Franey had been killed. This soil, this farm—it had become more than a plot of land. It was sacred ground. His family was surely buried here somewhere, and he longed to know where.

Jacob felt the sting of tears on his face as the losses of the past year, combined with the relief of being home, pushed him toward the ground. He sank heavily to his side in the fading light, heaving heavy breaths to slow his sobs.

He was home.

PART III

-25-

Jacob had just gotten to his feet when the barking of a dog made him spin around, searching for its whereabouts. Could it be? . . .

A dog bounded out of the orchard toward Jacob, his tail wagging. "Fritz? Fritz! I'm home!" Had he been waiting all this time?

Jacob knelt down to embrace the dog as he leaped to cover Jacob's face with licks, shuddering with joy. He stroked the dog's back and felt his gaunt ribs. "You poor thing. Hasn't anyone been feeding you?" Petting Fritz brought tears to Jacob's eyes again. Christian and Joseph had loved playing with Fritz, tossing him sticks and holding his paws in their hands. Jacob hugged the dog a little closer and put his cheek against his scratchy fur.

Fritz trotted behind Jacob as he started down the path toward Barbara and Cristy's house.

The dog bumped Jacob's hand with his cold nose, as though urging him to keep going. He would have to come back to the homestead later. For now, he needed to let Barbara and John know he was home.

As he walked the short path to his daughter's house, the unknowns of the future began to crackle in his brain. After his escape, Jacob hadn't thought much about what he would do after he got home. He would have to decide where to stay in the Northkill, since his house had been destroyed. John's family lived close by, and John and Katie would surely let him stay with them, if he asked. On the other hand, it might be best to stay with Barbara. She had loved Lizzie the longest and knew best how Lizzie had cared for his needs. She'd be less likely than Katie to mind that he was there.

As he walked toward Barbara's house, Jacob prayed that she and her family were safe and that they hadn't moved away.

When he saw a buttery light coming from the windows of their home, he hurried to reach it.

Jacob rapped three times on the door. The door swung open just a crack, revealing his son-in-law in the dim light. A moment passed as Cristy looked him over from head to toe.

"Cristy. It's me. *Yacob*," he said in a raspy voice.

Cristy gasped. "Oh! *Dat*! I didn't recognize you." Cristy swung the door wide open and stepped forward to embrace him.

Barbara laid down her embroidery and put her hands tightly over her mouth. She stood up and hurried to her father, throwing her arms around him. "*Dat*! I'm so glad you're alive. We were afraid—."

Jacob's eyes filled as he hugged her close. "I almost didn't make it."

Barbara held onto his forearm tightly as if she didn't want to let him leave her grasp. "You must be very hungry," she said. "Here, sit up to the table and I'll fetch you something to eat." She led him toward the table. "I'll get you some soup."

She paused. "Oh, you haven't seen the baby! He was born in January." She moved toward the crib. "The girls are already in bed. They'll be so surprised to see you tomorrow."

"What month is it now?" Jacob had forgotten to ask the people at the fort.

"June. The baby will be five months old next week."

Jacob reached out his arms. "May I hold him?"

Barbara looked at his unshaven face and dirty clothing. "For a minute." She handed the child to Jacob.

Jacob gazed into his baby grandson's eyes as he cradled him in his arms. He had missed so much. Jacob swallowed hard to think that Lizzie would never know this child. "What is his name?"

"Christian. We named him after his papa and Grandpa Stutzman." She paused. "And his uncle."

"*Du bisch da Christlich* (You are Christian)." Jacob stroked the child's pink cheeks with his forefinger. *Christian*. The gentle curves of the child's face took him back to the last time when he had seen his own son by that name. He could still see him being led away, his eyes full of fear, his shoulders, so small. *Oh, my Christian.*

Jacob's muscles tensed and the baby squirmed. When he began to yowl, Jacob handed him back to Barbara. "He is a lovely child."

"*Jah*, we love him dearly." Barbara rocked the child in her arms and then handed him to Cristy so she could heat up water for tea. Eyes down, she asked the whereabouts of her brothers.

"I last saw them taken from Presque Isle, by different parties."

Her head jerked up. "Then they're still alive?"

"I hope so. I pray so."

"We missed the three of you terribly. *Mam*, Franey, and Jakey too."

"It's been very hard . . ." Jacob couldn't finish his sentence. There was silence.

"I suppose you stopped at the farm on the way to our place?"

"For a few minutes." Jacob's eyes stung with tears, which prompted more tears from Barbara.

Cristy, bless him, made an effort to lighten the mood. "Tomorrow morning we can show you what we've done at the home place."

Barbara nodded. "And you'll want to see where *Mam* is buried."

The mood fell again. "*Jah*." He looked down at the table. Everyone fell silent for a few moments.

"You can stay here with us," Cristy said, anticipating the question that Jacob was about to ask. Jacob glanced at his daughter, whose eyes still shone with tears as she gave a vigorous nod.

❖

Barbara swung the kettle over the fire to heat up water for tea and a bath for her father. She soon saw that it would take more than tea to quiet his persistent cough. Cristy fetched a bottle of whiskey from the cellar and poured a bit in a cup.

"Here's some medicine, *Dat*," Barbara told him, "made from rye in our still. Should cure what ails you."

Her father took a small swallow and almost choked as the strong drink bit the rawness of his sore throat.

"Go slow, *Dat*," Cristy said. "No need to hurry."

"I think I walked a little too long in the rain. Got too cold for my own good." Jacob's voice was hoarse.

Dat sipped the drink through thin and cracked lips. The hair on the crown of his head was matted and tangled, looking as though it hadn't been washed in months. The hair on the rest of his head was perhaps the length of Barbara's little fingernail. His beard was short and patchy, with a couple of weeks' growth. Barbara kept staring at the strange sight but held her tongue. She couldn't imagine what he had gone through during the past year.

"I'd want a warm bath if I were you," she told him. "The water in the wooden tub is nice and warm. And I put a bar of soap right there beside it."

Her father coughed. "I haven't had a bath in warm water since the day we were taken from this place. I can just sleep in my clothing." His raspy voice was barely more than a whisper.

"No, you need to take a bath. Here are some night clothes you can wear to sleep."

Her father slipped into the back of the room and Barbara heard the sound of splashing water.

"You can leave your old clothing lying beside the tub and I'll wash them tomorrow," she called out. "I'll give you some of Cristy's clean clothes to wear in the morning."

As soon as her father went to bed, Barbara took his dirty clothes and put them outside the cabin. His leggings appeared to be made of buckskin, so they couldn't be washed. Barbara didn't know just what all of the smells were in that clothing, but she couldn't bear to have it in her house.

Dat coughed on and off during the night, so Barbara didn't get much sleep. The baby fussed more than usual that night. To keep his crying from bothering her father, she kept the baby at the breast more than usual.

The next morning, Barbara awoke tired but with a peace spreading through her. With her father home, the world felt more right today than it had yesterday. She asked him how he was feeling.

"Okay. A little tired, I guess." He coughed weakly.

"I'm afraid you haven't been eating enough," Barbara said after her father had eaten only a bowl of vegetable and beef soup. He said he was finished.

Barbara dipped another cup of soup into his bowl. "No, you eat this. You need it to get stronger." She was acting like her mother, trying to get *Dat* to eat even when he said he was full. Watching people eat the food she had prepared had always made *Mam* feel good. And she'd often said, "If you eat all of your food, it will rain." That was a good thing, since they needed the moisture for the crops.

Her father coughed. "I'm sure I'll feel better soon," he said. "Then I can work outside and get out of your way."

"That's okay, Papa. It may take a little time to get well." But what if the cough was a sign of something worse than a cold?

"Should we look for a healer to bring us something for *Dat*'s cough?" she asked Cristy later, when they were alone. "*Dat* doesn't want to take whiskey, and it doesn't seem to be helping much anyhow."

"I think we should do something," Cristy said. "Let's call on Anna Yoder. She knows about these things and probably has some remedy that might help."

Barbara stiffened. "I'm not sure we want to invite Anna into our house."

"Why not? We need to do something." The look on Cristy's face told Barbara that he thought she was being unreasonable. "I'm going right now."

He was back within the hour. "*Dat*, I brought Anna Yoder to help you with your cough," Cristy said, avoiding Barbara's eyes. "She brought something along."

"Good," *Dat* said. He reached out his hand to greet her.

"*Es is so gud fa dich saana* (It is so good to see you)," Anna said. "And I'm sorry you got sick on the way home. I brought you some of the cough syrup I made. I also brought some homemade salve to rub on your chest. It should help." She set the items on the table.

"Are there any instructions for taking this?" Barbara poured a bit of cough syrup into a cup and gave it to her father.

"About a tablespoon at a time," Anna said. "You can take it several times a day if you need to. It won't hurt you if you take more. It's good for you."

"Thank you," *Dat* said to Anna. "I know you're good with herbs."

They passed the next minutes in small talk, standing around Barbara's father as he sat in a chair.

"I notice that you're holding your neck as though it's a little stiff," Anna said. "Coughing often makes it sore, just like it does your chest. Maybe your neck could stand to be rubbed a little."

"That would be just fine," Jacob said. Anna stood behind his chair and gently massaged his neck and shoulders. Magdalena stood nearby, watching wide-eyed as Anna worked.

Barbara kept herself busy with the baby. What would *Mam* have said if she had seen Anna working on *Dat*'s neck?

Anna either noticed Barbara's discomfort or felt she was finished and announced that she was ready to leave. "That bottle of medicine is yours to keep," she said as she headed for the door. "Take it as often as you need to keep from coughing."

"I am much obliged. Come back again," Barbara's father said in a weak voice as Anna slipped out the door.

Barbara rubbed some of the salve on his chest before he went to bed that night. They all slept through the night. Even the baby, who often woke up wanting to nurse, slept until the first rays of the sun shone through the kitchen window. Barbara had nearly forgotten what a blessing a good night of sleep could be.

-26-

The day after Jacob got home, Barbara's family walked with him to the homestead. The sun rose warm in a cloudless sky, with a slight breeze stirring the trees. The maple leaves were nearly full size now, and the blackberry bushes were sprouting buds along the path. The family walked slowly alongside him, pausing several times as he coughed and took a minute to catch his breath.

As they neared the farm, Jacob turned to Barbara. "Was anyone else taken during the attack on our family?"

"The Indians killed a soldier at the fort. And they shot at John Miller—"

"John Adam Miller's son?"

"*Jah*, over toward the mountain, the same day they took you away. John was chopping wood, and the bullet hit his hand when he raised his ax. He ran and they didn't come after him."

Jacob nodded vigorously. "I was walking near the end of the line with my hands tied when I saw them shoot at a settler in the clearing, but I couldn't tell who it was."

"John's hand is crippled now. We call him Indian John."

"At least he wasn't killed, like his *Dat* was."

Jacob glanced at his grandchildren. It might not be good for them to hear so much talk about Indians and killing. How could they sleep at night?

They walked along in silence until they neared the foundation of what had been their home.

"I am so glad you're back home," Barbara said as they stood close to the ruin.

"It's so good to be home."

Without a word, Jacob walked to the place where Lizzie had been tomahawked. Barbara stood quietly as he looked over the scene.

"Where did you lay *Mam* and the children to rest?"

"Right here beside the house. I wanted to bury them by the edge of the orchard, but John thought they should be buried here."

Jacob glanced at the edge of the orchard. Had they buried the bodies there, they would likely have dug up the tin he had buried with their savings. He hadn't even thought of the hidden money until that moment.

"Do you know where each one is buried?"

"We marked the place with these rocks," she said, pointing to a small heap of field stones at the head of each of the three mounds. "Mam is buried here in the middle. Franey is buried on this side, and Jakey on that side." She pointed to the small mounds as she spoke.

"Was there a funeral?" The Reichards and Meyers hadn't had any.

"No. But the bishop said a few words at the burial. A few neighbors saw the fire and watched the Indians take the three of you away. They helped John and Cristy dig the graves."

Jacob nodded. "You never know when they might show up." Knowing that Indians were planning an attack on Fort Augusta made goose bumps sprout on his arms. That was only a few days' walk from the homestead. He was so weary of fear, but it seemed his constant companion, even now that he was home. What if the Indians came on another raid to the Northkill and found him? Would his daughter's family be at risk if he stayed with them?

Barbara stood nearby holding baby Christian, with Annie and Mary at her side. Magdalena was picking some flowers that grew in the meadow at the edge of the wood.

Jacob crouched on the ground and rubbed his hand on the round stones at the head of the graves. It felt comforting, in a way, to feel the coarseness of the stones that marked Lizzie's grave. Even though he couldn't see her, Jacob could sense her presence. Her body was resting in peace beside the garden, while her soul was rejoicing in heaven. Sometimes the space between earth and heaven seemed very thin.

Jacob's breath came in shallow gasps as he cleaned a few leaves off the top of the middle mound. He gently rearranged the stones at the head, his belated mark on the memorial mound. He wanted to lie down on the small knoll, to feel the soil and get as close to Lizzie's body as possible. He resisted the urge, which seemed much too private for Barbara and the children to see. Just then Magdalena came running up to him. "Here, Grandpa, I picked some flowers for you." She held out her hand with a bunch of tiny yellow flowers. Lizzie would have known what to call them.

Jacob rose to his feet to receive her gift. "Thank you. Shall we put them on Grandma's grave? She always liked flowers."

Magdalena nodded solemnly, so he knelt down and laid the bunch right next to the stones that marked Lizzie's grave. Jacob took his granddaughter's hand in his.

Magdalena gazed at the three graves. "Grandpa, we should have some flowers for Uncle Jakey and Aunt Franey too. I'll go pick some for them."

Jacob nodded. "Of course." His eyes watered as the young girl scurried off.

The rest stood in silence as Magdalena picked a large handful of flowers. She brought them back and laid them beside the small piles of stones on the two outside graves as she had seen her grandfather do.

Jacob patted her on the head. "Let's go see Uncle John and your cousins." He headed toward John and Katie's home not far to the west. Magdalena skipped ahead and found John in the barn.

John stepped out of the barn with a bucket in his hand. "Papa! You're home." He set down the bucket and strode up to Jacob with open arms and tears in his eyes. They held each other tight for a few moments. How good to see his oldest son in good health and safe.

The sun slanted over the brim of John's hat, casting a shadow over his face. "We sure missed you. We didn't know if you were dead or alive."

"*Jah*, I was kept in a camp with other prisoners. But the good Lord allowed me to get away from there."

"And the boys?"

"They were taken to other places. I don't know where they are."

John looked down. "We'll have to keep praying."

"I'm going to do everything possible to get them to come home."

John stood silent for a moment. "I'm afraid I'm not able to keep up with the farm the way you did."

"How could you? You're working by yourself."

By this time, Magdalena had fetched the rest of John's family. Katie came out carrying baby Fanny. The two little boys, Jakey and John Jr., clung to her skirt. She was large with child.

Jacob stepped up to greet Katie with a hug. Little Fanny turned her head, and the two boys hid their faces in Katie's skirt.

"This is Grandpa," John said. "He just came back from the Indian camp."

They peered at their grandfather but held on to Katie's skirt.

John saw Jacob looking at Katie's extended belly. "We're expecting another one this summer. Maybe July."

The boys kept their eyes on Jacob for a time and then started to play as both families walked back with him to the homestead.

"Someone should let my *Dat* know that you're back," Katie said as they walked along.

Jacob nodded. "*Jah*, I would like that." He had missed his conversations with Jake Hertzler.

"I'll go," Cristy said.

John nodded. "You can take Blitz. The bridle is hanging on the peg beside the barn door."

Jacob's eyes widened. "So Blitz came back? Last I saw him, he was running from the Indians."

John nodded. "*Jah*, a neighbor brought him back the next day. He was skittish for a while but he's back to normal now."

"Whatever happened to Bessie?"

"We found her in the woods. She's due to calve in a month or so."

Jacob sighed. "Thank God."

Cristy strode back toward John's place as John led them toward the ruins of Jacob's barn. "You can see that we still have some cleanup to do around here."

Jacob glanced at the circle of ashes. "I want to rebuild this barn. But first I must get the crops in the ground. It's soon too late to plant corn."

"*Dat*, you need to rest. You look worn-out."

Jacob suppressed a cough with his hand. "I see your corn is up."

"But you've had a hard winter without enough to eat."

Fritz stood beside Jacob, wagging his tail. "Looks like Fritz suffered too. Didn't anyone feed him?"

John shrugged. "We tried. Most days he sat by the path watching for you. This morning was the first time he ate much since you were gone."

Jacob reached down to pat Fritz's head. "You're a real friend."

Barbara stepped back into the circle of conversation. "We'll feed both of you all you can eat."

"Thank you," was all that Jacob could manage to say. To be at home on the farm and eat familiar food again with his own family was a gift from the hand of God.

Jacob was back at Barbara's home when Cristy returned with Jake Hertzler on a mount trotting beside his. Jacob stepped outside and waited as Jake rode up to the spot where he was standing.

"I'll tie your horse," Cristy volunteered as Jake dismounted.

"Thank you." The bishop reached out to shake Jacob's hand and then greeted him with a solemn kiss, according to the church's custom. They stood there for a few moments, hands clasped, each holding tightly to the other's shoulder. They spoke no words; it was enough just to be together.

"Come inside and sit for a while," Barbara said. "I have spearmint tea from the garden and dried apples to eat."

The children played quietly in the background as they sat at the table—Cristy and Barbara at one end of table, and Jake and Jacob at the other.

"I am so glad that God brought you back safely," Jake said. "You have suffered much at the hands of the Indians."

Jacob swallowed hard and nodded. How could he even begin to describe his experiences in the last year? "God was with me."

"We prayed for you often, in our home and also in the church fellowship. We had no idea where you or your sons were. Or if you were alive."

"I got separated from the boys after we got to the French fort at Presque Isle. I don't know where they are now, but I trust they're alive."

A worried look crossed Jake's face. "I hope both of them will return soon."

"That is my constant prayer."

Barbara brought the pitcher. "*Dat* will sure miss the boys when it comes to the farm," she said as she refilled cups with tea.

Jake cleared his throat. "I'm sure you'll be able to use some help to get your crops planted."

Jacob nodded. Was he planning to call for a workday? "I know this is a busy time of year, but I would be thankful for all the help I can get. It's going to be a lot of work for one man to do."

"We should never be too busy to help someone in need. I know the brethren will consider it a privilege to be able to help. I'll ask the deacon to set up a day to help you get the crops planted, and then we'll talk about a time later on to rebuild your house and barn."

Relief washed through Jacob's limbs. He was no longer alone.

Later that evening Barbara showed Jacob up the stairs to a room on the second floor of their small log house. Jacob had helped his daughter and Cristy build the place just before they had gotten married. The cabin was well built, resting on a stone foundation. They had two rooms downstairs, with a large fireplace at the south end, and steps to the right of it that went up to the second floor. The well-fitted pine boards that made up the floors and walls had very few knots. There were four small rooms upstairs, so they gave Jacob a little one at the far end. He could see Northkill Creek out of his little window to the west.

Jacob blew out the candle and lay down on a small rope bed. He wondered how long it would be before he was back in his own bed, in his own house, with a companion at his side.

The following Sunday, Jacob went to the church service with Barbara's family. Jake Hertzler's family was hosting. Jacob's spirit soared as they bounced along in Cristy's wagon. The rhododendrons were in full bloom along with the lilacs. The air was perfumed with blossoms. Jacob's eyes welled with tears as birds flitted in the trees alongside the rutted roadside. It all seemed too good to be true, a vivid contrast with the life he had lived just a few weeks earlier.

They were about halfway there when Magdalena scooted to his side. "Will you hold me, Grandpa?"

"*Jah*, of course." She crawled onto his lap. Jacob gave her a big smile and a warm hug. In the days since he'd been in their home, she'd mostly kept her distance.

"Grandpa," she said, as they passed through a dense wood. "Were you ever afraid when you were walking in the woods on the way home?"

"Sometimes, but not too much."

Her sweet little face turned serious. "What were you most afraid of: bears or wolves?"

"Bears are big and scary, but they usually won't bother you

if you leave them alone. Wolves can be dangerous if they're hungry."

"I hope I never meet a hungry wolf." The little girl shivered and leaned back against his chest. Jacob wrapped his arms around her and squeezed her tightly to himself. "You don't have to worry. We have a heavenly Father who takes care of us. And you have your Grandpa too."

She curled up tightly against him. He closed his eyes for a few moments, pretending she was his little Franey. When he opened them, he glanced over to see Barbara wipe a tear from her cheek.

"*Dat*, sometime you'll need to tell us about your trip through the woods, and also your time with the Indians," Barbara said. "You haven't told us much about it so far." She had mentioned it before, and he had found a way to change the subject.

"One of these days when my voice is better." How long could he put her off? She didn't need to know about the way their captors had marched him and her brothers along as prisoners, tied them up, and beat them. Or about the way they had burned two of the prisoners. Why should he relive that pain just to satisfy her curiosity?

As the wagon rolled into the Hertzlers' yard, Hans Beiler hurried over to greet Jacob. "Welcome back, Jacob," he said, shaking his hand and thumping his back. "I see you don't have an *Ausbund*. I imagine you lost yours in the fire."

"*Jah*, I had it with me in the cellar when the house burned down."

"I would like to give you my copy," Hans said. "We just happen to have two of them."

"Thank you. It will be good to have my own copy again." Jacob took the *Ausbund* with him to his seat, greeting people all along the way who stood in line to welcome him home.

It wasn't until the congregation started singing that morning that he realized how much it meant to him to hold a worship book in his hands. Through all the months at the Indian camp, he hadn't seen anything in writing. Jacob didn't read well, but it meant a great deal to have the church's hymns in front of him at worship. Having gone through his own trial of faith, he identified more deeply with the lyrics written by his spiritual ancestors in times of persecution.

Even so, he couldn't sing that day. It was partly because his voice was hoarse and raspy, but mostly because of the lump that formed in his throat as he looked at the people in the room. *My people!* Having been a prisoner and a stranger for months on the trail or at Buckaloons, Jacob sat there and soaked in the sense of being known and loved.

Still, he realized that he must look like a stranger to the assembly that day. His hair and beard were still very short, and every time he glanced around, someone was looking at him. Most looked down right away as though embarrassed, but Anna Yoder held his gaze for a few moments as she sang. It was as though she was singing to him.

Jacob studied her. She had fine-textured skin, strong cheekbones, honey-brown hair, and features that weren't at all displeasing. It wouldn't be long before some fellow started to court her. She would make a fine wife for some man.

After the service, Anna came to shake his hand. "I hope the cough syrup is helping. I'm so glad to see you are back in the fellowship. But I know that not having your boys home with you must be very hard. And I'm sure you miss Lizzie very much."

Jacob tried to speak, but the lump that rose in his throat barred his words. He simply nodded and quickly wiped away the tear that fell on his cheek. These days it seemed like the simplest gestures of kindness could make him weep.

Anna's eyes moistened. "I shall pray for you."

The next day Jacob felt strong enough to spade up parts of Barbara's garden. She warned him not to overdo it, but he wanted to get out and do something in the sunshine. Lizzie used to say there's nothing better for your health than working in the sunshine. The fragrance of the peonies and lilacs only made it better.

The spade Jacob was using had a crack in the blade that got worse as he worked. "If we don't get this shovel fixed now," he told Cristy at dinnertime, "it'll break apart and be good for nothing. Let me take it to the smithy's shop this afternoon to get it welded."

Cristy agreed, so Jacob rode there on their horse, carrying the shovel crossways on his lap. He pulled the horse up to the blacksmith's shop and tied it at the hitching post. The familiar smell of sulfur and burning charcoal stung his nose as he carried the broken spade through the double doors.

The smithy looked up from his work. "What can I do for you?"

Jacob handed him the spade. "I can't work in the garden with a shovel like this."

"I can take care of that." The smithy nodded to his assistant, who began pumping the bellows, and then he looked at him more closely. "Aren't you the man who got taken by the Indians last fall when they killed the scout at the fort?"

Jacob nodded. "They killed my wife, Lizzie, and two children. Took me and two of my boys captive. I was held at the Seneca village at Buckaloons all winter."

The smithy whistled through his teeth. "Whew, that must have been an ordeal."

"Wouldn't wish it on anybody. God helped me get away."

The steady whoosh of air from the bellows fired up the coals to a bright orange glow.

"Did the boys come back with you?"

"No. They got taken to other places. I'd do anything to get them back."

The smithy laid the blade of the shovel on the glowing coals. "Shall we send out a posse to rescue them?"

"I don't know where they are."

"So how are you going to get them back?" The smithy poked the blade of the shovel into the fiery coals, along with a small strip of metal.

"Colonel Bouquet says the army will eventually make the Indians return all of their captives. I trust that the good Lord wants to set them free, and he'll make it happen at the right time."

The smithy took his tongs and laid the strip of hot metal on the broken blade. Then he swung the blade over to a large anvil and beat it with his hammer until the pieces melded into one. After the red glow dimmed, he dipped the blade into a bucket of water and handed the shovel back to Jacob with a satisfied look on his reddened face. "There you are, strong as ever."

"Thank you, sir. How much do I owe you?"

"Nothing. It's the least I can do for you. If there's anything else I can do to help you get back on your feet, just let me know. Hope your boys come back soon."

"Thank you," Jacob said. "I'm much obliged."

With the shovel in hand, he mounted his horse and rode home. It would be wrong to send a posse after the boys, which would surely result in bloodshed. But what else might he do? Maybe he could negotiate a ransom with their captors. If needed, he could dig up the savings he had hidden in the yard. He and Lizzie had intended that money to use for Jakey. He didn't need it any longer, but someday his younger brothers might. But before Jacob could think of negotiating their release, he'd need to find out where they were being held. *Who could help me find them?*

Suddenly an idea came to him. *Conrad Weiser!* No one knew more about such things than the seasoned Indian agent for Pennsylvania.

Colonel Weiser had a tannery as part of his large estate. Jacob had dropped off a hide for tanning at Weiser's place not long before the attack. If he were to go there and pick up the

hide, he could ask Weiser where he thought the boys were being kept. If necessary, he could help Jacob negotiate for them
too.

As Jacob dismounted his horse and led him toward the
barn, he determined to go see Weiser as soon as possible.

-27-

The following Saturday, Jacob prepared to set out for the large farm where Conrad Weiser lived when he wasn't staying in the town of Reading.

Barbara wasn't happy about Jacob's plans. "*Dat*, won't you run into Indians—"

"I'll be on the lookout. I need to pick up my leather." This couldn't be any more dangerous than anything he'd encountered in the last months. It was only about twelve miles, an easy day's journey down and back.

He mounted Blitz and started out into the fresh spring air. The mayflowers burst forth along the path, and the mountain laurel was so thick in a few places that he got off of the horse to lead him through.

Jacob arrived at Weiser's estate at noon. Unlike New York, which had designated Sir William Johnson as their superintendent of Indian affairs, Pennsylvania hired negotiators as needed to manage its interactions with the Indians. Weiser was their most able mediator. German by birth, he also spoke English and a couple of Indian dialects.

As Jacob guided the horse into the rutted drive that led up to Weiser's home, he spotted Weiser walking from his house to the barn.

"Hello! What can I do for you?" the colonel said.

Jacob led his horse up to him and dismounted. "I'm Jacob Hochstetler. I came to pick up my leather."

"Ah, yes. We've been holding those hides of yours for a long time."

"I got taken by the Indians last September," Jacob said.

"I'm sorry to hear that. They've taken hundreds of people from the area."

"They stabbed my wife to death. Killed two of my children."

Weiser wrinkled his brow. "She was stabbed with a knife?"

"Yes, why?"

"They must have had a grudge against her. Indians don't usually kill people with knifes, except for revenge. I told you Amish folks to move away from the Northkill. Too dangerous."

He motioned toward the tannery and started walking. Jacob followed him on the path, with the horse following him on the path. Why would Weiser take the time to get the leather himself for a peasant like him? As the first president judge of Berks County, he ranked high among colonial leaders. The tannery stood at the far end of the estate, so they made their way along the edge of a verdant orchard of peach, apple, and cherry trees.

Jacob stepped up his pace to match Weiser's long strides. "My sons and I were taken captive in the attack. I escaped the village at Buckaloons. I just got back home last week."

"Whatever happened to your sons?" Weiser made a sighing sound. Was he genuinely interested in knowing, or just being polite?

"They are still being held."

"You know where?"

"I last saw them at Presque Isle. I was hoping you could help me find them."

"Not much I can do right now. Some prisoners might be released if the western Indians join with Chief Teedyuscung in a peace treaty. He sent negotiators with the calumet peace pipe to the Ohio territories just a few weeks ago."

"Will you help negotiate that treaty?" Jacob asked. "I'm praying my boys will come back before fall."

"I'm getting too old to go on those missions." He stroked his graying hair. "Don't get your hopes up for the boys. The Indians have likely adopted them." Weiser spoke with the confidence and authority of a provincial leader.

"But I'm certain my sons would come home if they had the chance. I'm sure they'd rather farm than live with Indians all their lives."

Weiser shrugged his shoulders. "Maybe not. A lot of whites don't want to come back."

How could he think that way? Perhaps Jacob was making a poor impression with his hair of different lengths and his unkempt beard.

"In my seven months at Buckaloons, not a day passed that I wouldn't rather have been at home."

"It's different for the younger ones. How old are your boys?"

"Joseph was thirteen when he was taken. Christian was eleven."

"Don't mean to discourage you, but they might enjoy living with the Indians. My father sent me to live among the Mohawks when I was their age so I could learn to interpret between our German people and the Mohawks."

Jacob shook his head in wonder. By that time, they had arrived at the tannery. Weiser found the two sides of leather with Jacob's name on them. "That will be eighteen shillings and nine pence."

Jacob stroked the soft leather in his hand. "I appreciate it." He reached into his bag and pulled out the coins for payment. "Thanks for your work. And your advice."

Jacob slung the leather over his shoulder and mounted his horse. He wasn't thankful at all. Weiser had blamed Lizzie for doing something wrong, and he had no interest in helping get Jacob's sons home. How could Weiser think his boys would rather stay with Indian families than come home to help him farm? Weiser only had to look at himself. Even though he had lived with the Mohawks as a child, he owned a large estate now. What boy in his right mind would prefer to stay with the Indians if he had the chance to inherit a farm?

Jacob wasn't about to give up hope for his sons' return— that they were alive and well and that they'd gladly come back home if given half a chance. He was going to do everything in his power to give them that chance.

❖

In the third week of June, men and women from the neighborhood came to the Hochstetler farm for a workday. Beyond the volunteers from Jacob's congregation, a few Lutheran neighbors came to help. Several carried rifles along with their tools. And of course John and Katie were there, as well as Cristy and Barbara. With instructions from Deacon Stephen Zug, they all went to their assigned tasks.

Four men joined Jacob's son John, guiding their horses and plows toward the plot where he hoped to plant corn. The field was thick with weeds, since it had not been plowed in the fall, and the heavy winter snows had left plenty of moisture in the ground. The plows tore up many of the weeds, preparing the soil for surface cultivation.

Jake Hertzler and several other men tossed the charred remains of the house and barn onto a pile and burned them. Jacob's throat constricted as smoke swirled from the site. How could he ever smell wood burning without reliving the awful scene when Lizzie was stuck in the window? He shook his head to shake the memory from his mind.

Stephen Zug set to plowing the garden plot in preparation for the women to plant a garden. Barbara hovered nearby, giving instructions to Anna Yoder, who had come to plant some herbs.

Barbara gave direction as several women prepared the meal for the day. Malinda Stehley, a widow, supervised the baking. She ordered several children to gather sticks in the nearby woods and then told Jacob to light a fire in the outdoor oven to bake bread for the noon meal. As the fire gained strength, Malinda mixed up the bread dough and let it rise, loudly calling out tasks to the children and youth who hovered about.

Jacob joined two men at the site of the barn. They removed the foundation stones that had been split by the heat and replaced them with others from the stone pile. Two young men pushed wheelbarrows back and forth between the building site and the stone pile, carrying stones suitable for the task. By noon, the foundation was ready for the first logs.

Hans Zook and several other men went to work in the nearby wood, chopping down trees to make logs for the barn. They worked in pairs, one on each side of a tree, chopping at the trunks with large felling axes. As the trees fell, the men moved in with crosscut saws to limb and buck the logs.

Peter Graybill stood nearby with a grindstone, helping to keep a sharp edge on the axes. Two young men worked with a team of horses to drag the logs from the woods to the construction site. With the help of the felling crews, they hooked a chain around the end of the logs, pulling them through the woods one by one. They brought them to a place near the barn where another man notched them and readied them for assembly on the walls.

When dinner was ready, Barbara rang a cowbell to call everyone to eat. The workers gathered around the buckets of water that had been brought from the creek. They splashed water on their faces and arms, and wiped them with linen towels. When everyone had cleaned up, Jake Hertzler invited them to stand in a circle.

"Shall we pause?" The bishop bowed his head and everyone followed suit. The group prayed silently as usual, each in their own manner of thanksgiving and devotion. *Perhaps others are praying like I am,* Jacob thought, after he had recited words that his mother had taught him. After a few moments the bishop quietly cleared his throat, and they were free to raise their heads.

Barbara stood at a table that had been brought from John's home. "Just help yourselves." On it were stacks of earthenware plates, a steaming kettle of cabbage, generous servings of peas and asparagus and chicken, along with a large bucket of Anna Yoder's spearmint tea.

The men went first in line, helping themselves to the food and then spreading out to find places to sit and eat. The women and children went next. The few chairs brought over from John's house were reserved for the older ones. Except for the children who sprawled out on the grass, the rest mostly sat on the foundation stones or the freshly cut logs for the barn.

As soon as the workers were finished eating, they went back to work. Most stayed until suppertime. The last to leave was Deacon Zug. "How do you feel about the progress?" he asked Jacob as he gathered up his tools and prepared to leave.

"Very pleased," Jacob said. "The crew got more done in one day than I could have in a month. I hadn't expected the woodsmen to fell so many trees."

"The church is meant to help at times like these."

"*Jah*, and I am thankful." Jacob's voice suddenly turned so husky that he could hardly speak. He had often helped others in need on such days, but now he was the one who desperately needed help. He would never think of a workday in the same way again.

Over the next few weeks, Jacob woke before dawn each day and hurried over to his farm. He plowed the soil and seed- ed the ground, and then his thoughts turned to putting the buildings back in shape. He and John worked alongside each other much of the time. John had always been the steady one among the children, and his calm, swift pace strengthened Jacob's resolve to rebuild his farm.

One morning when Barbara was visiting at John and Katie's place, Magdalena helped Jacob sift through the ashes of the house and barn, looking for iron nails. With nails so hard to get, they rescued every possible one. He gave Magdalena a little squeeze when they were done. "Thank you for helping me. When I have time this winter, I'll carve you some wooden animals."

"Oh, Grandpa, that will be so much fun. Can you make me a cow, like Moonface?"

Jacob nodded and gave her another little squeeze. "Yes, and a dog like Fritz to scare the bears away."

As the summer months went by, loneliness and memories often sent Jacob to Lizzie's grave. He missed her sorely. His grief, which he had worked so hard to contain during his time of captivity, now seemed endless, welling up at the smallest reminders. So many memories! Jacob sensed Lizzie's sturdy spirit everywhere on the farm. He heard her footsteps as he tilled the asparagus plants in the garden, the rows of peach and pear trees, and the hedge of raspberries.

Being around Barbara only stirred up more memories. The more Jacob observed his daughter at work, the more he saw Lizzie come to life in her manner. Jacob could see Lizzie's reach for perfection in all Barbara did—cooking, baking, gardening, caring for her family.

Some evenings, after the children were asleep in bed, Barbara would press him to talk about Lizzie. "What did *Mam* say when she found out the Indians were outside the house?" she asked one night.

Jacob's stomach shrank. Why must she ask such questions? "I don't remember. She was taking care of Jakey's leg. He got hit by a bullet when he opened the door."

"Did you shoot back to try to scare them away?"

"No. You know *Mam* and I don't believe in that." Jacob looked down at his hands.

"Then I think *Mam* is a martyr, like some of the women I read about in the *Martyrs Mirror*. She died because she obeyed your convictions."

Jacob wondered whether he had heard his daughter correctly. What would prompt her to say that Lizzie died because of *his* convictions, not hers? She had always supported his stance on nonresistance as though it was her own. Had she told Barbara about her parents' hesitance to bless the move across the ocean, or her reluctance to settle so close to Indian territory? What had she confided to Barbara about how she had hoped to move to a safer place?

Jacob didn't give Barbara the satisfaction of a reply. But as he mulled over the events that led to Lizzie's death, his conscience stabbed him for having persuaded her to move to the frontier. He wished he had been more open to her questions, more willing to take her fears seriously.

Some say it is wrong to talk to the dead, but Jacob wanted to be close to Lizzie, to feel her presence. One day in late August, Jacob knelt down beside Lizzie's grave and spoke to her aloud. "Lizzie, I'm sorry that I brought you to the settlement against your will. If I had it to do over again, I would have waited until you were ready." Jacob paused. "Or at least I would have moved farther away from the Northkill when the danger was so high."

Jacob lingered there on his knees until they got sore, wiping away the tears that kept blurring his vision. Was Lizzie hearing or seeing him? The bishop sometimes spoke of people in the afterworld as part of a great cloud of witnesses, mentioned in the letter to the Hebrews.

"Lizzie, if you can hear me, I hope you can forgive me."

And then it struck him—if he needed Lizzie's forgiveness, he needed God's forgiveness too. Jacob blurted out, "God in heaven, forgive all my sins. And please forgive me for not . . . for not . . . for not loving Lizzie as much as I loved myself."

Jacob took a long, deep breath. The air was purer now, the sunshine brighter. There was a lightness in his step as he walked away from the grave. It had been such a simple thing to do; why had he waited so long?

The sun shone brightly on the small meadow where John and Jacob were cutting the last hay of the season. A year had passed since his return to the Northkill, and Jacob and his son were doing most of their farming together. They took turns with the scythe, which wore on the body more than raking. John did more than his share, drawing on the strength of his youth.

Working in the field always reminded Jacob that they were short on farmhands. Two years before in the summer of '57, there'd been five menfolk to bring in hay, and now there were only two. Before, whenever something needed to be done, Jacob could say, "Jakey, you do that," or "Joseph, you run after that." Now it was just the two of them. But the war with the Indians was mostly over now, or so it seemed, so Joseph and Christian should be released to come home soon.

John must have been thinking about the same thing. He paused in his work and leaned on his scythe. "Do you think Joseph and Christian will want to farm when they get back?"

Jacob whipped his head to look at him. "Of course! Why not?" Whatever would make John ask such a question? What else would they possibly do? Start up a trade?

"I mean, to have their own farms."

"I've always planned for all of you boys to have your own farm. I was saving up for Jakey when—"

"I know. But Jakey showed more interest in the farm than Joseph or Christian. And now that the boys have been with the Indians for a while . . ." John looked down so Jacob couldn't see the expression on his face. Was he serious? But John was more like Jacob than Barbara; he didn't talk unless he had something to say.

Jacob shrugged his shoulders. "They're young. I wasn't interested in having my own farm until I started courting Lizzie. That's when I first got interested in coming to this country, so I could own my own land."

"I just wondered. We're having a hard time keeping up with all the land we've cleared. Maybe we could let some ground lay fallow." Was this John's way of telling him that Jacob was expecting too much of him? Perhaps trying to farm the same land without the boys' help was wearing them out.

"We could hire someone to help us," Jacob said. "Maybe one of the young men in our church."

"Like who?"

Good question. There were a number of young men in the fellowship, but most of them were needed on their own farms. It was hard to find an extra hand for something more than a week or two, especially during the busy seasons of planting and harvest. Just the time when Jacob and John most needed help, so did everyone else.

John took a step toward Jacob. "Rather than plant corn next year in that northern patch, let's scatter some grass seed. When Joseph or Christian comes back, we can plow it up again."

"Sounds good." As usual, John was being reasonable. And wise. Jacob had probably expected things to get back to being normal too quickly. And it was wearing on his son.

Jacob reached out for the scythe and handed his son the rake. "John, it's time for me to get out of Barbara's house. I'd like to rebuild my house by next summer."

John pulled off his hat and wiped his brow with his hanky. "Has Barbara been complaining?"

"No, no. I'm just eager to get back to the way it used to be. And it would save me walking back and forth from her place to mine every day."

"Will you build on the same spot?"

"*Jah*, I want to prove we can live here in the Northkill. I plan to build a house just like the old one. When Joseph and Christian come back, I'll have a place for them to stay." Jacob knew some would say it was foolish to rebuild before the war ended, but why wait?

"Can you afford it?"

"*Mam* and I had some money laid by that I can use. It's buried in the orchard. We were saving it up to help Jakey get started. Now that he's—"

"When do you want to get started?"

"I'd like to start cutting up logs this fall. Sometime in the spring, we can go to Philadelphia to get supplies and build as we have time. I know the folks in our church will help me. God willing, I'd like to move in by the end of the summer."

John pulled his hat back on his head and stuffed his hanky in his pocket. "That sounds like a good plan."

-28-

March 1759

It was a cloudy day when Jacob headed for Philadelphia with John. It was the best place to get nails, hinges, and latches for the doors in the house and other outbuildings, frames for the windows, and tool handles to replace ones that got burned in the barn. Jacob took along with him a gallon of whiskey from the distillery and the money he and Lizzie had saved in the orchard. He figured that should be plenty for everything they needed.

After they finished at the market, Jacob took a detour to see Christopher Sauer in his print shop. "I want to see what he knows about the progress of the peace treaties."

"I'm glad to see you," Mr. Sauer said when Jacob and his son stepped into the print shop. "You met with some misfortune since you were last here. Lost some family members in an attack, if I remember right. We wrote about it in the monthly paper."

"They killed my wife and two children. Took two of my sons captive."

"I'm so sorry to hear that. I believe I met your wife and two children the last time you were here, when you bought the *Martyrs Mirror*."

"Yes." The memory was clear as spring water in Jacob's head. "Conrad Weiser says my sons can't come back until the proprietors make peace treaties with the Indians. Can you tell me what happened at the recent peace treaty in Easton?"

"They've had four peace treaties there since Chief Teedyuscung called the first one in '56. The one last October was the biggest, so they're calling it the Grand Council. Had thirteen tribes represented—the six nations, the eastern

Delawares, the western Delawares—five hundred Indians. Worked out some land disputes."

Jacob's heartbeat quickened. "Will it help my sons get free? They're being held by the Delawares or the Shawnees."

"Maybe. The western Indians don't want the English to settle west of the Alleghenies. That's why a number of Indian chiefs were in Philadelphia in February to meet with General Forbes. They came down from the Indian town of Buckaloons, on the Allegheny by Brokenstraw Creek—"

Jacob shivered. "I know that place! I was held captive there for seven months. Those chiefs must have come quite close to the Northkill on the way."

"Likely. They want to make sure the English keep their promise to leave the Ohio territories as soon as the French are forced out."

"What are the chances of a peace treaty to make them release the prisoners?"

"It could still happen. Last fall, Frederick Christian Post led a peace mission to the western Indians and got them to agree to give up their support of the French. That's why General Forbes was able to take Fort Duquesne, which they now call Fort Pitt. I think it's only a matter of time before the English take the rest of the Ohio Valley. And then they'll demand that the prisoners be allowed to come back home.

"Who is this Frederick Post?"

"He's a Moravian missionary," Sauer said. "Worked among the Indians for years. Married a Christian Delaware woman. After she died, he married a second Indian woman. The Indians love the man. Trust him."

"Did he visit the western Indian camps? That's likely where my sons are being held."

"*Jah*, he made two different trips to places in the Ohio territories—Venango, Fort Machault, and Kuskuskies, near Fort Duquesne. He met with chiefs like King Beaver and Keckenepaulin, who were responsible for the bloody raids in the settlements. Even Shingas, the man whose head would

have brought two hundred pounds from Governor Denny in
'56."

Jacob's mouth dropped open. "My sons and I were held in
forts at Venango and Machault on the way to Presque Isle. Do
you suppose Post met any white captives in his travels?"

"*Jah*, he said he met several English captives—shook hands
with them."

"Then he could have met Joseph or Christian." Jacob and
John held each other's gaze for a moment. "I need to talk with
him!"

"Post was here in Philadelphia a few weeks ago in March,
but I don't know where he is now." Sauer fidgeted with the
newspaper in his hand. "Is there anything else I can help you
with?"

Jacob nodded. "I need another almanac. I lost mine in the
fire."

Sauer pulled an almanac off of the shelf and handed it to
him. "I hope your boys come back soon."

Jacob paid for the almanac and walked back to the wagon
with John. "I want to meet Frederick Post. If the Indians trust
him, he may be able to have Joseph and Christian brought
home. I'd much rather talk to a Moravian missionary than to
colonels like Bouquet and Weiser."

John nodded. They rode for a time in silence, taking in the
sights and sounds of the countryside and imagining the pos-
sibilities that Post might open up.

"*Dat*, are you planning to live in the house by yourself?"

"Who would live with me?"

"It will take a lot of extra work for you to do the cooking
and keeping up the house, plus the farming. It might be easier
to stay at Barbara's house."

"I expect that I will get married again, eventually. I should
have a house ready for a new wife."

"Have you been looking for someone?"

Jacob glanced at John out of the corner of his eye. "No. I
wanted to get the house built first. Do you have someone in
mind for me?"

"No, no. But there are a few widows in the area." John paused. "It might be good to talk to Barbara about your plans. If she's like Katie, she likes to know what you're thinking."

"Lizzie was that way too. Always wanting to know how I felt about something before I'd thought it through myself."

Jacob and his son lapsed back into silence. John was being unusually forward. Jacob didn't mind, but he did take notice. Had he been talking to Barbara? Or had Katie pressed him to talk to Jacob about it? How was he supposed to listen to his grown children?

With the help of people in the church fellowship, Jacob finished his house by the end of August. Jacob moved out of Barbara's house with mixed feelings. On the one hand, it was a step forward toward the life he'd lived before the war. On the other, it was lonely at times, and he missed his daughter's cooking.

Now that he had moved back into the home place, every day brought some reminder of a way Jacob had depended on Lizzie as a helpmeet. Whenever he got a stain on his shirt, Jacob could hear Lizzie say she would have been able to get it out. She used to do wonders with the lye soap she made every year at butchering time.

Lizzie always had a little something like flowers to spruce up the house or make it smell good. So Jacob thought of her whenever he smelled the honeysuckle, the lilacs, or the peonies.

Lizzie had always remembered their children's birthdays. Their grandchildren's too. And the anniversaries of their children and other couples in the fellowship. Jacob had forgotten Barbara's birthday last fall, even though he had been living with her and her family at the time.

He knew that no one could ever replace Lizzie. But living by himself pushed Jacob to think of marriage and to look around for a companion. At church, Jacob's eyes often drifted toward Anna Yoder. She was quite a bit younger than he, but she could make a wonderful companion. Not only was she a healer, but he enjoyed talking to her. Yet whenever Anna came to mind, Jacob's mind flew back to the difficult conversation with Lizzie after Anna had given him a massage. What would Lizzie think if she knew he had his eyes on Anna? If he married Anna, would it spoil his fond memories of Lizzie?

Shortly after Jacob moved out of her house, Barbara brought up the subject of marriage while she was helping him in the garden. "*Dat*, I think *Mam* would want for you to get remarried."

"Oh? What makes you think that?"

"*Mam* knew you needed a woman in your life."

"Do you have someone in mind?"

"Well, now that you ask," Barbara said, "what about Malinda Stehley? She's a good cook and housekeeper. It's been more than a year since Sol passed away." She had obviously been mulling this over.

Jacob raised his eyebrows. "She likes to take charge."

Barbara grinned. "That's true. But so do you."

Jacob frowned. "What would *Mam* think of Malinda?"

"She would want you to be happy."

True, but what if that meant marrying Anna Yoder? Jacob wasn't about to ask Barbara that question.

That evening, Jacob went to Lizzie's grave. Lizzie had always loved Queen Anne's lace, so he stopped in the meadow to pick some sprigs to toss onto the grave. He stood there for a long time, reliving the events of the past two years. *If only we had moved away from the Northkill, our family might not have been attacked. If only the attack hadn't happened, and Lizzie hadn't been killed, I wouldn't be in such a tough spot.*

Who could ever take Lizzie's place? What would people say if they saw him courting a younger woman like Anna? Some might know about Lizzie's bias against Anna and think less of him. Maybe he should follow Barbara's suggestion to court Malinda Stehley. That would definitely be the safest thing to do. No one would have any doubts about Malinda. But Jacob wasn't sure he was that interested in her.

The next Sunday, Jacob studied Malinda at the church service. Nearly fifty, Malinda had a dignified look, although her face seemed a bit worn. Thin too. After living with Lizzie's plump figure for two decades, he'd have to get used to that. Maybe Malinda wasn't a good cook.

Malinda seemed to look on the serious side of life as well, not as quick to laugh aloud as Lizzie had been. Did she take herself too seriously? Would she understand Jacob when he was making a joke?

He glanced at Malinda several times during the service and then again during the church meal. Jacob tried not to be obvious about it, lest someone notice and start gossiping about the two of them before they even talked to each other.

That week, Jake Hertzler dropped by Jacob's home to return the bucksaw he'd borrowed. The two of them chatted for a moment at the edge of the meadow where Jacob was fixing a fence.

"*Jakob*," he said, "have you thought of remarrying? I know that's a personal question, but I think it would be a good thing."

Jacob looked into his friend's eyes. What had brought about all this marriage talk? First John, then Barbara, now Jake Hertzler. "Are you thinking of someone?"

"Last Sunday at church I saw you look at Malinda Stehley a couple of times. She might make a good wife for you."

Maybe this was more than a coincidence. "Did you talk to Barbara this week?"

"No. Did Barbara say something about Malinda too?"

"*Jah*."

Jake seemed pleased with that news. "That's very interesting. What do you think of her?"

Jacob leaned against the fence post that stood between them. "She seems like a nice lady, but how can I get to know her without having everyone in the fellowship find out about it? I don't want to start rumors that we're getting married when I'm not even sure I'm interested in her."

"Why don't you come to our house for dinner next Sunday? Catharine and I will invite Malinda to come too. No one would give that much thought."

"*Jah*, if—"

"We'll plan on that," the bishop said as he mounted his horse. "You can come even if it doesn't suit Malinda. We've been meaning to have you over."

The following Sunday, Jacob joined Jake and Catharine in their home for dinner. Malinda Stehley was there too, as planned. Their hosts gave no hint that the dinner had been arranged to bring Malinda and Jacob together, except that they gave them seats next to each other at the table. As Jake invited them to bow their heads for the prayer of thanks, Jacob wondered what Malinda had been told about the occasion.

After the prayer was ended, Malinda turned to Jacob. "I just appreciate the way that Jake shepherds our flock. Don't you?"

"*Jah*, I appreciate his emphasis on obedience to the Scriptures—"

"But I noticed that the young people don't always pay attention to the sermons. It seems to me that they don't listen the way we used to when we were young. Don't you agree, Brother Jake?"

Jake was chewing on some food, so Malinda turned toward Jacob again. "I always thought your boys were such good examples, Jacob. I'm so sorry they were taken away. Have you heard where they are?"

Jacob was chewing too, so Malinda went on. "You must miss them so much." She turned to Catharine. "It would be so hard to have children go missing, wouldn't you think?"

"It is very sad," Catharine said. "Katie tells us how much John misses his brothers on the farm. John and Katie have a lot of extra work these days. We often pray—"

"And I just wonder if we pray enough," Malinda said, nodding vigorously. "The Bible says we should pray without ceasing. Of course we need to pray for God's will to be done. I prayed every day for Sol to get better, but the good Lord saw fit to take him home. We tried some different remedies but nothing seemed to help. He just kept getting weaker and weaker. Now I'm by myself. I try not to complain; the children help me out as they can." At that she took a few bites of her potatoes.

Catharine looked at Jacob and pointed to a dish in front of him on the table. "Help yourself to the corn in that dish, Jacob, and then pass it on around."

"Good fresh corn," Jacob said, hoping to keep his part of the conversation alive. He helped himself and handed the dish to Malinda. She dipped herself a spoonful and passed it on.

There were a few moments of quiet before Malinda spoke again. "Some people say we should have tried some other medicine. We could have asked Anna Yoder to treat him, but Sol never liked having his feet rubbed, and I agreed that it's not good to have a woman doing that kind of thing for men. Of course if Sol had wanted a foot rub I would have been right there too, but I can't see how it helps and I don't know about Anna's herb medicine. Now, Jacob, I know you wouldn't go to see her, because you're very stable, but some of our younger men might be tempted by her. And so it might be good for the church just to discourage it, to keep rumors from being spread. You know how misunderstandings can get started that way, and it's so unkind when people spread gossip in the neighborhood, especially the older women. The Bible talks about gossips and busybodies. Sister Catharine, I'm sure you've seen how rumors can divide the church." Malinda paused to take her first bite of corn.

Catharine glanced at her husband. "Rumors can really hurt people—"

"I know what you mean!" Malinda said, putting down her fork. "If people would just learn not to pass things on that aren't true, that would take care of it, don't you think? One day Henry Zimmerman told Sol that he liked the way the Dunkard minister preached obedience to the Word, and the first thing you know, people were saying that Henry and his wife were leaving our church. I only told people Henry liked the Dunkard preaching and the way it draws young people. And I think it's sad that the young people don't pay more attention in our church."

Jake nodded. "We need the young people to stay in our church. Jacob, please take a second helping of potatoes and pass them around again."

Jacob helped himself and passed the bowl to Malinda, who had barely started eating her first helping. She passed the dish on to her hosts. Now he understood how Malinda stayed so thin. She didn't eat; she talked. "I know that the Dunkard preacher spoke against powwowing too," Malinda said. "That's why Henry told Sol to be careful about herb remedies. Henry told about an herb book full of magical arts, something about the Egyptian mysteries. The Dunkards are against it, which is a good thing, don't you think, Brother Jake?"

Jake nodded. "*Jah*, we don't believe in powwowing—"

"The Indians powwow, don't they?" Malinda said, turning toward Jake. "And I'm told they use herbs too. Jacob, did you see this in the village where you were being held?"

He nodded. "The Indians use different ways of healing. They gather herbs from the woods to make tea and other remedies." Jacob thought for a moment about the masked man who had said incantations over him but decided not to mention it.

"Do you suppose the Indians are teaching your boys to powwow?" Malinda asked. "I imagine the boys are learning lots of things you might not like. Do you suppose they dress like the Indians, or do they get to keep their Amish clothes? I saw an Indian one time with tattoos all over his arms and chest, but of course your boys wouldn't do such a thing. I'm sure they'll face many temptations. I'm sure you pray often for God to protect them. I do too, every day."

Jacob shifted in his chair. "I often pray for them."

"Speaking of Indians," Malinda went on, "I heard that the Indians came to your house one time and Lizzie chased them away. Is that true, Jacob?"

"Well—" Jacob started.

"I know one time they came begging to my house, and Sol said I should give them some of my fresh sweet corn that I had planned to use for dinner. I gave it to them and they ate it right off the cob and finally left. And that reminds me that I need to take some fresh corn over to Jacob Beiler's house. He didn't look so good in church today. I wonder if he's not declining. Catharine, don't you think he looked a little pale? I can tell when people's color isn't so good, and I try to help people out with the little that I have. I know I brought something to Lizzie one time when she wasn't feeling well."

"Lizzie appreciated that," Jacob said.

"I try to remember the words of Jesus, that it is more blessed to give than to receive, but of course I'm always glad when I get a little bit of help myself. The roof on my house needs fixing, and my son said he was going to get it done but he hasn't yet. I just put a bucket under it to catch the drips when it rains. I'm not one to complain, but I do get a little tired of it, and I thought maybe I should talk to Deacon Zug about it, to see if anything could be done."

Jacob felt suddenly tired, like he could take a nap. Listening was harder work for him than chores, notwithstanding the prohibition of labor on the Lord's day. When they had finished eating, Jake and Jacob chatted in the living room as the women washed the dishes. From time to time, Jacob cocked an ear to the women's conversation. He mostly heard Malinda talking and thought about how Catharine must be a good listener.

When the two women were finished with the dishes, they joined the men in the living room. The four of them chatted for a time before Jacob excused himself to go home.

On the way home, he fretted about what he was going to tell the bishop the next time he saw him. Of course Jake would ask him what he thought of Malinda. Jacob didn't want to disappoint him, but he was convinced that Malinda was not the one for him. *I would never get a word in edgewise.* He was still tired from the attempt to keep up with Malinda's end of the conversation.

As Jacob approached the house, he picked a pear from the orchard and then stopped by Lizzie's grave to eat it. When he was finished with the fruit, he threw away the core and knelt quietly by the grave for a few minutes, remembering the Sunday afternoons that he and Lizzie had spent quiet times together.

I'm not going to marry anybody I don't love like I loved Lizzie. There, it was decided. That would be a good thing to say to the bishop when he asked him about Malinda. Jacob nodded his head for emphasis as he got up from his knees and headed for the house.

It brought to mind the saying he had repeated to John when he and Katie were thinking about getting married: "The marriage state is a like a coop built stout, the outs would fain be in, the ins, be out." At this point, he didn't want to be cooped up with Malinda. He just wasn't that good of a listener.

-29-

A few weeks after dinner with Malinda at the Hertzlers, Jacob made a call on Anna Yoder. He walked there on a Sunday evening, well after the sun had gone down. The stars were beginning to come out, with few clouds in the sky to hide them. The moon was bright enough that he did not light the lantern he was carrying by his side. Ever since his escape from the Indian village, walking the paths near home seemed easy and safe.

Jacob strode up to the door of Anna's home and knocked boldly. He paused for a moment and then rapped again. A few moments later, Anna opened the door. Her eyes widened in surprise, then she smiled. "Come in," she said. "I'll take your hat."

Jacob took off his straw hat and handed it to her. She hung it on a peg by the door and then pointed to a rocking chair. "Have a seat."

"Thank you." Jacob sat down and watched as Anna lit a lantern. The light of the flame flickered against her round cheeks and cast her shadow against the wall.

"I baked some apple pie yesterday," she said. "Would you like to have a piece?"

"*Jah*, that would be very nice."

Anna got up from the chair and walked toward the cupboard. She took a knife from the drawer, pulled the linen cover off of the pie, and cut a generous slice. After she put the slice onto a small plate for Jacob, she cut a smaller piece for herself.

"I hope you enjoy the apples in this pie," she said as she handed him the plate and sat down at the table. "They came from my orchard."

Jacob took a few bites. "This is good. The best I've had in a while."

She blushed. "Thank you."

"You're probably wondering why I came by this evening."

"*Jah*, I am a little curious. It's not so often that men come by here at night."

Jacob nodded and cleared his throat, which suddenly felt clogged with words. "You know that I'm living alone these days. I know that you're alone too. I thought we might enjoy each other's company. I'm certainly enjoying your pie."

Anna smiled and nodded her head. "I like to bake for others."

Jacob's heart leaped. "I was walking in the moonlight on the way over here tonight. Maybe we could take a little walk together."

"You mean right now?" Her voice rose a little in pitch.

"*Jah*, we needn't walk far. Just enough to breathe the fresh air and enjoy the full moon. The weather's so nice that we won't need our coats. And you won't have to bother with shoes. I didn't wear mine."

"I would enjoy that," she said, although she sounded a little hesitant.

They finished their pie and then Jacob stepped outside and held the door for Anna. They paused for a moment by the door to let their eyes adjust to the darkness.

Anna turned toward him. "Won't we need a lantern?"

"I'll light a lantern if you wish. I brought one with me but I didn't need it. The moon is bright enough."

Anna paused. "That will be fine. I'm just not used to walking in the dark without a lantern. But since we're together, I'm sure it will be safe."

"Okay, then, let's walk this way." Jacob stepped into the rutted path that led toward the Tulpehocken trail. They walked side by side in the moonlight.

"It's almost a full moon," Anna said. "I always love it when the moon comes up over the trees and lights up the path like this."

Jacob gazed up at the sky. "Me too, especially in the fall when the sky is so clear."

They walked in silence for a time and soon came to a place where the branches reached over the path, blocking out the moonlight. As they walked through the dark place, something rustled the brush near the path. Anna gasped and grabbed Jacob's sleeve.

"It's all right," he said, taking her hand. "It's probably just a rabbit or a squirrel. I got used to hearing those night sounds when I walked those many miles home through the forest."

"You must be very brave. I'm scared to walk through the woods alone."

"It was a bit dangerous to be in the big woods alone, mostly because of the Indians. But I don't worry much here."

Anna gripped Jacob's hand tightly. He didn't mind it at all. In a few moments, they had passed through the dark overhang and came into a clearing with the full light of the moon. Nearing the creek now, they could hear the sound of the running water that rippled through the cool night air.

"When I was a little girl, I spent lots of time playing in the creek that ran through our farm in the old country."

"Then why don't we sit on the bank?" Jacob led the way through the trees to a soft place at the water's edge. Jacob held her hand as she found a comfortable place to sit. They sat close together, letting their bare feet dangle within inches of the water. The moonlight glistened on the surface of the creek. A frog croaked nearby and another splashed into the water.

Jacob gathered up his courage. "I still remember the way you rubbed my feet when you came to our house with your peach pie. My feet never felt so good."

"I do it because it makes people feel better. My mother taught me."

"It certainly worked for me," Jacob said. "And with that neck massage you gave me, I felt good in my back too. I think you must have a gift from God for healing."

"Maybe so. But God is always the one who heals people."

"Would you be willing to give me a foot rub again?" Jacob knew he was being forward, but he longed for her touch.

She paused. "I don't usually work in the dark."

"That's okay. I shouldn't have asked." *Why was I so forward?* Jacob chided himself.

"Oh, I don't mind that you asked," Anna said. "Just not right now. I'm happy just to sit here and soak in the sounds of God's creation."

They sat in companionable silence for some time, listening to the night noises around them.

"You went through hard times in the last couple of years," Anna said softly, "and I admire the way you came through it. You must be very strong."

"Only because God helped me. I could easily have died."

"I'm so glad you made it through. Now I pray that God will bring your two boys back home. You must miss them very much."

"*Jah*," Jacob said, his voice husky. "I don't know if I'll ever see them again." He'd never said that out loud, although the thought was never far away.

"I miss seeing them," Anna said, "especially Christian."

"Oh?" Jacob leaned forward to hear more.

"He's so smart. And eager to learn. Remember that day when your family helped trim my trees after that big storm? Christian came up to me in the garden and asked me about my herbs."

"He was naming them on the way home."

"Really? He showed an interest in something that interested me. Men don't often do that, especially young boys."

Jacob sat up and took note of her words. "How did you come to know so much about herbs?"

"When I was quite young, my father got very sick. Everyone thought he was going to die. A neighbor woman came by with a potion made of herbs that helped him get better. From that time on, I started growing herbs."

"That's interesting. Someone helped you at a time of need and now you are helping others."

She chuckled. "I practiced on my family. Sometimes my *Dat* made outlandish faces when he drank my concoctions. I wasn't always sure if he was just teasing me or if it tasted that bad."

"It probably was good for him, even if it tasted bad. At least that's what my mother used to say when she made me take medicine."

"Mine too. But I like it best when the drinks help people and taste good too."

"I liked the drink you made the day we trimmed your trees. Some kind of tea."

"Thank you. I make different kinds of tea. God makes the plants, and I've learned how to use them."

"I admire people who know about plants. When Christian comes back, maybe you can teach him to use herbs."

"Do you think he'll come back soon?"

"It's possible, if the British win the war and make the Indians give up the prisoners."

"I'll be eager to see them again," Anna said. "I like to watch boys growing up. I had always hoped for a son of my own. I guess it wasn't God's will."

Jacob wasn't sure what to say. It could be difficult to put into words what one longs for but can't have. They were silent for some time, and then he said gently, "You did have a child, didn't you?"

"*Jah*, a little girl. But she died at two months of age. Ulrich and I never had any others."

"Children are a gift from God," Jacob said. "Grandchildren are even better."

"Look, a falling star," Anna said. Excitement edged her voice as she pointed to the sky. "It's a little hard to see through the trees."

At that, Jacob grasped her hand and helped her get up. "Maybe we should go back to the meadow. We could see the stars better there." They walked hand in hand back into the clearing.

"We could sit on this old log," Jacob said, and pointed toward it. They sat down close to each other and looked into the night sky.

"I can see the North Star now," Anna said. "A little while ago it was hidden by a cloud."

"My son Christian loves to watch the stars," I said. "You know how curious he is. Now the Indians call him Stargazer."

"They gave him a new name?"

"*Jah*, and they called me Fruit Grower."

They sat for a while without saying a word. A comfortable silence welled up in Jacob's soul as he held Anna's warm hand in his. He longed to stay until the moon dropped in the sky, but he knew that would be overdoing it.

Finally he said, "I'm getting a little sleepy. Maybe it's time we go back." He was wide awake, but it seemed like a good thing to say.

They walked across the clearing and down the path to Anna's home. Jacob paused at the door. They stood for a moment facing each other. He squeezed her hand. "Thanks for going on a walk with me."

"Thanks for inviting me. I really enjoyed it."

He stuffed down the urge to plant a kiss on her cheek. "Maybe we could do it again sometime."

"That would be lovely."

"Goodnight," he said as he squeezed her hand one final time. "I'll wait for a moment until you get a candle lit inside."

"No, that's okay. The moonlight is bright enough that I can find my way. And don't forget to take your lantern. Goodbye." She swung open the door and stepped inside.

Jacob picked up his lantern and headed toward home, his heart full of joy. Being with Anna renewed his soul. A new wind was stirring in his heart. It was the first time since he had lost Lizzie that he felt so drawn to a woman.

Jacob went to bed as soon as he got home, but it took awhile for him to fall asleep. He reflected on the things they'd talked about. Anna had shown strong interest in his boys, especially

Christian. Her memories of Christian's sweetness and curiosity, and her concern for him and Joseph now, moved him.

Turning on his side, Jacob longed to be with Anna again. Perhaps he could go see her again in the next week.

The next Sunday afternoon, Jacob finished his chores early and hurried to Anna's house again.

She seemed genuinely glad to see him as she opened the door. "Hi, Jacob, come on in."

Jacob stepped inside her cabin and doffed his hat. She pointed to a peg on the wall, and he hung the hat on it.

"May I get you a cup of tea?" she asked. "I just heated up a kettle of hot water."

"*Jah*, that would be nice."

"Peppermint or spearmint? I have both kinds in the garden."

"I prefer peppermint."

Anna took a knife from the kitchen and headed for the door.

"May I go with you? I'd like to see your herb garden."

"Sure. I'd love to show it to you." Jacob followed her into the garden where she cut a handful of peppermint stems. Her garden was laid out in squares, with small paths between patches of herbs so that she could make her way around the garden without pressing down the soil. She told him that she fertilized the garden with compost made from fallen leaves and the manure from her animals.

"You have lots of different plants in here," Jacob said. "Do you know the names of all of them?"

She chuckled. "Now I know where Christian gets his curiosity. He was asking me the same kinds of questions you are. Yes, I know the names of all of them. I have an herb book that my father passed down to me." Anna led him through the garden, naming each of the plants and telling him how she used each one as medicine. "I learned a lot from a book my father gave me. It has a lot of natural remedies."

The sun was setting in the sky when they finished going through the garden. "Feel free to come in and stay awhile," Anna said. "I'll make your tea. And I've got a bit of pie if you would like."

Jacob smiled at the invitation. "Thank you. I would love to have some of your pie."

The two of them sat in the small kitchen and chatted. Jacob tried to keep his mind on the conversation, but he kept thinking how much he wanted to feel Anna's touch on his feet. *How silly of me*, he thought to himself. He remembered that she had refused the last time he had asked. Should he wait for her to volunteer?

The evening wore on, and Anna never mentioned a foot rub. Jacob finally got up the courage to ask. "Would you be interested in giving me a foot rub?" He held his breath.

"*Jah.* I'll do that for you" she said, to his great relief.

"My feet might stink a little."

"That's not a problem," Anna said. "I'll use a little lotion, and that will make them smell better." She pulled up a chair and began massaging his feet.

Jacob could feel his heart pounding in his ears. Anna's warm touch was even better than he had recalled. And her gentle manner helped him relax. He settled back in the chair and savored the sensations that shot up his legs.

Anna hummed softly as she worked, so Jacob remained quiet, soaking in the tenderness conveyed by Anna's touch. He watched the expression on her face. Only once during the massage did she meet his gaze, and then only for a brief moment. As she finished her work, she stood up and said, "Is that what you were looking for?"

"*Jah*, and more. I don't understand how you can make it feel so good."

"Thank you. I have a lot of practice," she said with a smile. She seemed pleased by his words of affirmation.

"Would you like to take a walk again this evening? I know it's rather dark, but I could carry my lantern."

Jacob was pleased when she agreed. They made their way back to the same log they'd sat on the previous week and chatted for a while before he walked her back home and they bid each other goodnight.

As Jacob walked home, his heart sang for joy. He no longer cared what looks he'd get when he showed up in public with Anna. In his heart, he'd crossed the bridge from widowhood to marriage. He'd give Anna a little more time to know and trust him, but he was confident that if he proposed marriage, she would say *jah*. Why worry about the opinions of people at church?

The next morning, Barbara arrived at his house with a basket of small cakes and a frown on her face. "Cristy said he saw you walking toward Anna's cabin." She set the basket on the table and busied herself with rearranging the cakes inside. "Have you been seeing her?"

Jacob weighed his words carefully. "I've talked to her a couple of times. Is that a problem?"

"I just wondered if it was getting serious. I know it's none of my business, but I keep hearing things about her among the women at church. I don't know what they'd think if they knew you were courting her."

"Courting hasn't been discussed."

"What else would you call it?"

"We're getting acquainted."

"What do you think *Mam* would say?"

"*Mam* never said much about her, other than admiring her herbs."

"What about the way she gets men to do things for her by giving foot rubs?" Barbara seemed worked up about something.

"She seems like a nice lady to me. She's a good cook." Jacob hoped that Barbara could see something positive about Anna.

"Well you'd better be ready to answer some questions." Barbara's eyes added weight to her words. Clearly, she didn't want Anna as a substitute for her mother.

"I'll think about it."

After Barbara stormed away from the house, Jacob slumped down in a chair. *Why must courting be so difficult?* First Barbara suggested he see someone whom he didn't care for, and then she got upset about the one that he did care for. Who was he trying to please, anyway: a new companion or his daughter?

Jacob knew his choice would affect not just Barbara but the whole family, including his grandchildren. It would be best if they were as happy about their new stepmother as he was about his new companion. Jacob had prayed daily about his various difficulties during the past several years. He shook his head. This was a new type of challenge to bring before God.

-30-

It bothered Barbara that her father kept seeing Anna over the next several months, since he knew she didn't like it. *Doesn't he care what I think?* She talked to Cristy about it one Sunday afternoon.

"Don't you think *Dat* should quit seeing Anna?" she said, after they had finished lunch and all the children were napping or playing outside.

"How come you're so worried about it?"

"I just think *Mam* would be really upset if she were alive. She told me that Anna is too free with her foot rubs. She uses that to get whatever she wants."

"*Dat*'s got his head on pretty straight."

"But aren't you worried about what people will say? I can just hear some of the women talking about it when they find out." Cristy shrugged his shoulders and got ready to go outside. Since Cristy wasn't being helpful, Barbara decided to talk to her brother John. Maybe the two of them could talk some sense into their father's head. John saw himself as the reasonable one in the family. He didn't easily get stirred up, like she did, and rarely poked his nose into other people's business. He was so practical about courting, in fact, that Barbara wasn't sure he understood romance. But maybe he could help their father see that romance sometimes stands in the way of clear thinking.

Cristy watched the children while she went to see John by herself. She walked over to John's house in the afternoon sun, determined to head off *Dat*'s plans. On the way, she walked past *Dat*'s house. It was mid-April and she noticed that he'd been working in the garden lately. Was he lining the nest for Anna? The garden looked better than it had for quite a while. Barbara couldn't remember her father ever getting that excited about the garden when *Mam* was living.

What if it was Anna who was working in the garden? Why else would there be varieties of herbs *Mam* never had? *How brazen! Working in* Dat's *garden before they are even married.* Didn't they realize that people notice these things?

When she knocked on the door of their house, Katie answered.

"I wanted to talk to John without the children listening in."

"He's taking a nap. But I can wake him up."

Barbara shook her head. "No, don't bother." If they woke him, her brother might not be in a good mood.

Since John wasn't available, Barbara took up the matter with Katie. They stood outside in the warm afternoon air. "I guess you know that *Dat* is courting Anna Yoder?"

"*Jah*, John and I talked about it. And I know that others have noticed."

"Really? Other people know?" It was worse than she had imagined.

Katie laughed at her shocked look. "You can't keep that kind of thing a secret."

"What do you think of their romance?"

"I don't mind. It's up to *Dat* what he wants to do."

Barbara rolled her eyes. "I don't mind if *Dat* gets married, but not to Anna."

"John says it's *Dat*'s business to decide who he wants to marry. I agree."

"But *we* have to live with his choice," Barbara said. "After all, she'll be our stepmother. And she's still young. They might have children who'd be part of our family."

Just then the door opened and John stepped outside to join them.

Barbara chuckled at her brother's tousled hair and the sleepy look on his face. "I didn't mean to wake you. I just stopped by to ask how you felt about *Dat* courting Anna Yoder."

"*Dat* asked me about her awhile back," John said, yawning. "I told him I'm glad he found somebody that suits him. He's quite smitten by her."

Were they as blind as *Dat*? "It looks like she's been working in *Dat*'s garden. That's pretty forward of her."

"I'm not so sure about that," John said. "I think she just gave *Dat* the herbs from her garden. He's sprucing things up a little."

"She has a bad reputation. Men come to her house alone, supposedly to get a foot treatment. *Mam* said she does it to get things done around her place."

"Let's go a little easy here," John said. "*Dat* talked to me about this. Anna's a healer, so you'd expect that people would come to her if they need help. But that doesn't mean she gives men everything they might want."

"But I'm concerned for *Dat*'s reputation. And ours too."

"Let's let *Dat* take care of his own reputation. He's a man of deep convictions. I'm not worried about what people think."

Barbara could see this was getting nowhere. "I'd better get home."

She turned and left. Why was she the only one in the family with enough sense to worry about *Dat*'s romance with Anna? Even Cristy didn't think there was anything to worry about. *How come they can't see something that's so obvious?*

In early April, Jacob made a trip to the blacksmith's shop to have him weld a hinge. As he walked out of the shop with the hinge in hand, Hans Kurtz, a neighbor, approached the shop. He reached out a hand and they greeted each other.

After a few comments about Jacob's misfortunes with the Indians, Hans said, "*Jakob*, it's been more than two years since you lost your wife. Have you thought about marrying someone else?"

"Can't say I've never given it a thought." Why had he brought it up?

"Good. There's Malinda Stehley and Franey Zug, although they're both a bit older than you are. Of course there's Anna Yoder, but you wouldn't want to marry her, not with the reputation she's got. And then there's the two sisters who were never married who might be suitable—Lizzie and Mary Detweiler."

"*Jah*," Jacob said with a frown. "I know those women." Jacob had eyes to see, just like Hans did. And why did he have to comment about Anna?

Hans wouldn't let the matter rest. "Like I said, any of them but Anna would make a good wife for you. Silas Burkholder told me she's a witch."

"Oh?" Jacob tried not to appear shocked. In as casual a tone as he could muster he said, "I didn't know Silas was seeing Anna."

"He went to her for a foot treatment and she tried to get him to drink some concoction—a witch's brew she got from the Indians."

"I wonder how he knew it was a witch's brew."

Hans's eyes flashed. "Are you saying he's a liar?"

Jacob fidgeted with the hinge in his hand. "No. It's just that I know that Anna wouldn't have anything to do with witches."

Hans raised his eyebrows and cocked his head. "You must have your eyes on Anna. Just wait until Silas hears about that."

Jacob shifted on his feet. What made Hans accuse him so? "She's a friend of our family. Lizzie started visiting her after she lost her husband. And I don't always believe the rumors I hear about people."

Hans didn't back down. "If a man like Silas tells me what a woman did to him, I'm going to believe it. Even plain people can be witches in disguise."

Jacob's neck got warm up to his hairline, but he responded in the calmest voice he could muster. "I must go now. I don't think it will do any good to talk more about this."

Hans nodded, said goodbye, and walked into the blacksmith's shop.

On the way home, Jacob pondered what to do about Silas's accusation. It sounded far-fetched, ridiculous. Why had Silas made such a strong accusation? Who was spreading that rumor?

Jacob's mind went back to the conversation with Malinda Stehley at the bishop's home. Hadn't she mentioned something about Anna and a witch's brew? And about the Egyptian mysteries? Had Malinda been talking to Silas? Or Hans? Perhaps he could mention Silas's name to Anna. Or Malinda's. But how could he do that without upsetting her?

If he was going to keep seeing Anna, Jacob knew he must hear her side of the story that Hans had just told him.

The next Sunday afternoon he walked to Anna's house. She welcomed him warmly and invited him to sit down. After a cup of tea, they went on a walk. It would be easier to talk about difficult things in the growing darkness.

As they sat on the log by the creek making small talk, Jacob tried to muster the courage to bring up the matter of the rumor. When Anna mentioned that one of the hinges on her door was developing a crack and might soon come loose, Jacob saw his opportunity. "I could take that hinge to the blacksmith shop for you."

"That would be nice of you. I miss having a man around here to fix things."

"I was just there the other day. I got a hinge welded. I ran into a neighbor who was talking about another neighbor named Silas Burkholder. I don't know the man, but he mentioned that Silas knew you."

Anna stiffened. "What did he say about me?"

Jacob searched for the right words to say. "I don't remember exactly what he said, but something about making him drink. A concoction—a witch's brew."

She jumped to her feet. "Silas Burkholder is a liar!"

"So you know him?"

"He came to my house for a foot massage." Anna paused. She seemed uncomfortable talking about these things. "It's just that I'm cautious when men come for a treatment. I didn't like the familiar way he approached me, so I refused to treat him. When he explained his symptoms, I told him that an herb remedy might help. When I looked it up in my herb book, he called it a handbook for witchcraft."

Jacob sighed in relief. It seemed like such a simple misunderstanding that could easily be corrected. "Perhaps he didn't understand herbal remedies."

"It's ridiculous. I know there are church people who have herb books with magical formulas associated with the Egyptian mysteries, like powwowing. Mine is not like that at all. But he wouldn't listen to reason."

"The neighbor said you tried to get him to drink some witch's brew you got from the Indians."

Anna's voice trembled. "Who is this neighbor? What does he know about it?"

Jacob shrunk back. "Hans Kurtz."

"Hans might not know it, but he is passing on a ridiculous lie. I didn't even make a drink for Silas. I just offered to make him an herb drink if he wanted it. When he asked how I know so much about herbs, I said that the settlers had learned a lot about the use of herbs from the Indians. Silas is spreading lies because he was upset that I wouldn't massage his feet or shoulders. When I told him no, he stood and threatened me. I ran out of the house and over to the neighbor's place. I stopped running when I saw Silas carrying his lantern in the other direction."

Now it was Jacob's turn to get angry. "That was wrong of him to treat you that way," he said.

Anna stood up and walked a few steps away. "I want to go back to the cabin."

Jacob stood up. "I'm sorry I brought it up. I shouldn't have said anything."

"You're not the first person who has said something to me about Silas Burkholder. The deacon came by here one day to ask me about it. He said Malinda Stehley talked to him. I told him what really happened, but I don't think he believes me." Anna sniffed and then blew her nose into her hanky.

Jacob stood there feeling as helpless as he always had when Lizzie used to cry. He reached out his hand and gently touched her shoulder. "I'm sorry."

"Now why does the deacon believe Silas instead of me? The man's not even a member of our church. And Malinda Stehley is a gossip, plain and simple."

Jacob shrugged his shoulders in the darkness and sighed. "I don't know. She likes to talk."

"Way too much. Men will always believe a man before they believe a woman. Unless it's gossip about another woman. That's just how it is and it's not fair."

"I suppose that's true sometimes," Jacob said in a low voice. He had never thought about it before.

She studied Jacob for a long moment in the lantern light. "Do you believe me?"

"*Jah*, I'm sure you're telling the truth. I just wonder why the deacon took Silas's side."

"Why do men always take the men's side? I'm going back to the cabin." With that, she spun around and walked away.

"Can I walk with you?" Jacob picked up the lantern and hurried after her.

"I guess so. I need the light to see." Her voice was trembling.

Jacob led the way with the lantern until they arrived back at the cabin. He lifted the lantern to the top hinge of the door. "You're right. That hinge is getting a crack in it. If you want, I'll get it fixed for you."

"No," she said firmly. "It can wait. Good night." She stepped inside and closed the door with a thud.

Jacob stood there for a moment and then turned to walk into the night. He plodded toward home, accusing himself with each step. Why had he brought up Silas Burkholder? Or Malinda? He swung his lantern in the darkness, reflecting on what to do next. Should he speak to Silas? No, Silas would surely mock him, especially if Silas knew that he had an interest in Anna.

Perhaps I should talk to the deacon, he thought. At least he'd keep it confidential. But if the deacon did believe Silas instead of Anna, he wouldn't want Jacob to marry Anna.

After his nightly reading from the prayer book, Jacob crawled into bed. He lay wide awake for a time, weary but unable to fall asleep. He searched in vain for the right words to frame an apology for Anna, and then fell asleep with the disconsolation that she might not give him the chance to share it. It was a long and troublesome night.

A few weeks later Jake called for a church council meeting. It was a time when the adults stayed seated after the worship service while the children were dismissed to go. Jacob shifted in his seat as the bishop called the meeting to order. Jake's voice was trembling. Something was afoot.

"Beloved brothers and sisters," the bishop began. "As you know, we live in danger of attack from the Indians. A number from our fellowship, both parents and children, have been affected. We lost the Meyer family and several members of our beloved brother Jacob Hochstetler's family. They were either were killed or taken captive. Through the Lord's goodness, Jacob made his escape and walks among us, yet he is missing two sons. Only the Lord knows where they are."

Jacob's throat felt tight as Anna Yoder glanced in his direction.

Jake continued. "Some time ago, Colonel Conrad Weiser warned us that as nonresistant people, we shouldn't live so close to Indian territory. A number of families have already moved to the area near Chester. I have been giving oversight to that small fellowship. Colonel Jacob Morgan has invited some of us to move down toward Caernarvon, where he lives. There's a little village there called Morgantown. One of our families moved there last fall. Now several more families are making plans to go there as well."

With these words, he cast his eyes in the direction of John Mast, a man of good repute in the fellowship. "John, do you want to speak?"

"*Jah*, I can say a few words." All eyes turned toward the tall, slender man who stood up to address the congregation.

"As Jake said, a number of families have decided to move to Morgantown, which is about thirty-five miles south and east of here."

Jacob's heart sank. Was the church going to split in two?

"We certainly don't want to divide the church," John continued, as though he was reading Jacob's mind. "We intend to stay in fellowship with this congregation. The main purpose for leaving is to move to a safer place. We have found good land to support a number of families, so we can live together in a settlement, much as we do here. Much of the land is forested but suitable for tilling."

Jake looked around. "Are there any questions?"

Benedict Miller raised his hand. "How many families are going?"

"Several families for sure, and one is undecided."

Benedict raised his hand again and addressed his question to the bishop. "Are you planning to move with this group, or will you continue to serve here?"

Jacob was glad that someone had the courage to ask the question.

Jake paused and looked over the group once more. "I do not plan to leave. Catharine and I named our farmstead 'Contentment' for a reason. Unless the Lord changes our minds, we plan to stay here. I will be the bishop for both this fellowship and the new group, at least for now. It's quite a distance to travel on a regular basis—about thirty-five miles each way."

"Are you ready to announce the names of the people who are moving?" It was Benedict Miller again.

"I think that would be in order," Jake said, "although there are a few who have not made a final decision. Will all those who have decided to go please stand up?"

Four couples rose to their feet. Jacob had heard hints from several of them to this effect.

Jacob saw Anna take a hard look at the couples who were standing. Was she thinking, like he was, that they were losing an important part of our fellowship? Soon there'd be no one left at the Northkill.

A week later, on Sunday afternoon, Jacob worked up the courage to see Anna again. He walked to her house with a heavy heart, rehearsing what he might say to win back her trust. He was relieved when she greeted him politely and invited him to have tea. Jacob didn't feel the sense of warmth between them that he had felt before. But neither did she turn him away coldly, as he had feared.

"I'm so sorry about the misunderstanding last Sunday," Jacob said. "I want you to know that I don't believe the rumor Silas is spreading around."

"Thank you, it's just that . . ." Anna's voice trailed off.

Jacob waited for her to say more, but she remained silent. He tried again. "It's a hard thing when you are misunderstood."

She nodded silently.

"Shall we go on a walk?"

"We can." She looked away rather than meeting his gaze.

Jacob made some small talk as they walked toward the evening sun. And then their conversation turned to the church meeting that had taken place the week before.

"I'm a little disappointed that several families plan to move away."

Anna sighed but said nothing.

"I just don't see why they want to move away from here."

"They're tired of the danger. They want to feel safe."

"I heard that. But there are several Indian paths that go right through Morgantown. You never know where or when the Indians will decide to attack. Who's to say they won't attack there?"

"Well, John Mast's group is convinced that it's safer there than here. I'd sleep better at night if I lived there too."

What? Jacob had been getting ready to ask Anna to marry him, and now the Morgantown group might pull her away. How could he possibly convince her to stay? It might be now or never.

Yet he couldn't afford to ignore her fears. If they were to get married and the Indians attacked, how could he possibly forgive himself?

"Would you feel safer if you didn't live alone?" Jacob was fumbling with words but didn't know how to express what was in his heart.

"Maybe. I'm sad to see Fanny Mast go. She's one of the few women who support me when people make false accusations."

"I see." He reached over to squeeze her hand but she drew it back.

"I'm not sure I want to stay here when so many people believe rumors about me. I'm thinking about moving to Morgantown with the other families. A fresh start."

Jacob's eyes widened. Anna was slipping away from him. He might have to do something risky. "Hans Kurtz is moving down there. Do you want to be that close to him?" He smiled to soften his comment.

She remained silent.

"John's and Barbara's families are planning to stay around here. Otherwise I might consider moving to Morgantown myself." Was there any other way to keep the door open a little longer?

"They need your help on the farm."

He held his breath for a moment. "You'd make a good companion."

"I was afraid you were going to ask." She kept her pace and looked straight ahead as she spoke.

Jacob felt a weight pressing down on him. "You wouldn't consider marriage?"

"No."

"May I ask why?"

"Indians seek revenge. They could come after you at any

time—here at the Northkill, at Morgantown, anywhere." She spoke as if it was a matter of fact.

Jacob walked beside her in silence. What could he say? Was she really that worried about revenge from the Indians, or was she taking her own kind of revenge against him for having listened to Malinda Stehley and Hans Kurtz? Or was there another suitor?

Anna stopped walking. "If the Indians make a peace agreement and return your sons, that might be different."

"I'd give anything to make that happen."

"I know. But until it does, my answer is no." Anna's tone softened. "I'm sorry, Jacob."

They walked back to her cabin in silence. Jacob bid her a quiet goodbye. He noticed that the hinge was bent worse than before, making the door scrape when it closed.

He walked home with his shoulders drooping, rehearsing all of the ways he could yet try to bring his sons back home. Wasn't the heartache of missing his sons each day enough? Now he would have to endure the added pain of missing Anna too. As long as his sons were gone from home, Anna—the woman he was coming to love—would be out of his reach as well.

-31-

August 1761

Jacob had just leaned back in his chair for a Sunday afternoon nap when he heard a knock on the door. It was Jake Hertzler.

"Come in," Jacob said. "Always glad to see you."

They made some small talk and then the bishop pulled a newspaper out of his leather pouch. "I read something in the newspaper this week that I thought might interest you."

"Oh?" What news was big enough that Jake would come to tell him about it?

"There was an Indian treaty conference at Easton last week and it looks like they're making some progress. There were eight tribes represented. The war may soon be over."

Jacob went stiff. He couldn't breathe for a moment. "Were the Delawares and Shawnees there?"

"*Jah*, the Delawares, but I didn't see anything about the Shawnees."

"How about the Senecas?"

Jake glanced over the paper. "No, I don't see the Senecas in this list." He took off his hat and rolled the brim in his hands. I came to tell you about a speech made by the governor. He mentions the need to return all the prisoners."

"Can you read it to me?" The words came out choked, husky. He could hardly believe this news.

"This comes from the governor's speech at the conference on August 7, 1761," the bishop said.

I have frequently sent messages into the Indian Country, to put them in mind of their promise to return to us our Flesh and Blood, who are prisoners among them, and to press them to fulfill that promise; and it is possible, that the Belt sent with the messengers for that purpose, may have been forwarded to the Six-Nation Council by mistake; I therefore now return you the belts, that you may make further enquiry of the Oneidas about them.

"Can you read it again?" Where was the good news that Jake was seeing?

Jake read the paragraph again and then dropped the newspaper on the table. "I don't understand what the belts are about, but it appears that whatever they are, the governor is using them to get the prisoners home."

Jacob leaned forward in his chair. "The Indians communicate with belts or string made of wampum, which is what they call the purple and white shell beads. It seems that the governor sent a belt to the Indians to remind them of the agreement to release their prisoners. But they didn't take it to the right people or give them the right message."

Disappointment rose like bile in his throat. Familiar. Discouraging. He sighed and looked down at the newspaper on the table. "It's been the same news all along. The Indians come to a treaty conference and the governor tells them they need to return all of the prisoners. Time goes by and they have another conference where they are told the same thing."

The bishop had sympathy in his eyes. "Maybe this news isn't as good as I thought it was."

A mist came over Jacob's eyes. "It's one thing for the Indians to talk about returning the prisoners, but it's quite another to actually do it."

"At least they're meeting to talk. That's a good sign."

Jacob shrugged and swallowed the lump in his throat. They talked for a moment about the summer weather and the crops, but his heart wasn't in it. Jake soon took his leave. After he was gone, Jacob lay down to rest, but he couldn't sleep. It would have been better not to have heard anything about the Easton conference than to hear this disappointing news.

Not that the news was so bad; there hadn't been any set-backs or new attacks on the settlers. It's just that there was nothing new, no cause for hope.

Jacob got up to take a walk. The sun was hot that day, so the creek and the shade of the trees would surely help him feel better. He sat by the bank, soaking in the pity that welled up inside. The summer would soon be gone—the fourth season that he'd needed to farm without his boys. Every year that went by would make it more difficult for the boys to adjust back to Amish life.

What worried him most, however, was that he was beginning to forget his sons' faces. How could it be? He closed his eyes and pictured Christian and Joseph as they had looked the last time he saw them without paint on their faces. It was as though he was gazing through a thin piece of fabric that rendered their features fuzzy and indistinct. How would he remember them if they were gone for another four seasons? Or more?

The longing to embrace Joseph and Christian was like a stone in his stomach, the weight of which seemed to grow with time. If only something could be done to hasten their return.

A year later Jacob learned that there was to be a council between various Indian tribes and Governor Hamilton in the city of Lancaster. The Indians promised to bring prisoners with them this time, so he determined to attend and meet his sons.

Jacob walked to his daughter's house to tell her about it.

"Oh, *Dat*, that is such good news," Barbara said. "I'll make a new shirt for each of them. I've been saving some fabric that *Mam* gave me."

"How will you have time, with the children?"

"I'll make time." Barbara's enthusiasm spiked Jacob's hope that this was indeed God's time to fulfill his daily prayers for his sons' return. Did he dare say something to Anna Yoder about it, or at least ask for her prayers? No, it would be better to surprise her by bringing the boys to a church service with him.

A week later, he sat waiting at Barbara's house as she finished stitching up the second new shirt. Two-year-old Jacob clung to Barbara's skirt as she ran her needle through the hem of the second shirt.

She must have felt his impatience. "*Dat*, if you hold little *Jakob*, I might be able to get done quicker."

"Of course." Jacob picked up his little namesake and carried him outside into the sunshine. The toddler babbled and tugged on his beard, bathing in his attention. Jacob was surprised that Barbara had volunteered to make the shirts in the first place. With five children and another one well on the way, it was a wonder that she had the time to sew something for the boys on such short notice. But she was like Lizzie; once she got her mind on something, she pressed until she got it done.

He was bouncing little Jacob on his shoulders near the barn when Barbara stepped outside. "Here they are, *Dat*."

Jacob carried the toddler to the house and thanked Barbara for her efforts. He tucked the two linen shirts into a bag and mounted his horse for the ride to Lancaster City. What might his sons look like by now? Likely they'd both have their heads shaved except for a scalp lock. They would be old enough to grow beards, so they'd need to shave regularly, unless they plucked out the hair instead. Indians didn't wear beards.

Would they have tattoos? Perhaps Jacob had never explained the scriptural teaching against tattoos, so they might not see anything wrong with it. Surely they'd have the common sense not to make permanent marks in their skin, especially with ungodly symbols. If they did have tattoos, maybe they could be covered with a long-sleeved shirt and trousers.

What would they be wearing? It was late August, so they might be wearing only a loincloth around the Indian camp.

But on a trip to a treaty center like Lancaster, they'd surely be dressed in their best clothes. Maybe leather breeches and a leather jacket, with European shirts. At least the chiefs would be dressed up in their best clothing to make a good impression on Governor Hamilton.

Would they be wearing gaudy ornaments? Surely they knew the biblical teaching against jewelry. They'd never seen Lizzie or Jacob wear jewelry of any kind and knew the way of the plain people. What would it be like to see his boys wearing nose rings or large earrings stretched on loose rings of skin dangling on their ears? Joseph would have a bass voice, since it had already started to change at the time he was taken captive. Jacob could imagine his Adam's apple bobbing slightly as he talked. On the other hand, Christian would likely be singing with a tenor voice. His voice had always sounded somewhat like a girl, and more than once Jacob had rebuked his older brothers for teasing him because he sounded like Franey. Of course, he was much older now.

Would he recognize them? Jacob would surely recognize Christian because of his blond hair and blue eyes. All of the Indians he'd ever seen had dark hair and dark eyes, except for the "white Indians" at Buckaloons.

All the questions made Jacob want to see his sons even more. He urged his horse to a faster pace. He was both afraid to hope and afraid not to.

As he rode into the center of the city of Lancaster, people were streaming into the city from all directions. On the outskirts of the city, hundreds of Indians were staying in a makeshift camp made up of huts constructed of boards, poles, or branches. It looked like a small town of its own.

Dignified Indian sachems showed off their regalia with women accompanying them. Energetic young warriors jumped, danced, and beat their drums. Children ran everywhere in the camp, playing hide-and-seek among the huts, laughing and shrieking with delight.

Judging by their dress, Jacob supposed the Indians had come from different tribes or at least different places. Some wore clothing much like the colonists, with linen shirts and breeches and plain hats like the Quakers. Others wore laced hats and colorful coats that were trimmed with gold and silver, likely given to them as presents at another treaty conference. Some appeared quite poor, with dirty shirts and ragged coats. And even if they wore European clothing, they wore the traditional scalp locks and their bodies were decorated with paint, tattoos, and jewelry.

Quakers walked about in their plain black garb, eager to show their readiness to make peace with the natives. In several places around the camp, Quaker men gathered in small groups for conversation with the Indians. Other white people milled about too, some camping in their Conestoga wagons parked on the other edge of the clearing. Others set up tents with little campfires surrounded by blankets lying on the ground. Perhaps some of them, like Jacob, were waiting for the release of a family member. Others were curiosity seekers eager to witness the making of historical treaties.

Jacob tied his horse at the edge of the grove and took a little walk around the camp to stretch his legs. There were several hours of daylight left when he arrived, so on impulse he looked around for Joseph and Christian. Small groups of Delawares came and went on a dusty road to the west of town, so Jacob headed in that direction. Before long, a group of huts that looked like a Delaware camp came into view. Jacob strode toward the encampment with a measure of fear. As an escaped prisoner, it might not be safe for him to be seen alone. But he was so eager to get a glance at Joseph or Christian that he kept going despite his trepidation.

It wouldn't have been wise to make a direct inquiry of his sons' whereabouts, lest he appear to be prying, or even worse, spying. So Jacob strode along as casually as he could with so much at stake, glancing here and there but trying not to stare. Jacob wasn't much good at faking. He had always been taught to let his "yea be yea" and his "nay be nay," a practice that must be as true for the eyes as for the tongue.

Jacob wasn't the only one looking around. A dozen white onlookers walked nearby, staring at the natives in a manner that embarrassed him. The treaty conference had brought out throngs of curiosity seekers, with the Indians as the main thing to explore.

As Jacob walked the hot, dusty street toward the temporary quarters set up by the Delawares, his insides started to churn. Was it fear or anticipation? Perhaps both. He'd dreamed a hundred times about the reunion with his sons, but it was unsettling to think of what they might have become during the long separation. Was Joseph still angry with Jacob for making him put down his gun? Was Christian still interested in astronomy?

Despite the butterflies in Jacob's stomach, he kept up his pace. When he arrived at the encampment, a deep familiarity gripped his soul. A dozen Delaware men stood conversing in small groups in the small clearing in front of the makeshift homes while several women huddled over a cooking fire. Children chased each other with abandon, laughing and waving sticks at one another.

And then—he drew in his breath—Jacob saw what seemed like a familiar figure. He looked like Scar Face, the tall warrior who had carried Franey's scalp on his belt all the way from the farm to the fort at Presque Isle. What would he be doing here?

The man that Jacob now spied in camp seemed much more relaxed, standing quietly with two other men. All three were bare-chested with war paint streaking their faces. They wore leather thongs around their necks with the usual pouch and scalping knife.

Might Scar Face be returning my sons? Jacob searched for memories of his interaction with Joseph and Christian. On the trail, Scar Face had always seemed distant from Jacob and his sons, never speaking directly to them. Just the opposite: it was as if Scar Face had ignored them on purpose. He'd usually marched close to the front of the war party. Whenever the party stopped to rest, he seemed impatient to move on.

When the Indian turned his head toward Jacob, all doubt fled his mind. This was indeed Scar Face, the man who had murdered his beloved little daughter. Jacob would never forget that man's face, easily identified by the scar that ran from the top of his crooked Roman nose across his left cheek.

At that moment, a little girl with long black pigtails ran up to the man and wrapped her brown arms around his legs. He reached down and stroked the top of her head with affection. Jacob's face flushed hot with grief and anger. He trembled all over. Jacob pretended not to have seen the man and turned to make his way back toward town. His thoughts ran apace with his pounding heart. Was it safe for him to show his face at the treaty conference or even in the town? What if the Delawares decided to recapture him and use him for ransom or to strike a bargain at the negotiating table?

Jacob tried to slow his thoughts. He took a deep breath. Surely these Indians wouldn't have the gall to take revenge on him or to reclaim him as a prisoner when the purpose of the treaty conference was to release the ones they already had. He slowed his pace and nearly turned around for another look at the warrior who had given his family such immense and overpowering grief. But he thought better of it and kept moving to the place where he'd tied his horse.

By the time Jacob got back to the wooded place where he'd decided to stay, it was dark enough that he lit a fire. He pulled a flint and a small iron from his pocket and struck them, directing the sparks against some dried leaves and a few dead boughs. Not that he needed the warmth. The setting of the sun brought little relief from the stifling heat of the mid-August day, and it would have been much cooler without a fire so close by. Yet he needed the comfort of a flame.

As the leaves caught fire and the flames spread through the tinder, Jacob recalled that night on the trail when he'd watched Scar Face clean the flesh off of Franey's scalp by the light of the fire. The years that passed had done little to soften the awful effect of that scene. Though he tried to push the sight from his mind, his stomach churned at the memory. Other scenes also shoved their way past his attempt to forget those years. Tears coursed down his cheeks as he recalled the sight of Franey's beautiful braids dancing from the warrior's belt as he swaggered along the trail.

He could still see Scar Face hoisting Franey's scalp onto a pole at Fort Presque Isle and claiming his bounty from the French officer. Jacob had fooled himself into thinking that he'd forgotten those things, or at least that time had dulled the horror. Now it was clear that it hadn't.

As he lay on the ground mulling over those images from the past, hatred rose in his heart for the tall man and his young daughter. Jacob contemplated running to a constable to tell him that his daughter's murderer was camping in town. Or to shout the news aloud to the agitated settlers waiting for the return of loved ones, with the hope that vigilantes would take the law into their own hands.

Jacob was tired and wished for sleep, but sleep would not come. He tried counting sheep but they quickly turned into barking dogs that lurked around the Indian camp, their gaunt ribs reflecting the desperate hunger and sickness in the Seneca camp during the height of that awful winter.

Jacob repeated the Lord's Prayer and Psalm 23 twice. Each time he came to the part in the Lord's Prayer about forgiving others as God had forgiven us, he wanted so much for the words to be true for him, but he didn't mean them. It didn't matter that God was asking him to forgive the man. It was simply beyond his ability to do it.

In the wee hours of the morning, Jacob heard the sound of little girls at play. He turned his head as they skipped into the clearing, the waning crescent moon glowing on their faces. The girls must have been about six years old, lithe and strong. They twirled and danced, giggling as they swung each other in circles. They sounded like Franey and Magdalena, playing in the yard on Sunday afternoon in years gone by. As they drew closer to Jacob, he could see that one was white and the other was Indian. In the dim light, the Indian girl looked to be a Delaware. She tossed her long black braids with careless abandon as she and her companion spun in circles. The white girl had pigtails too, only brown and not quite as long.

And then the two suddenly stopped their twirling and held each other's hands. They looked solemnly at each other, repeating words to each other that Jacob couldn't understand, and then joined in a long embrace.

At that moment the little white girl noticed Jacob. As she turned toward him, he suddenly recognized her.

"Franey!" Jacob lunged to reach her hand as she reached out toward him. But just as his hand touched her warm flesh, she was gone.

Jacob's heart thrummed hard in his chest. Was it real, or had it been a dream? A calm assurance came over him, bone-deep. He took the dream as a message of comfort from God. *Thank you God*, he prayed. Jacob soon fell asleep and didn't wake until dawn.

-32-

For breakfast, Jacob ate a few bites of dried corn he had brought with him. Perhaps the entire evening had been a figment of his imagination. Not only the vision of his daughter, but also the warrior who had killed her.

God, he prayed, as he readied his horse, *if that really was the man who killed Franey, and you want me to meet him again, make our paths cross somewhere on the treaty grounds. And if that happens, tell me what to say to him.*

Jacob made his way toward the center of town where a crowd was gathering. It seemed to be the most likely place for the prisoners to be delivered to their families.

When he found a place in the treaty grounds to watch the proceedings, Jacob stood beside a man who introduced himself as Horace Martin. Horace spoke good German, and he understood English as well. Jacob asked him if he'd mind translating for him, since it was hard for him to understand, especially when the speaker talked fast. Horace gladly agreed. He told Jacob that the *Engellanders* in Lancaster thumbed their noses at the Germans and insisted that they learn English. What presumption! Why did they think everyone had to speak their language?

As they waited for the conference to begin, Horace told Jacob a lot about Lancaster City and the Indians. He had come to the treaty conference to find his daughter, taken a year before Jacob's sons. She would be fifteen years old.

The formal meetings took place in the county courthouse, a two-story brick building topped by a cupola. At first Horace and Jacob were too far away to hear what was going on at the center of the negotiations. But they wormed their way to the front of the crowd and found a place to stand within earshot of the proceedings. The Indians gathered on one side of the council fire, and the provincial councilors on the other.

Indians from different tribes sat on boards, benches, or steps at the front of the large room. The headmen sat closest to the front, backed by warriors, women, and children. Horace whispered to Jacob that some of the chiefs had not come to the conference, insulted by the lack of a proper invitation. Chief Custaloga, whom Jacob most wanted to see, was one who had stayed away. Jacob looked at the ground for a long moment. Did that mean the prisoners from Custaloga's village, perhaps Joseph, would not be returned?

Governor James Hamilton and other provincial officials, all dressed in their finery, were seated on chairs opposite the Indians. The governor wore a powdered wig and a ruffled shirt accented by the brass buttons on his coat. With the advice of his councilors, he could speak for the province on behalf of King George III of England.

The governor opened the conference with a string of beads in his hand: "With this string I clean your bodies from the dust and sweat, and open your eyes and ears, that you may see your brethren with cheerfulness, and hear distinctly what I have to say to you at this conference." And then he laid a string containing hundreds of beads onto the table.

He paused after each sentence as the Moravian missionary Frederick Post translated his words into the Delaware language. This was the man who had taken his life into his own hands, negotiating with the Ohio Delawares on behalf of the province in 1758. It was possible that he had seen Joseph or Christian. Maybe he would have a few moments to speak to Jacob after the conference.

The governor continued his formal welcome: "Brethren, with this string I open the passage to your hearts, that you may speak freely and without reserve, as brethren ought to do when they meet together." And then he laid down a shorter string of beads.

After more such speeches, he brought his welcome to a close: "Having now wiped your eyes, opened the way to your hearts, and cleansed the council seats, I, by this belt, take you by the hand and bid you heartily welcome, and assure you that I am ready to do everything in my power to strengthen and preserve that brotherly love and friendship which so long subsisted between your ancestors and His Majesty's subjects of this government." With those words he laid a wampum belt on the table and said he was finished.

King Beaver of the Delawares responded on behalf of all of the Indians present: "Brother, we all rejoice to hear what you have said to us, and are glad that you have cleansed us, and have spoken to us in the manner which our forefathers used to do to one another. As we speak different languages, we shall be glad of an opportunity of consulting among ourselves, and shall deliver what we have to say to you tomorrow morning."

Jacob turned to Horace. "Is that all that's going to happen today? I thought we'd see prisoners returned."

Horace nodded with a glum expression on his face. "Nothing moves fast at a treaty conference." No wonder it took so long for the prisoners to be released after the war had ended. He would have to learn patience.

As soon as the formalities were over, Jacob pushed his way to the front to speak to Frederick Post, but he slipped away before Jacob could reach him. *Was it prideful of me to think that such an important man would have time to speak to me?* Jacob wondered. *Or that he would have met Joseph or Christian?*

The next morning, Jacob found Horace Martin again. It was nice to know someone in the press of the crowd, and he was grateful for Horace's translation. King Beaver began his speech with a word of thanks for the governor's welcome and the hope that they could speak freely to one another.

Jacob leaned forward as King Beaver spoke of their desire to return the prisoners of war: "And we have been likewise ever since endeavoring to bring in your flesh and blood, as you required it of us. Mr. Croghan, and the captain at Fort Pitt, know that we have delivered many of them, and now we bring a few more of them to you. There are some behind yet, and they meet with good usage, and live as we do, and choose to stay with us, but I hope they will come to you after some time, because you live better than we do." With those words, he laid a wampum belt on the table.

Jacob's feet felt suddenly heavy, as if he were rooted to the spot where he stood. Did this mean that not all of the prisoners were being returned at this conference? His mind numbed with the realization that his sons might not be in the delegation.

The chief went on, telling about the good peace they had negotiated with Sir William Johnson, the Indian agent of New York. He held up the belt that had been given to them by Johnson. "With this belt, I collect dry wood to put to the fire and make it bigger, so that the smoke may rise to the skies; when other nations see it they will know by the light that I have been in council with my brethren."

When the chief finished his speech, the governor rose to say that he was well pleased with the desire of the Delawares to hold fast the chain of friendship between them, and to hold his request in their hearts. Jacob's heart was in his throat as the Indian brought forth their prisoners for exchange. The governor stepped forward to receive them, one by one, from the hands of King Beaver. Jacob counted seventeen prisoners returned that day. They named nine men and seven women, captives from Maryland, Pennsylvania, and Virginia. And there was one little boy; no one knew his name or from whence he had been taken. Jacob could hardly bear to watch the reunions taking place around him. His sons were not part of the group.

Horace was disappointed too. No news of his daughter. "I'm going to write to the governor," he said. "I have an attorney friend who'll do it. Want him to write one for you too? We can go talk to him about it now."

Horace's offer was a ray of hope on a cloudy day. "*Jah.* Whatever it takes to get the boys back home."

Together, Jacob and Horace walked a few blocks to the attorney's office. The office was on the first floor of a large, three-story brick house, with rich wooden paneling on the walls and ceiling. Horace explained their interest to a secretary, who bid them sit on chairs in the lounge. After a time, a young assistant came and plied them with questions about their missing children. He scratched down the information with a gray quill.

Close to the supper hour, the attorney called them into his office and handed letters to them. Horace carefully looked over his letter and said it was fine. Jacob looked at the English script on his. "Will you read it to me?"

Horace nodded and started out,

To the Honorable James Hamilton, Esquire, Lieutenant Governor of Pennsylvania,

The humble petition of Jacob Hochstetler of Berks County,

Humbly Sheweth: That about five Years ago your petitioner with two Children were taken Prisoners, and his wife and two other children were killed by the Indians, that one of the said children who is still prisoner is named Joseph, is about 18 years old, and Christian is about 16 and a half years old, That his house and improvements were totally ruined and destroyed.

He glanced at Jacob with eyebrows raised.
"*Jah*, that's right," Jacob said.
He continued,

That your petitioner understands that neither of his children are brought down, but the Ambassador of King Custaloga, who has one of his children, is now here.

Jacob nodded.

*That your Petitioner most humbly prays your Honor to in-
terpose in this matter, that his children may be restored to
him, or that he may put into such a method as may be ef-
fectual for that purpose. And your Petitioner will ever pray.
Aug. 13, 1762.*

The attorney looked at Jacob with inquiring eyes. "Is everything said accurately?"

"Yes."

He laid the letter on his desk. "Then just make your mark
right here." He pointed to the line with his name and handed
Jacob the quill pen.

Jacob made his mark. "When do you suppose we will hear
from the governor?"

"Hard to say. Might be months from now."

Jacob tried not to look too disappointed. More waiting.
"Thank you for your assistance."

After they had paid for the attorney's services, Jacob and
Horace walked back toward the treaty grounds.

Jacob turned to Horace. "Do you think our letters will do
any good?"

"They can't hurt. It's always good for the governor to know
if someone is missing. I'm sure he'll keep a record of it."

"I hope so." Jacob's head drooped as he walked back to the
place where his horse was tied. Should he return home now?
No, there was something more that remained to be done, if
God opened the door.

On the way back to the treaty grounds from the attorney's
office, Jacob spotted Scar Face again. He stood near the edge
of a crowd of Delawares. Jacob took a long look at him. No
question; he was the man who had killed Franey. And likely
the one who had earlier made the mark on the door after
Lizzie had shooed the Indians out of the house.

Should he reveal himself to this man? Jacob ruminated on
it all evening. The way Scar Face treated his own little daughter showed that he could be gentle and loving, not merely

the cruel and vengeful man Jacob had seen him be. Had he changed? Or was Jacob just seeing a different side of him?

Jacob thought of Scar Face as he prayed the Lord's Prayer before he went to sleep. When he came to "Forgive us our debts, as we forgive our debtors," he wondered if God took Scar Face to be one of his debtors. Could Jacob truly extend forgiveness to the man who had taken his daughter's life, especially when he wasn't even sure he wanted to try?

When Jacob got to the treaty grounds the next morning, he heard someone say that more prisoners were to be exchanged that day. Although representatives of the Six Nations were present for the speeches, that day the governor addressed the western Indians who held most of the captives: "For the prisoners that you have delivered at Fort Pitt, as well as for those you have now brought along with you, and delivered to me, I return you my hearty thanks; but you must remember, that on reestablishing and renewing the ancient chain of friendship with us, you repeatedly engaged to deliver us all our flesh and blood, which you have taken from us, by the instigation of the Evil Spirit."

Jacob nodded, for the governor was right. The Indians had promised to return all of their flesh and blood. That meant Joseph and Christian.

The governor continued: "I must insist on your taking every measure in your power to deliver them up, agreeable to your engagements, which will be the only means of strengthening and establishing a lasting peace, to us and our children yet unborn."

That's right. How could I live in peace with my sons in an Indian camp?

The governor's face reflected his earnestness. "This matter lies so near to my heart that I should not act as your true and sincere friend, if I did not speak with the greatest freedom and plainness to you about it, and tell you again that it is impossible we can look upon you as our brethren, if you detain from us our flesh and blood; we cannot sleep quietly in our beds till we see them all; our very dreams are disturbed on their account; we demand of you nothing more than the right which God and nature has given us."

Jacob could have shouted "Amen." How many hours had he lain awake in his bed, thinking of what was happening to his two sons?

After the governor had finished speaking, he held up a wampum belt for all to see. "To signify our sincerity to make peace, I offer you this large belt. There are thirteen rows."

Jacob cocked his head, noting that the governor spoke of the prisoners as British subjects. They were like stolen property, taken from the British and kept in Indian camps. *So that's what my family became when we landed in Philadelphia in the fall of 1738.* All the men had been made to sign papers declaring their loyalty to the British crown before they could get off of the ship. It had bothered him then, but it could be an advantage now.

Since his sons were British subjects, the Indians would need to release them before the peace treaty could be completed. The Indians had no choice, even if the boys had chosen to become white Indians. They were his own flesh and blood, and no Indian had the right to claim them. It was time to return them—now.

Jacob's heart pounded with anticipation after the governor's speech ended and it was time for another prisoner exchange. Joseph and Christian hadn't yet appeared in the crowd. Perhaps they were concealed from view.

First a young Indian woman stepped forward to return a young boy, perhaps three years old, to a woman who claimed to be his birth mother. But instead of going to his rightful mother, the little boy clung crying to his Indian mother's neck. The white mother beckoned gently to the boy, holding out her arms and speaking softly to him.

Could the child understand what she was saying? Did he remember her? The crowd watched enthralled as the child refused to let go. Finally the boy's Indian father pried the child's arms loose and handed him to the white mother. The boy kicked and screamed as the white woman took him into her arms.

At that, both of the adoptive parents began to cry. In all his months at Buckaloons, Jacob had never seen such tears. A lump rose in his throat. Their love for that child was clear.

Jacob shifted his gaze to the next prisoner to be released, a young white woman carrying a baby boy on her hip. Her young Indian husband held the woman and her child in a long embrace. A tall, white man with a beaver hat stepped from the crowd and beckoned to the young woman. He claimed to be her father.

The tall man stood waiting as the couple kissed and embraced each other. Suddenly they turned their back on the tall man and headed away. The tall man quickly ran ahead of them and blocked their way. Another white man aided him by coming up with a flintlock and pointing it at the young couple.

Jacob held his breath as the Indian man reached over and took the child from his wife. He kissed the little boy and hugged him to his chest, speaking softly into his ears. And then he handed the child back to his wife. He stepped back as the young woman and her child moved toward her father. She looked sullen and angry.

The father wrapped a rope around his daughter's waist and tied it with a knot. And then he began to walk to the other side of the clearing, forcing her to follow him. The man with the flintlock strode alongside, speaking roughly to the woman and making threats. Her Indian husband stood at the edge of a group of Indians with a stony face, his hands crossed in front of him. What was going through his mind?

As Jacob gazed at him, a Scripture came to mind. "What . . . God hath joined together, let not man put asunder." Did that verse apply to this couple? Should they have been allowed to stay together? If Joseph spent more time with the Indians, he could soon marry an Indian woman. What if they had children? Would he be willing to leave his wife and children to come back home to the Northkill?

Jacob shuddered as he realized how few of the prisoners wanted to come back to their white families that day. Hadn't they loved their white families before they were taken? Or had they just gotten so accustomed to Indian ways that they didn't want to come back home?

As the crowd left the grounds that day, Jacob found an interpreter who could speak to the ambassador representing King Custaloga. After a short exchange, he learned that Joseph was indeed in Custaloga's village.

"Swift Foot is content to be part of our Indian family," the interpreter said as he translated the ambassador's words. "He does not want to go back to the white man's ways."

Jacob's stomach clenched. "He is my flesh and blood, and I want him to come home."

He waited for the interpreter to speak the words to the ambassador, who shrugged his shoulders. "Why should he have to leave if he wants to stay?"

Jacob could have grabbed the ambassador by the throat. "Your people took him from me by force, and I need him back on my farm." This was the closest he'd gotten to Joseph in years, and yet he was so far away.

"I will tell Chief Custaloga," the ambassador said. "And I shall tell your son that I met you. Perhaps he will choose to come home. I do not know."

On impulse, Jacob reached into his bag and pulled out the two shirts Barbara had made. "Please take one of these shirts as a gift to the chief. The other one is for Joseph, I mean, Swift Foot. Tell him that his family would like for him to come home."

The ambassador reached out and took the shirts. "Thank you."

Would he really speak to Joseph? Might the gift help to move Custaloga to action? But what if Joseph himself didn't want to come? Perhaps nothing but a treaty agreement could pry his son away from his captors, now his adopted family.

There was one more thing that Jacob had to do before he was ready to go home. It was the season for peaches, so he walked to the market and bought a small basket full of the ripe fruit. He carried it down toward the Delaware camp, and found Scar Face there with his young daughter. Jacob swallowed slowly. Then he held the basket out to the warrior and spoke to him in both German and English. "These peaches are for you, from our family. God bless you."

Scar Face took a long look at Jacob. When his eyes drifted from Jacob's eyes to his beard, a glimmer of recognition showed on his face. He looked at the basket of peaches in Jacob's hand. And then he beckoned to his daughter, who stood nearby. With a cautious eye on Jacob, she moved to her father's side.

"*Anishik* (Thank you), Fruit Grower," Scar Face said as he took the basket from his hand and offered a peach to his daughter. She smiled as she reached out to take it.

Scar Face leaned over and said something to his daughter that Jacob could not understand. And then he reached down and untied the strings on the ends of the small belt of wampum that was wrapped around her arm.

He motioned for Jacob to hold up his arm. When he did so, Scar Face tied the little belt around Jacob's wrist. He bowed slightly, and said "*Wulanguntowoagan* (Peace)."

Jacob bowed in return. "Thank you."

His heart welled with astonishment as he turned to walk back toward the treaty grounds. What had just happened? He glanced over his shoulder to see Scar Face and his daughter each chewing on a fresh peach, the juice running down the sides of their mouths.

Peaches. A wampum belt. And a little girl's smile. This was reconciliation beyond Jacob's wildest imagination. This was not what he had come to Lancaster for, and his heart still ached for his sons. But it was a miracle all the same.

-33-

It was one of those days when nothing was going right. First, Barbara had trouble getting the fire to burn. It smoked up the house before she finally got it going, and then it got so hot that she burned the stew in the kettle.

Worse yet, the children were cranky all day. Little Christian kept tugging at his ears, so Barbara figured he had an earache. It got so bad that he screamed whenever she touched his ear. It tore at her heart, but there was nothing she could do to help besides rock him.

Cristy said he was going to fetch Anna Yoder. He knew how Barbara felt about Anna, but he wanted relief for the children. He was back with Anna in less than an hour.

"I'm sorry to hear that the children aren't feeling well," Anna said.

"*Jah*, they've been fussy all day, and I don't know what more I can do. Christian is the one who is really sick. I think he must have an earache."

"That's common for children his age," Anna said, as she took the child into her arms.

Christian began to wail as Anna kissed his forehead. She sat the child on her lap and held him close. And then she looked into the child's eyes as she held her hands over his ears. Barbara saw Anna's lips moving, whispering so quietly that she couldn't hear what she was saying.

In a few minutes, Christian settled down and quit crying. Anna kept her hands over the child's ears, all the while speaking softly to him.

With a handkerchief she wiped the tears from Christian's eyes. Barbara went back to making supper. She glanced over from time to time to see how the child was doing. He seemed quite relaxed now, with his head on Anna's bosom.

"I think he's much better now," Anna said after some time had passed. With that, she handed the little boy back to Barbara.

She took him and cradled him in her arms. He wrapped his arms around her neck and lay quietly against her. She rubbed his back and spoke quietly into his ear.

"Do you feel better now?" Barbara asked. "Your ears look red."

He nodded. "*Jah, Mam,* I feel better, but my ears feel hot."

Barbara took him over to the bed and laid him down. "Just rest here for a little while," she said.

She looked at Anna. "What did you do? I can't believe he got better so quickly."

"I don't understand it," Anna explained. "Sometimes when I hold my hand over someone's ears, or another part that is hurting, it draws out the pain."

Cristy nodded, triumphant. "That's what I thought. You must have a gift."

"If I do," Anna said, "it is a gift from God."

Christian drifted off to sleep, and the other children quieted down as well. It was the first time in two days that Barbara had a sense of peace. Who would have thought that Anna Yoder would be God's way to bring healing?

Anna was gathering her things to leave when Barbara blurted out an apology. "Anna, I have something to say to you before you go. I've had bad feelings about you for a long time. Will you forgive me?"

Anna turned toward her, her eyebrows raised. "Of course, Barbara, I will gladly forgive you. And if I've offended you, I'll try to make it right."

"No, Anna, it was my problem, not yours." At that, Barbara wrapped her arms around her and gave her a hug, the first time she'd ever shown Anna any affection. They each had tears in their eyes as they embraced, and when Barbara glanced over at Cristy, he was dabbing at his eyes too.

"I'm sorry it didn't work out between me and your *Dat*," Anna said. "You would be a wonderful daughter. I admire your *Dat* for all he's gone through, but I'm worried the Indians might come back and—"

"*Dat* has a strong faith in God. He's at the treaty conference in Lancaster this week where the Indians are supposed to bring back their captives. We're all hoping Joseph and Christian will be returned."

"I often pray for him and for them."

"Thank you again," Barbara said.

That night she lay in bed reflecting on the goodness of God. It wasn't just Christian who had been healed that day. She had been healed too. Maybe Jake Hertzler was right about the need to forgive others. It was so hard to do, but it felt so good to have done it.

Barbara lay wide awake, listening to Cristy's light snoring and the children's quiet breathing. The moonlight shone through the window as though it were beckoning her outside. She slipped quietly out of bed and opened the front door. The night air was warm but pleasant.

She stood there gazing at the small clouds drifting across the crescent moon. She had always thought that God showed his love by giving people the things that they had asked of him. For the first time, she felt God's comforting love through a painful event she'd tried so hard to avoid.

Jacob stopped by his daughter Barbara's house first thing when he got home from Lancaster City. She met him at the door, her face full of hope until she saw that he was alone. "*Dat*, where are the boys?"

Jacob shook his head, so sorry to have raised her hopes. "Not all of the prisoners were returned."

"Did you find out where they are?"

"Joseph is in Chief Custaloga's village. I sent the shirts with his ambassador."

"Can't the province make Custaloga set him free?"

Jacob paused, not sure how to form the words to answer her question. "He claims that Joseph wants to stay."

His daughter's pained look was almost more than he could bear. He added quickly, "I'm not sure it's true. I wrote a letter to the governor to see what he can do. I hope it helps." Jacob held his head in his hands.

"Maybe I spent all that time for nothing." Barbara shook her head and blinked back tears. "I hope Joseph gets to wear the shirts."

Jacob reached into his pocket and pulled out the wampum belt. "One good thing happened. I met the man who killed Franey. He gave me this peace belt after I gave him a basket of peaches."

Barbara mouth dropped as Jacob swallowed the lump in his throat. "God showed me that I had to forgive him for murdering Franey. It was the hardest thing I have ever done."

Barbara held the wampum in her hand. She fingered it gently as she led Jacob inside the house and showed him to a chair.

The two sat in silence on opposite sides of the oak table. "Papa, I must ask your forgiveness too," she said. "I've had a bad attitude toward you ever since the Indian attack. I've blamed you for letting *Mam* and the other two die. I thought you should have gone to the fort, or moved away, or . . . something. I realize now that it wasn't your fault. Will you forgive me?" Her eyes glistened.

"Of course I forgive you," Jacob said. "You and Cristy have been so good to me, helping me get back on my feet after my escape from Buckaloons."

"And *Dat*—" She blew her nose and wiped the wetness from her cheeks with her hanky. "I've been wrong about Anna."

Jacob cocked his head. "How is that?"

"After she came by here this week and healed Christian's earache, I came to see how wrong I've been about her. She's very nice. I shouldn't have tried to keep the two of you from getting together. She would make a good wife for you."

Jacob wiped his eyes with his sleeve. What was he to say? Barbara seemed so much softer toward him than she had ever been before. "I think she's afraid to marry me. Afraid of what the Indians might do to us."

"Still, I'm sorry about my part. Will you forgive me?"

"Of course." Jacob stood up and hugged his daughter.

He walked home that evening with a lightness in his chest. It was as if each act of reconciliation during the past week had made it easier to breathe. Now if only he could repair what had happened between him and Anna. But how could that be possible?

It seemed too soon for the monthly church service when it came a couple of weeks later. If only Jacob had better news to share about the boys. If only people didn't know about his trip to Lancaster so they wouldn't ask him where the boys were. Surely the people at church were as tired of hearing the bad news as Jacob was of sharing it.

But then, they hadn't heard about Scar Face and the wampum bracelet. They might be interested in hearing about that, if they could grasp its meaning.

Jacob headed for the church service with the wampum in his pocket but said nothing about it until they were seated for the noon meal several hours later. As he sat down to eat his serving of bean soup, he reached into his pocket and laid the little belt on the table beside him. Bishop Hertzler sat across from him and spied it first.

"What is that?"

"A wampum belt. The Indians used it for a bracelet."

The other conversations at the table quieted as people glanced at the unfamiliar object. They leaned forward to hear Jacob explain how he had gotten the belt at the treaty conference in Lancaster.

"Do you mind if we pass it around?" Deacon Zug asked, motioning for the bracelet.

"Go ahead. Just so I get it back."

Some of the women and children, who were waiting to eat in the second round at the tables, crowded around to listen.

"*Jakob*, as soon as the men are finished eating, please stand up and tell us the story from the beginning," Jake said. "This is important enough for us all to hear."

In a few minutes, the men moved away from the tables and the women and children sat down to be served. After the food was passed, Jake gave him the signal to speak. Jacob stood up and cleared his throat. How was he to begin?

"One day in September of '54," he said, "the Indians came to our house. They had often come before, but this time it was different. They wanted a peach pie Lizzie had just taken from the oven. Since she was saving it for someone else, she shooed them away. The Indians got very upset, so one of them with a big scar on his face took a stick from the bake oven and made a black mark on our front door. Lizzie was always afraid of what that meant."

Jacob saw Catharine Hertzler's eyes widen. Hadn't Lizzie told her friend about the incident? Or was she surprised that he was telling the story to the whole church?

"Now that I've lived with the Indians, I understand that they were offended when Lizzie didn't share her food with them, regardless of what she had planned for it. The Indians always share their food with their guests, even if they have very little." His knees shook as he looked into the faces of the people whose eyes were locked on him. "Maybe we could learn from them."

Barbara's mouth hung open as he described the time he spied Franey's scalp swinging on Scar Face's belt. Jacob cleared his throat again. Hadn't he told her about that?

A heavy weight pressed on his chest. "It was terribly hard for me to watch the men clean the three scalps around the fire that first night." What more should he say, since Magdalena and the other children were listening so intently?

Anna Yoder sat in a corner of the room, listening with her head cocked sideways, the way Lizzie used to when she wasn't sure she could believe what Jacob was saying. On the other hand, Malinda Stehley leaned forward with open mouth, drinking in every word. Who all would hear the story from her?

Jacob plunged on as a wellspring of feelings came unstopped, bursting forth in testimony. He told them about the long march to Presque Isle, his imprisonment and escape, and finally about the chance meeting with Scar Face at the treaty conference. "I bought him a small basket of peaches at the central market," he said. "I hoped that it would bring peace between us. And he gave me the little wampum belt that his daughter was wearing that day."

Jake took out his hanky and blew his nose. Every eye was fixed on Jacob. No one was looking at their hands, or out the windows, as they sometimes did during the long church service.

"Now I know that God was with me all the way through this trial. Even though I couldn't see it, God's hand was guiding me. I give thanks for all he has done for me."

Jacob glanced at the mantle clock to see how long he'd spoken. *What?!* Nearly an hour, as long as the bishop's sermon that day.

Several men reached out to shake Jacob's trembling hand as they prepared to leave. Anna was nowhere to be seen.

Jacob took a deep breath. Suddenly he felt as naked as the time when the Indian women plucked the hairs from his beard. How could he have been so foolish, revealing such deep feelings to the whole congregation?

"Thank you, *Dat*," Barbara said to him as she prepared to go home with her family. "I've been wanting to hear about some of those things for a long time."

Jacob walked home alone, worried about what he'd done. Why hadn't he told his daughter these things privately? It would have been better for her to hear it before the rest of the fellowship.

It was late afternoon when he got home. He stopped by Lizzie's grave, where he could talk with her about what had happened.

Jacob reached into his pocket to pull out the wampum bracelet. It was missing. *Where could I have put it? When did I last see it? Why did I pass it around?* If some child had taken it outside to play with it, it might well be lost. *How could I have been so foolish?* First he had made a fool of himself by giving such a long testimony. And then he had lost the only proof of his time with Scar Face.

-34-

The next day, Jacob plowed up a small patch of stubble. As he followed Blitz around the field, his mind drifted to Joseph and Christian. If they didn't start for home soon, they wouldn't make it back in time to help with the harvest. If they waited several months longer, they'd be in danger of the big snows. Was it too much to hope that they'd be home by late spring?

Jacob breathed deeply of the fresh earth, a smell that kept him putting one foot in front of the other. Each time he and Blitz made a turn in the field, he tried to name something aloud that he was thankful for. It wasn't hard to do, since God brought many things to mind.

He thanked God for the rich bounty of the Northkill soil, for the good weather and sufficient rains in due season, for neighbors who had helped him in times of trouble, for the love of children and grandchildren, for delivery from captivity in the Indian camp, for the church fellowship who helped him walk in the ways of God, for good health, for the healing grace of forgiveness, and for the way Barbara had come to accept Anna.

He thanked God too for the freedom to worship God in this new land, for the faithfulness of his father and Jacob Amman in the old country, for his distant Anabaptist forebears who stood their ground during the great trials of the Reformation, not counting their lives more important than their testimony of faithfulness to Jesus Christ. He thanked God for the faithful writers of the *Dordrecht Confession of Faith*, for the *Martyrs Mirror* and the *Ausbund*, for *Die ernsthafte Christenpflicht* and the *Wandering Soul*. Most of all, he thanked God for the promise of eternal life in the hereafter.

As he breathed out his prayers of thanksgiving, he did not tire of watching the plow tear up the rich brown soil. The implement ripped out the spent stalks and weeds, putting Jacob to thinking about the way the earth replaces the old with the new. His life was like that soil, plowed up by the terrible events of the war. Lizzie and two of his children had been ripped out of his life and covered up by the soil. His house and farm buildings were ripped away too, burned to the ground by those who declared him their enemy. But in just five years after the attack, the buildings had all been replaced with structures as good as the ones that were burned. Some were even better.

"And we know that all things work together for good to them that love God, to them who are called according to his purpose." How often Jacob had heard his father recite that verse from the book of Romans. Now it was full of meaning for him as well. Would to God that he and his family and people would walk in faithfulness to God's purpose throughout the generations—even centuries—to come. Someday, the bodies of his loved ones—Lizzie, Jakey, and Franey—would be raised up. Their bodies lay like seeds in the ground, waiting to burst forth with heavenly bodies at the sound of God's holy trumpet, to be gathered up with all of the faithful.

Jacob turned the plow at the end of a row. If only it was part of God's good purpose to give him another companion like Lizzie. Maybe God could still change Anna's mind, or bring someone else into his life whom he could love as much. If only God would spread his wings of protection over Joseph and Christian and bring them back home.

Why had God chosen not to answer those prayers? Was he still testing the commitment Jacob had made on bended knee that evening by the barn—to follow God no matter what the cost? Was God testing his faith as he had tested Abraham, whom he asked to give up his favorite son?

"Vater im Himmel (Father in heaven),"* Jacob prayed, as he pulled the plow out of the soil and guided his horse to the spring for a drink. *"Thy kingdom come. Thy will be done in earth, as it is in heaven"—whether it be about Anna, or about the boys, or anything else.*

When Jacob got back to the house, he found a handwritten note pinned to his front door. He unfolded it and read the German scrawl: "Dear Jacob, I heard your testimony on Sunday. If you come to my house, I have something for you. In Christian love, Anna Yoder."

Jacob read the note twice, out loud. What did Anna have to give him?

That evening after a few bites of supper, he hurried to Anna's house. She answered his rap at the door and invited him to come in.

"I got your note," Jacob said, not sure what else to say.

"Good." She nodded toward her rocker. "Please sit down. Would you like a cup of spearmint tea?"

"No one makes it any better."

"I'll need to heat the water." She dipped some water from a bucket into her kettle and hung it over the fire. "You're probably wondering what I have for you."

Jacob nodded. "Your note made me very curious."

Anna went to the mantle to pick up something and brought it to where he was sitting. But instead of handing it to him, she stood there in front of the chair, holding it in her hand. It was the wampum bracelet.

Jacob's eyes widened. Why had she taken it? He got up from the chair and searched for clues in her face and eyes.

"I brought it home by mistake. I put it in my pocket while you were speaking on Sunday. I was listening so hard that I forgot to return it to you."

"You left very quickly. Did you—"

"I'm ashamed—"

"It was foolish of me to talk for so long. Almost an hour! I am so embarrassed."

"You spoke from the heart—"

"I'm afraid I said too much."

Anna stood only a step away from him, her gray-green eyes locked with his. Jacob held his breath. Would he be able to bear the words she was about to speak? Was she about to remind him that his experiences with the Indians had forever branded him as a marked man, too dangerous to be her companion?

"*Jakob.*" She spoke so quietly that he leaned forward and took a step toward her. He took hold of the wampum, but she kept it in her grip. "After I heard your testimony on Sunday, I was ashamed of my attitude toward you. I hadn't understood the depth of your trust in God. I have been looking through the eyes of man."

She dropped her eyes from Jacob's gaze and swallowed deeply. Her cheeks flushed a rosy pink in the lamplight.

Jacob stood in awkward silence. Should he offer forgiveness? Should he embrace her and say it was all right? Or might that lead to misunderstanding?

A gurgle rose from the fireplace. "Oh, the kettle!" Anna left the wampum in his hand as she moved to pull the boiling water away from the flame. And then she steeped the tea leaves, poured them both a cup, and set them down at the table. She sat down and pointed to the chair opposite her.

Jacob took the tea and seated himself with a word of thanks, but his mind was lost in thought. He sipped the tea without a word, sensing that she had something more in mind, but afraid to hope for what it might be.

"I never did get that hinge fixed," she said.

Jacob wrinkled his brow. What was she talking about?

"You offered to fix the hinge on my front door," she said.

It was as though sunlight had burst into the room. The last time he had volunteered to fix that hinge, she had pushed him away. Now she was giving him another chance.

"I'll take care of that hinge first thing in the morning," he said, leaning toward her over the table. "I may have one that matches. Is there anything else you need done?"

"My firewood pile is getting a little low."

"I'll take care of that too."

"Thank you." Anna stood up. "Again, I'm sorry I kept the wampum belt."

"That's okay. I understand." Jacob walked home in the growing darkness with his mind whirling. Could he dare to believe what had just happened? It wasn't the door to her house that most interested him, but the door to her heart. Was she ready to let him back inside? Had the gift from Scar Face touched Anna as much as it had him?

The sun had barely risen the next morning when he strode to Anna's house with a used hinge in his hand, a couple of tools in his pocket, and a freshly sharpened ax on his shoulder. He hummed the tune to a Swiss love song that he and Lizzie had sung together when they were newly married.

Anna greeted him with a smile and the usual offer of hot spearmint tea. He drank the tea but didn't linger in conversation. Sometimes deeds speak louder than words.

He quickly replaced the old hinge with the one he had brought. "What do you think of this?"

She swung the door open and then closed it. "That is so much better." She flashed him her brightest smile.

So far, so good. "Glad I just happened to have that hinge in my barn. Now it's time to chop wood." He left the house and went to work at the woodpile, chopping without a break until Anna beckoned him in for dinner several hours later.

The kitchen smelled of fresh mint, cooked vegetables, and something baking in the oven. "It smells mighty good in here," he said.

"That's quite a pile of wood you made. That will keep my house warm for a long time."

"Glad to do it."

"I suppose your neck muscles are a little sore," Anna said. "You might need them rubbed a little."

Jacob grinned. "I would enjoy that."

She smiled in return. "Right after dinner."

At the end of the meal, Anna surprised him with a piece of peach pie she had baked while he was working outside. After he enjoyed the pie, he settled into a chair. He leaned forward and breathed deeply as Anna worked her magic on his neck and shoulders. "If you promise to rub my shoulders every time I chop wood, I'll keep you supplied all winter."

"Well, I'd have to think about that."

Her playful tone beckoned him to say more. "I could help you with other things too. I could plow your garden, trim your orchard trees, help with butchering." Jacob paused. "The things I used to enjoy doing for Lizzie."

Anna paused her massage but kept her hands on his shoulders. "That's a lot for a busy man like you to do for me."

Jacob couldn't see the expression on her face, but the tone of her voice and her touch suggested that it might be time to move toward the big question he was hoping to ask.

"I could use some help myself," Jacob said. "Maybe God is waiting to bring my boys back home until there's better cooking at my house. My boys loved pie."

"I love baking pies."

Jacob shifted in his chair so he could look into her eyes. "So, Anna . . . will you marry me?"

Anna's eyes beamed with delight. "*Jah*, I would love to marry you."

"Shall we get married yet this fall?"

Anna flashed her brightest smile. "I'll be ready just as soon as we can make the plans."

Jacob walked back to his house as the slanting light of late afternoon glowed on the greenery of the rolling hills. Flush with eagerness for his new life with Anna, Jacob breathed the earthy fragrance carried by a gentle south breeze as he passed his freshly plowed field.

How was he to understand the ways of God? The days were getting shorter, and it would only be a few months until the snow began to fly. Alongside his joy at Anna's acceptance of his proposal ran the familiar vein of grief for his lost family, both the living and the dead. Jacob breathed a prayer, as he did every day, that God might return his sons to him. The home that he and Anna would create would be different from the one he and Lizzie had made together, but it would be a place of love and care for his sons. He closed his eyes and hoped against hope that he could wrap his arms around the two of them before winter—better yet, in time to attend the wedding.

Jake Hertzler had recently quoted the words of the prophet Isaiah to the congregation, declaring that God's ways are higher than our ways and his thoughts higher than our thoughts. In the same way the rain and the snow from heaven make the earth sprout and grow, bearing seed for the sower and bread for the eater, God's word will accomplish the thing for which he sent it. As Jacob walked toward the barn to feed Blitz, rubbing his hands together against the slight chill in the air, he prayed that it might be so.

Historical Background

Jacob Hochstetler's family was but one of thousands in colonial Pennsylvania whose lives were shattered by the events of the French and Indian War. The Seven Years' War, as it is often called, was international in scope, encompassing eleven nations on four continents. Scholars have documented the immense legacy of this clash of empires, which forever altered the social and religious landscape of America.

It would be difficult to overestimate the significance of two developments in the aftermath of the conflict. One was the forcible and widespread displacement of Native American peoples and disruption of their way of life. The other was the levying of taxes to pay for the war's expenses, which, among other vexations, provoked the colonists to revolt and eventually establish the United States of America.

The account of Jacob Hochstetler's experiences was first written as an essay by William F. Hochstetler as part of the introduction to Harvey Hostetler's massive genealogy book listing the descendants of Jacob Hochstetler and his first wife, whose name remains unknown. The 1912 edition lists 9,197 families, largely descendants of Jacob's three sons who survived the attack.

In 1938, Harvey Hostetler printed an even larger genealogical record of the descendants of Jacob's daughter, Barbara Stutzman, listing 15,550 families. Amish families are generally aware of their genealogical ancestry; their shelves often house several books tracing their ancestral lineage through various family lines.

Descendants of Jacob Hochstetler formed the Jacob Hochstetler Family Association, Inc. in 1988, which publishes the quarterly *Hochstetler/Hostetler/Hochstedler (H/H/H) Family Newsletter*. Historical researchers regularly publish their family research in the newsletter, including articles with corrections to William Hochstetler's account.

Online genealogical databases now make it possible for many people to quickly determine if they are a descendant of the Hochstetler clan, and if so, their relationship to their thousands of cousins. Because marriages to relatives within the Amish community are common, many people can trace their lineage directly to Jacob Hochstetler by several different paths, at times through all four of his children who had descendants—Barbara, John, Joseph, and Christian.

One serious downside of the close intermarriage among Jacob's descendants is the occurrence of two peculiar forms of dwarfism among the Amish that have been traced by gene studies directly to Jacob Hochstetler and a neighbor, John Miller. Geneticists have suggested that the two men may have been in-laws with a near common ancestor who carried the gene that produces this genetic malady.

The most visible public reminder of the story of Jacob Hochstetler is a Pennsylvania Historical and Museum Commission marker located just south of Interstate 78 near Shartlesville, Pennsylvania. It sits right next to old Route 22, where the road runs behind a Roadside America Inn. The sign says: "The first organized Amish Mennonite congregation in America. Established by 1740. Disbanded following Indian attack, September 29, 1757, in which a Provincial soldier and three members of the Jacob Hochstetler family were killed near this point." Although not entirely true to fact, it stands as silent testimony to a significant era in the spiritual landscape of the land we call America.

Acknowledgments

This book is the culmination of much research and many invigorating conversations with people along the way. A number of people deserve my sincere, written acknowledgment.

Thank you to John Ruth, an interpreter of history who early on pointed me to good sources. He also engaged me in helpful discussion about my project at key points in the writing process, and helped me to understand the Hochstetler story as one small strand in the web of relationships in the colonial clash of empires.

Thank you to William Unrau, distinguished professor emeritus at Wichita State University, who helped me to understand the colonial context of the Amish interaction with Native Americans. His strong support of my endeavor was a keen encouragement.

Thank you to Beth Hostetler Mark, a librarian at Messiah College, who gathered the archival sources relating to the Jacob Hochstetler family in the context of the French and Indian War. I often drew on her bibliographic instincts when searching for historical sources. At times she served as a sleuth for me, employing her librarian's tools and Internet connections to help me track down the arcane details needed to properly document the historical background for this book.

Thank you to Daniel E. and Arie Hochstetler for the hospitality in their home when I was doing research for this book. They both gave feedback on an early version of the manuscript and encouraged me in this writing project. Daniel is the founder and longtime editor of the *H/H/H Family Newsletter*, and serves as the vice president of the Jacob Hochstetler Family Association. Not only did he supply me with a copy of the entire collection of the newsletter, he also shared other sources he had collected.

Thank you to Lois Bowman and Cathy Baugh of the Menno Simons Historical Library and Archives of Eastern Mennonite University, who assisted me on several occasions. They faithfully stand guard over a treasure trove of historical materials, and readily gave me access to its riches.

Thank you to Rolando Santiago and Becky Gochnauer of the Lancaster Mennonite Historical Society, who took an interest in my project and helped me make vital connections that strengthened my story. I particularly admire the work they have done in the construction of an authentic replica of a Native American longhouse. Even more, I admire the conciliatory spirit in which they interpret the history of the Mennonites in the colonial context, including their role in the displacement of Native Americans in Pennsylvania.

Thank you to the editors who encouraged me and shepherded my work toward publication through various stages: Amy Gingerich, Suzanne Woods Fisher, Byron Rempel-Burkholder, and Valerie Weaver-Zercher. The marketing staff at Herald Press, particularly Ben Penner and Jerilyn Schrock, also deserve my gratitude for their belief in and enthusiastic promotion of this book.

Thank you to readers James Hershberger, David L. Miller, and Sam S. Stoltzfus, who responded to my manuscript from an Amish perspective, and to William Unrau, Rusty Sherrick, and Iris de Leon-Hartshorn, who provided feedback on the basis of Native American studies. Thanks also to Joanna Swartley for reading and responding to an early version of the manuscript.

Thank you to J. Richard Thomas and Elizabeth Soto Albrecht, my supervisors in Mennonite Church USA, who supported me in this significant diversion from my daily work. Together we hope that the book will promote the vision we share as members of our denomination: "God calls us to be followers of Jesus Christ and, by the power of the Holy Spirit, to grow as communities of grace, joy, and peace, so that God's healing and hope flow through us to the world."

Thank you to my wife, Bonita, for her loving forbearance throughout the process of researching and writing this book. She listened with grace to my preoccupied musings about this project through its various stages and often served as a caring companion when I was slogging through rocky terrain. I do some of my best work when I approach my writing as a medium of word painting, complementing the visual mixed media that grow out of her creative imagination.

Above all, I give thanks to God, whose redemption through Jesus Christ makes possible a peace that transforms human relationships. Without such marvelous grace, my life would be deeply impoverished and this book would have little depth. *Soli Deo Gloria.*

The Author

Ervin R. Stutzman was born into an Amish home in Kalona, Iowa, and spent most of his childhood in Hutchinson, Kansas. He serves as executive director for Mennonite Church USA and has also served the Mennonite church in the roles of pastor, district overseer, mission administrator, area conference moderator, seminary dean, and moderator of the denomination. He holds master's degrees from the University of Cincinnati and Eastern Mennonite Seminary, and received his PhD from Temple University.

Ervin's past publications include *Being God's People*, a study for new believers; *Creating Communities of the Kingdom* (coauthored with David Shenk); *Welcome!*, a book encouraging the church to welcome new members; *Tobias of the Amish*, a story of his father's life and community; *Emma, A Widow Among the Amish*, the story of his mother; and *From Nonresistance to Justice*, a book that examines the past hundred years of peacemaking in the Mennonite church. He has also published articles and contributed chapters to other books.

Ervin is married to Bonita Haldeman of Manheim, Pennsylvania. They live in Harrisonburg, Virginia, where they are members of Park View Mennonite Church. Ervin and Bonita have three adult children, Emma, Daniel, and Benjamin; and two grandchildren, Felix and Eva.

Read all the books in the Return to Northkill series by Ervin R. Stutzman

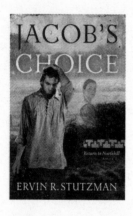

JACOB'S CHOICE
Return to Northkill, BOOK 1

PB. 9780836196818. $14.99 USD
HC. 9781513801681. $28.99 USD

Jacob Hochstetler is a peace-loving Amish settler beside the Northkill Creek in Pennsylvania when warriors, goaded by the hostilities of the French and Indian War, attack his family. Taken captive, Jacob finds his beliefs about love and nonresistance severely tested. After enduring a hard winter as a prisoner, Jacob makes a harrowing escape. Based on actual events, *Jacob's Choice* tells the story of one man's pursuit of restoration that leads to a complicated romance, an unrelenting search for his sons, and an astounding act of reconciliation.

Expanded Edition
HC. 9780836198751. $29.99 USD

The expanded edition of *Jacob's Choice* includes the novel itself along with maps, photographs, family tree charts, and other historical documents to help readers enter the story and era of the Hochstetler family.

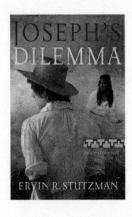

JOSEPH'S DILEMMA
Return to Northkill, BOOK 2

PB. 9780836199093. $14.99 USD
HC. 9781513801698. $28.99 USD
Amish teen Joseph Hochstetler is taken into captivity by Native Americans during the French and Indian War. Joseph finds himself pressed between his unfolding romance with a young Indian woman and the tug of his heritage. Based on actual events, *Joseph's Dilemma* traces the wrenching dilemma of a young man caught between his Amish past, his love for a woman, and an unknown future. When no decision seems like the right one, can the providence of God open up a new way?

CHRISTIAN'S HOPE
Return to Northkill, BOOK 3

PB. 9780836199420. $14.99 USD
HC. 9781513801285. $28.99 USD
When Christian Hochstetler returns after seven years of life with the Delaware Indians, he finds that many things have shifted. His father, Jacob, wants him to settle back into a predictable Amish life of farming, and Christian's friendship with Orpha Rupp also beckons him to stay. Yet Christian feels restless, and when he meets an outgoing preacher from another church in the area with a new take on the gospel message, Christian stands ready for a change. Will Christian choose to remain Amish, or will he depart from the faith of his childhood?

Discussion questions for all books in the series
available at HeraldPress.com/StudyGuides.